CAPTURING HIS HEART

REGINA BROWNELL

www.bloodhoundbooks.com

Print ISBN: 978-1-5040-8520-5

ALSO BY REGINA BROWNELL

The Two Week Promise

One Lucky Christmas

I would like to dedicate this book to all the readers who have taken a chance on my words. From the bottom of my heart thank you for being part of my journey and helping me live out my dream.

CHAPTER 1

I wake up on the wrong side of the bed every morning. Literally. The blankets are always overturned, my fluffy rainbow down comforter strewn about on the floor. It's like the exorcist slept in my bed. But still, no matter what side of it I wake up on, when I do open my eyes, I can't help being grateful at how I'm living in the greatest city in the world.

My teen years were spent doing everything possible to get off Long Island and into the hustle and bustle of Manhattan. I wanted to make a name for myself, be a big-time journalist and climb my way to the top of the journalism world. I made it to Manhattan, and almost to the top of the world.

I've been preparing for this almost my whole life. Writing for *Forever Twenty* has been a dream come true, but I want more. Like having my articles right on the front cover. Being well-known is all I've worked for and I'm not giving up now.

A gray veil of light peeks through the pale yellow curtains as I tug on my hip-hugging navy-blue lucky skirt. Makeup—check— cute white button-down blouse—check again—my sanity— double check! I wore this exact outfit when I landed the job at *Forever Twenty*. Who knows, it could be good luck.

It all started with a summer internship which turned into a role as one of their staff writers. Today I'm going in there with my head held high in hopes my article about having a sex bucket list will be enough to make its mark. I've been complimented on my articles, and it's gotten me a small following on my Instagram, and my blog, but I'm hungry for more.

I allow my golden brown locks to free themselves from the crazy mess of a bun I pinned up last night before bed. Waves of hair fall at my shoulders as I run a hand through to fluff it up.

A knock at the door gets my blood pumping.

"Millicent, we're going to be late." Cheryl, my friend, and co-worker, bangs harder at the door. There's no more time to doll myself up. My entire livelihood is in the one room of this loft, and it takes no longer than three seconds to cross the room to answer.

My stunning hazel-eyed friend is armed and ready with my favorite strawberry-banana smoothie, and poppy seed bagel, nestled in a brown bag. It's been our Friday routine for five years.

She hands it to me, I take it, followed by my keys and purse which hang to the left of the door. Slipping on the black ballet flats off the shoe mat, I tug the door closed and start walking.

With one hand I eat straight from the bag, while the other holds my drink.

The apartment building I reside in isn't the most chic of places. The old black-and-white tiled floors are chipped in various spots. Sometimes it feels like I'm living right out of *The Big Bang Theory*, because the elevator rarely works and when it does you don't want to be on that sucker—not even for a two-floor drop.

"So, did you finish the article?" she asks, as we descend the stairs.

"I did. Yesterday afternoon."

The August humidity squeezes us, and I wrinkle my nose at

the stench of urine and garbage. The scent is almost washed away by the spritzing rain, but not quite. It took me a while to get used to the sights and smells of the city. Although I'd visited many times before moving here, it's much different than being a resident.

We jog down the steps to the subway with several other people going in both directions. I stare up at her as we come to a stop on the platform. The subway stations are brutal this time of year and with all the bodies piled in, I'm melting.

Cheryl purses her lips and observes me. My self-doubt must be visible, like a cartoon character when they get angry, and you see the symbols circling their head.

The clickity-clack of a train comes roaring down the track on both sides. It's too loud to have a conversation. When it comes to a halt, us, plus the several other commuters push our way onto the train. We're like packed sardines in here.

"What was the article about?" She takes a bite of her bagel.

I grip my drink and the silver pole as the train lurches forward.

"I wrote a sex bucket list."

I swear the blue eyes of the man next to me flit to mine. His ears perked up when he heard *sex,* I guess.

Cheryl straightens her button-down. "Ah, that one. Are you going to check off any of those?"

I snort. Then grow quiet for a few seconds.

"Am I overstepping by asking?"

"Absolutely not. You deserve the chance. Don't second guess yourself. You write good shit," Cheryl says.

Aside from this I write a blog for fun, using ideas from work in hopes maybe someone would stumble upon it and love it. Like my boss. But it hasn't happened, so I have to step up to the plate.

"I know, but I've always wanted to be featured. My only concern is I'll go in there and she'll see right through me."

She nods. "I know. Honestly, with how you write no one would ever know you weren't banging every sexy creature in this city."

Flames flicker on my cheeks, turning them warm. I haven't had sex since I moved into my loft five years ago after I graduated from NYU.

She bumps into me. "I'm just playing around."

It's weird to think, but Cheryl was the last person I kissed. It was only a kiss. We were drunk. I panicked, thinking it would ruin our friendship because it wouldn't be the first time. I went through something similar in high school when I discovered I was bisexual. It didn't faze Cheryl and she said it was an enjoyable kiss, then we moved on from it. It was a relief to be on the same page with someone.

When we come to a complete stop, Cheryl and I squeeze our way out of the car and finally get some air to breathe. Not everyone gets off so it's an easy run up the stairs. Our office building is to our left. We pause outside, and dig into the contents of the paper bags, grabbing a few bites before we go in.

I stare at the entrance as people file in and out. Some have briefcases, others have backpacks or purses hooked over their shoulder. Nausea creeps up and the meal I love so much suddenly doesn't seem so appealing.

After a few minutes we make it to the seventeenth floor with seconds to spare. *Forever Twenty* has one of the biggest office spaces in the building and a nice view of Manhattan. My cubicle is next to the window, but there's not much to see as the skyscraper next to us is in my direct view. It's shaded from the sun, so it always feels like night in this one section.

I put all my things away, locked up safe in my desk. This is it, the moment I've been waiting for. I gather what I need, the printed article, the USB drive I stashed it on, oh—and my sanity, I grabbed that too.

My chest tightens as I knock on the door to Allison's office.

"Come in," she says, her deep voice rumbles, making my stomach churn.

She briefly lifts her head before returning to whatever paperwork is scattered on her desk. "Ah, Millicent, I was about to have Keith reach out to you. Perfect timing."

I squeeze the USB drive harder and hug the manilla folder containing my pride and joy to my body.

Her face is void of emotion. Not even a twitch of a smile, she's unreadable. "Please sit."

Her office is in the far corner of the office, but it overlooks more than the side of a building. She's got a street view. I don't know if I should look at her or keep my eyes out the window.

I take the seat in front of her desk as she glides in her office chair towards a cabinet to her right, tugging out a folder, then back to her desk. The silence in the room hurts my ears worse than the sirens echoing down a Manhattan block.

"Millicent, your articles are superb, really, they are. People enjoy what you have to say."

My face contorts, I feel the tug on my brow. There's a *but* coming. Maybe if I shove the article right at her the *but* will never come. The words leave her perfectly pink parted lips before I have the chance.

"But I hate to do this. Um, we feel like your articles have run a little... stale? Dry? They aren't spicy enough, it's like..."

She fixes her stare on me. She's suspicious. Is it that obvious I haven't had sex in five years, and I've been bullshitting my way through articles?

"Um, you catch my drift." She stammers for the right word, rolling her wrists so her hand makes a circling motion. "We had some cuts and you and three other staff members are being let go."

Shot to the fucking heart. Ouch! Not even Bon Jovi can save

me. My shoulders sag and I lower the folder and USB drive to my lap.

"I will email you a recommendation letter for all your work over these last few years. I'm sure you'll find something."

My conscience is screaming at me to fight back. *Show her the article, you fool.* My body though, refuses to move. I go through the motions, trying to make sense of it all. I sign a few documents and as if I were a zombie, I stumble out onto the office floor. I try to smile at Yvonne, one of the writers who I talk to a lot, but it probably comes out looking like a clown with lopsided lips.

Cheryl is sitting at my desk when I return. Her excitement drops and she pushes my chair back to stand and it crashes against an old puke green filing cabinet. I wince at the clang it makes when it hits.

"What happened?"

In silence I gather my things, aware of her presence. When I finish putting everything together and into my bag I stand straight. She's still there watching, lips pressed tight together. In one forward motion she scoops me into my arms. I can't cry here, but the tension is building. I feel it in my core. It tingles in my nose and burns my eyes. Stepping away, she says something, but I'm too stunned to actually hear it.

I hold it all in until I get to my apartment. With the door shut I lean against it, dropping all the contents in my hand as I slide down. The tears come in waves. First the sad ones fall slowly, then the angry hot fat tears that burn my skin, followed by hollowed sobs, then back to sadness. I barely register taking my phone out of my back pocket to call my brother.

"Hey, Mil," he says, in a chipper tone.

"Ezra?"

"You okay?" A serious calm takes over him.

Defeated.

"I think I want to come home."

It might be a rash decision, because I LOVE Manhattan, but if I can't find something right away, I'll never be able to afford this place, and I can't ask my parents for any more money. Maybe going home will help guide me in a better direction, even if it means living under my parents' roof until I figure it all out.

CHAPTER 2

ONE MONTH LATER

I stare at the crisp white ceiling and black walls that surround me. It's a reminder of my failure. Being back here in my parents' house on Long Island and being jobless isn't the worst scenario; but after living on my own since college being under their roof feels like a jail sentence.

I'd had to wait until September for the lease in my New York apartment to run out so I gave myself a month to find a job that paid well enough to stay. Leaving New York wasn't an easy decision and I hope it was the right one.

Beside me, on my unkempt bed, is my laptop open to a blank screen as I wait for inspiration to hit so I can write a blog post. Between job applications, dead-end interviews, and packing up the apartment, I'm spent; but I need to keep up my appearances on social media if I want to keep myself relevant.

The bedroom door flies open, and Mom strolls in holding a familiar black bag. *Shit.* I must have forgotten it in her van when we moved everything over.

Suddenly I'm seventeen again and Mom is standing at my dresser with my mini vibrator trying to open it, her reasoning, because she had never seen one so small. That was my first experience with a vibrator. My girlfriend at the time had gotten them and I was curious.

"Millicent, dear, you forgot a bag in the car," she says. Her wide brown eyes go from my face to the bag in her hand.

During my time at *Forever Twenty* I was given many samples, mostly toys, some condoms. I got the vibrators a week before they let me go.

I jolt up from the bed and take long strides across the room. I grab the bag from her, and somehow hit a button on one of them and the whole thing rumbles to life. *Oh God!* Reaching inside I search for the culprit. It's long, hard — I peek inside — pink, and very wiggly. A hot blush creeps up my neck.

"Oh. It's a bag of toys. I thought it felt kind of weird." Mom shrugs.

I smack my hand to my face, shaking my head. Mom's light laughter is a breath of fresh air. She was never the kind of mom I had to fear asking for advice. She even went as far as buying me a congratulations balloon when I got my period too and got one of those confetti poppers and shouted, "Congratulations you're a woman!" In fact, when I came out as bisexual, she took me out to dinner to celebrate. Which I was grateful for, because it was a hard thing to do.

People always used to mistake us for sisters. She was young when she and Dad got pregnant with me; they were just out of high school. She wanted to be in the know so I didn't make the same mistakes and wind up with two kids before I hit twenty.

"Got any good tips for your dear old mom?"

I groan. "No. I'd rather not know what happens under this roof, especially while I'm living in it."

She laughs, but her cheeks turn a shade of pink. My parents still act like they are in their twenties and look like they are in their thirties. They also have no filter.

It's weird being back here. The room that I spent eighteen years in is mostly the same. The only things missing are the band posters. Mom has given the space a fresh coat of paint, most likely due to all the peeling that occurred when I tore down my posters.

"So, I didn't only come to deliver your vibrators." She snickers. "I need you to run an errand for me."

My brows scrunch together. She's up to something. Her eyes have an evil gleam in them. I'm not falling for it. "What kind of errand?"

I only worry because once Mom nonchalantly set me up on a blind date when I came to visit one weekend during college. The kicker was she didn't realize the girl and I had already dated. The relationship had not been a good one. Her plan backfired and I spent the weekend inside my head going over everything I could have fixed in the relationship.

"You aren't setting me up again, are you? Like tell me there's somewhere you want me to go, and someone will just casually bump into me: 'Oh hey, what are you doing here?'"

She chuckles. "Me? No. I just need you to pick up a cake at the bakery."

I cross my arms. "And why can't you do it?"

She checks the invisible watch on her wrist and keeps her focus there for a good ten seconds before lifting it.

"Alright, I get it. I'll go. But don't think while I'm here you are going to try and set me up again. The single life is… nice."

She makes the sign of the cross over her heart. "Cross my heart, baby girl."

I scoff. "Right."

She steps towards me and rests a hand on my shoulder. "I love my strong independent daughter, who doesn't need a man—or a woman—to make her happy, but it never hurts to ya' know… get laid."

A snort flies out of my mouth and I cover it with my hands. Mom scoffs playfully. I want to be annoyed by her comment, but instead I can't help smiling.

Mom hugs me and gets on her toes to kiss my head. I'm a few inches taller than her. She holds me for a few seconds longer before retreating. "I want you to be happy."

It doesn't seem like it, but I am. This is a snag in the road, and I'm determined to get back out there and be someone again. For now, I'm looking forward to family dinners, and outings with my parents and Ezra.

"I know," I say.

"You're going to be just fine."

When she's gone, I peek at the bag of vibrators in my hand. I wonder if anything in there is worth writing about. I'll have to figure that out later: for now it's off to town.

THANKS TO DAD, my ancient Honda Accord runs like a champ. He has been driving it to keep her going while I've been in Manhattan. My parents are amazing; I honestly don't know where I'd be without them.

Town isn't too crowded today and I can pull up in front of a photography studio, two stores down from the bakery. The storefront awning has the name Parker Photography in big bold white lettering against a black background. My eyes scan the glass windows and signage hung in each pane advertising their specials.

I get out of the car, adjusting my tote over my shoulder. Stepping up onto the sidewalk my eyes settle back on the photography studio window. Hanging on the glass door is a HELP WANTED sign. It's not journalism, but it's something.

How much experience would I need to work for a photographer? It could be a good gig to save money and eventually get out of my parents' house. I could even learn the basics and take nicer photos for social media. Maybe this is a sign from the universe telling me to get back on the horse and saddle up.

Upon closer inspection, it says "Assistant Needed". *Oh, that could work.* I lean in to investigate further when two emerald eyes zero in on me through the glass. They are strikingly familiar. I jump back and the door opens with a ding.

CHAPTER 3

*L*uke Parker. Heat infiltrates my body. Our expressions match, either horror or shock, I can't tell which. The last time I saw him was at the graduation party. The night I started to lose my best friend. I can see the memory passing through his eyes too.

Minutes before Luke and I had a moment together, I was rejected by my best friend, Astra. She knew every one of my secrets. She had been out and proud since we were fourteen. I spent hours talking to her about how I thought I was bisexual, but always felt invalid since I liked boys too. I should have known then, when she told me I was most likely only looking for a place to fit in, and so I copied her.

One kiss to let her know my feelings left our friendship hanging in the balance and eventually she stopped talking to me. She said I was confused, and she wasn't interested in a romantic relationship with me.

Jason Geiger, whose house we were at, had called for a game of Seven Minutes in Heaven. I was still wiping my tears when he made the announcement. He lived down by the bay in a large mansion. Jason was the popular jock everyone flocked to.

With my emotions running high, I said fuck it, and joined them. I sat across from the boy my younger brother played *Dungeons and Dragons* with, Luke Parker. Luke didn't like me much then. I picked on him and my brother for playing the game, and for LARPING aka live action role playing. They'd dress up in these crazy costumes and gather at the park to pretend they were in a fantasy world.

His scowl said everything: he didn't need to mutter a word.

Jason stood in the center of the circle. He had us all write our names on strips of paper, then deposit them into a bucket. A few kids went in and out. With each passing name chosen, my pulse kicked into high gear. My name was in there somewhere amongst the others. I knew I was doing this to rid my lips of Astra's taste, to forget I ruined a thirteen-year friendship.

"Luke and Millicent."

When I looked across the circle at Luke, his face paled. His sights set on me. He had glasses then, black thick-framed, and reminded me of Squints from *The Sandlot* movie. I searched the room for any sign of my brother, but he was nowhere in sight.

"Are you guys going to do this or not?" Jason asked, annoyance clear in his voice.

Luke stood first, on shaky legs. I did the same, swallowing back the knot in my throat. I couldn't believe what was about to happen. We walked side by side into the living room closet. It was a tight squeeze with all the coats and jackets, Jason's family's shoes and even a vacuum.

The door shut with a bang, and I jumped. Luke and I were in the dark, but I could somehow see his outline. The only sound coming through was the pumping bass from the music outside and the soft hitch of our breaths.

"Don't tell Ezra," he said.

"Why would I tell him?"

"I don't know."

There were a few beats of silence between us.

"I can't see you," Luke said.

I reached out, touched him, and felt a bulge under my hand. Shit. I stepped back and pulled my arm to my chest. Emotions bubbled inside of me. Not because I was about to kiss my brother's friend, but because of why I was about to do it.

"Sorry."

"I– I– it's fine."

Telling him we could pretend it happened was on the tip of my tongue, but he stepped forward bumping our chests into each other. His hand found mine and slowly his fingers traced along my wrist and up my arm, like he was trying to find the perfect spot to rest his hand.

"Have you ever kissed a girl?" I asked.

My body trembled at his touch. I shivered even though it felt like nearly a hundred degrees inside the enclosed space.

"Shut it, Millicent."

"I'm not making fun—"

"No, you are. Have you ever kissed a guy?"

Ouch. It hurt, but I deserved it. Our exchange of words didn't stop him from continuing his climb up my arm. I closed my eyes, and thank God it was dark, or he would have caught me closing my eyes and enjoying the sensation.

When his hand cradled my face, I couldn't move. Somehow something that was wrong felt right, but then what was the whole thing with Astra? Panic consumed every part of me as Luke moved in for the kiss. His lips brushed mine and I leaped from his grasp and fled from the closet and the party.

That whole summer I avoided Luke, and if he came over, I'd leave. I went away to college after, so I haven't seen him since.

"It's you!" he says.

Luke is no longer a boy, he's a fucking man. He's a bit scruffy with a dark beard covering his cheeks and chin. It's trimmed neatly along the edges. My eyes linger on him, lowering to his shirt. With his new look I expect to find him dressed to fit the part of sophisticated, good-head-on-your-shoulders type of style. Instead, he's wearing an olive-colored shirt scrawled with the word *Paladin* and a symbol underneath, clearly from one of the online games he and Ezra used to play.

I snicker, some things never change. "That's some way to greet one of your oldest friends."

A manic laugh leaves his lips. "Friends? Did you want me to say something like, 'Oh Millicent, it's so wonderful to see you after all these years.'"

"You might want to try it with a smile," I say, crossing my arms at my chest.

He gives the cheesiest smile I've ever witnessed.

I can't help but laugh. "Long time no see, huh?" I say.

"You're telling me," he says. "Last time I saw you, you were causing chaos and using a fake ID to go clubbing every weekend with Astra Sullivan."

I raise a brow at him. He's still sour from our Seven Minutes in Heaven. Which is strange because it was years ago.

"And last time I saw you, you were running around in tights LARPING with my brother and his friends at the lake and eating Funyuns in my basement while killing fictional beasts in an intense game of *Dungeons and Dragons*. What's your point?"

The corner of his lip twitches. He wants to smile, but he's trying to hold back. It's hard to take him seriously while he's wearing a *World of Warcraft* T-shirt.

"So, what's with the sign?" I nod to the HELP WANTED words behind him, so we can stop rehashing the past and move forward.

It's probably not the best plan of action, since it's Luke, but I need something.

"Why?" he asks.

"Maybe we got off on the wrong foot again. I'm sorry, Luke." My eyes meet his. I'm trying to show him I'm not the girl who was in the closet with him. I've changed, no matter how much that night still haunts me. "I lost my job in the city and I'm back home for a while. I worked—" I can't bring myself to say I wrote about sex. "I worked as a journalist for *Forever Twenty*. I wrote about … uh … womanly things."

Yeah, I said "things." The words "sex" feels weird to say in front of Luke. I'm a little hot and bothered by the memory of the closet and what I touched. I'll keep that to myself.

He purses his lips and leans against the opened door. He still hasn't invited me in. I get it. I'm probably the last person he wants to work with.

"Is this your studio?"

"It's Dad's," he says. "He wants to retire and is trying to teach me the ropes. He is looking to hire an extra hand to help with bookings and some on-the-job stuff too. Like assisting me, so I'm not overwhelmed."

Luke lowers his attention to the sidewalk and kicks a pebble. He's having a hard time keeping eye contact with me. Another thing that's never changed. He's always been shy and easily embarrassed.

I can't tell if his sour mood is because of what happened that night or not. I don't know what happened after I left. It did cross my mind a few times. Did they ridicule him because we clearly didn't kiss? Ezra never said anything if they had.

"I know I'm the last person you want to see—" I don't allow myself to look away. I have to let him know I'm serious and I'm not the girl who used to tease him.

He almost nods, but stops himself, catching my eyes.

"But I was basically an assistant for several years while I interned. As an intern I did it all. I worked in various departments helping file papers. I pick up on tasks really fast. When I interned in the photography department, they showed me how to do basic edits, and I got to pick some images for articles."

I check his reaction, only to be greeted by a blank stare.

"I also fetched coffee, but in your case, you'd probably send me on a mission for—what was it?" I tap my index finger against my lips. "...Hot chocolate with a hint of cinnamon?"

His eyes widen, but he still refuses to look at me. I don't know how I remember. It could be the many winters I spent helping Mom make cups of hot cocoa for Ezra and his friends while they played.

"Luke, I'm sorry about—you know." Now it's my turn to find a pebble to kick, but mine is invisible.

"That was years ago and it's not that."

He remembers.

"Then what is it? Have you had any other people interested?"

"No. We put up the sign yesterday."

"Then you don't have to look any further. I'll sit down with your father. He can interview me. I have my resume. He can look it over." I sigh, feeling like I'm getting nowhere. "I'm kind of desperate to get out of the house and work again."

Still, I'm greeted with silence.

"I have a blog and it does well, but I'm kind of terrible at taking pictures for my entries. I dunno, maybe you can teach me some things..." I shrug.

"I uh— do you think you could handle taking phone calls and booking clients?"

A smile tugs on my lips. I wait for him to acknowledge me. "You know you want that hot chocolate..." I half-laugh and wait for him to as well, but he doesn't budge.

"If you'll give me a chance, I can show you I'm not the same person I was all those years ago."

He's silent as he mulls over all the possibilities of my offer. I can't believe I'm sitting here begging Luke Parker of all people to hire me, but desperate times call for desperate measures. Who knows, maybe he'll inspire me to write a blog post. Sitting around my parents' house while I wait for a job to come to me is the last thing I want to do. I need this.

He sighs. "When can you start?"

I smile, thinking maybe I got through to him. "Whenever you need me."

A flush forms on his cheeks. He clears his throat, looks down, then back up. "Can you come in tomorrow around nine? Dad will be here, and I can show you the ropes."

"Do you mean that?" I step forward, the space between us dwindling. He moves back and slams into the door with a bang. I wince and retreat.

"Yeah."

Without thinking I break out in a scream and wrap my arms around him. He doesn't move an inch locked in my grasp. His hands are still by his side. I somehow have my face buried into the side of his neck, getting a whiff of his clean scent. It's fresh like he stepped out of the shower moments ago.

"Thank you, Luke. I promise I won't disappoint you again."

When I pull away his scent lingers in my nose. I can't quite read his expression. His head tilts to the side, raising a brow.

"You— Millicent, I—"

"It's fine. Look, I have to go pick up something for Mom at the bakery, but I promise things will be different between us. See you tomorrow?"

He doesn't finish whatever thought was on his mind. It stays buried. Instead, he says, "See you tomorrow."

I turn away without looking back as I head for the bakery. Tingles tickle the back of my neck, like I know he's watching, but I'm afraid to check. Thank God the bakery is close by. I slip inside the store and take a moment to catch my breath. *This is going to be okay. It's just Luke Parker, Ezra's friend, nothing more.*

"MILLICENT, IS THAT YOU?" Mom asks from the kitchen.

I make my way through our living room, and the entryway of

the kitchen. She's standing at the sink washing dishes. She dries her hands and finds my eyes.

"Ah. You got the cake."

Mom being mom, ordered me a strawberry shortcake. My favorite. I don't know if it was the interaction with Luke, and the repercussions of my behavior when I was younger, but when the employee handed me the cake decorated with *Welcome Home, We Missed you!* written in pink cursive on the frosting, I almost lost it. Now here I am standing in front of her, and I can't help it. Missing my family was the hardest part about being in Manhattan, but I didn't realize how much it affected them. I was close by, but with conflicting schedules it was hard to make time.

"Oh, sweetheart."

I put the cake on the table, so I don't drop it. Being home is bringing memories back. Ones I've spent years repressing. Like losing my best friend over one kiss, and the way I treated Ezra and his friends, my failure at being an adult, and everything coming crashing down. It's stupid, and there's other things in the world more severe, but my subconscious has chosen this moment to break down.

She crosses the room and in seconds I'm engulfed in Mom's hug. It's warm and inviting and it makes me never want to leave the comfort of it. I sob into her arms until there's nothing left. Then she opens the cake box, and we devour most of it, while we talk about things.

"I kind of got a job while I was out."

"Really?" She wipes her mouth with a napkin, then places it down on the table.

"Yeah, do you remember Luke Parker?"

She chokes on her cake and sips her milk. It takes her a minute.

"Jennifer said they had been looking for someone at the studio. Tony has been having some health issues with his heart and she thought it would be best for him to start taking it easy."

Jennifer is Luke's mom. "You still talk to her?"

"Yeah, on occasion."

Mom's eyes pop. There's something she's not telling me. I'm too tired to push, so I let it go.

"I'm so glad you found something. I think it will be good for you to get out of the house and work."

"Me too. And it's not like I have to stay forever. I can use it to get back on my feet, put something more on my resume, learn some extra tricks on taking photos. It's overall a good thing."

She smiles through her next bite. "Definitely."

CHAPTER 4

*I*f I didn't need something to occupy my hours, I would have turned around the moment I pulled up to Parker Photography. The onset of a migraine isn't helping either. There's an ache in my sore stiff neck, and the sunlight burns my eyes. I forgot my pills, but there's no going back now.

Inside the studio, beautiful family portraits, wedding photos, and pictures of fancy engagements hang on the wall. There's one wooden Ikea-style desk to my right. It's nothing crazy, something you could easily slap together in less than an hour. On top are some papers, a laptop, a phone, and a few shelves with papers jammed inside. Towards the back of the room is a large empty space. A cream-colored tarp hangs from the ceiling. Cameras and lighting equipment are set up around the area.

A door creaking in the back of the studio catches my attention. Footsteps follow and a second later Luke appears.

"Morning, boss," I say.

"Can you refrain from calling me that?" He's not amused.

"Yes ... sir?" I can't help grinning.

His eyes are cloudy, shoulders taut, and there's tension rolling off him like life got too heavy. My lips part with the words on my tongue, the urge to ask him how he's been sits there, but is interrupted by the back door opening and closing again.

Tony Parker is the spitting image of Luke. His eyes are eerily the same emerald color but hidden underneath round frame glasses. "Millicent, it's so nice to see you again."

At least he smiles. He reaches his hand out for me to take and covers mine. He's taller than Luke by a few inches. I'd put him around six feet. When I release his hand, he adjusts the strap of a camera case over his shoulder.

"I'm heading out for a shoot. Luke will get you settled. I'm sure I'll see you around. Thank you for offering your help."

"It was no problem, Mr—"

"Tony. Call me Tony." He gives one last smile before heading out.

Luke is quiet. As he always was. There's an awkward silence in the room. I'm sensing the sourness from high school lingering, so I distract myself by getting a better sense of the studio and their images.

"I have some edits I have to do. Let me show you the ropes up here." Luke walks over to the desk and leans against it, stretching out his long legs. He was never toned or muscular, still isn't. He didn't play sports but was a part of a lot of school clubs. He mostly kept to himself, but he always worked his ass off for his grades and being president of various clubs and activities. I never told him, but I admired him for it.

"Did—"

"And—"

We speak at the same time.

"You go first," I say.

"What was your job at the magazine again?"

"Writer." I cough to clear my throat.

"What did you write?"

"Se— relationships." There's heat rising in my cheeks, hot as an easy-bake oven erupting into flames. Talking to my younger brother's friend about sex is not exactly a comforting idea. Why make this anymore awkward than it already is?

He narrows his eyes at me, like he's trying to read my expression. Shifting his weight, he crosses his right leg over the left.

"I also uh— I have my own blog and Instagram page. I post some of my articles that didn't quite make the cut for publication."

"Good, we need some social media presence too. Dad gets kind of lazy with it. He's always grumping about having to post, so the responsibility usually lands on me, but I'm not a social media guy. Um— aside from that, you'll need to book clients and assist me on a few photoshoots."

Hanging on the wall behind the desk I take note of some awards and newspaper clippings regarding the studio. There's also a corkboard with five-star reviews cut out from magazines.

"Wow, your dad is legit."

"Yeah, it's legit." He mocks my word-use. "So, do you think you can handle it?"

"Yes bo— sir— er Luke." I grin, hoping it will help him relax a little, but I think I've agitated him more.

He rubs the scruff on his chin with his thumb while combing over me. His wide eyes wander from the tips of my knee-high laced brown suede boots to the denim button-down. The top two buttons are popped open exposing some skin and the tiniest hint of cleavage. He coughs a few times before finally his attention lands back on my face.

"Well, let's get to it then."

He pushes off the desk and stands straight. His eyes find mine for a second before he waves me over. Holding out his hands, he gestures for me to sit in the large computer chair.

He hits a few keys on the black keyboard and the computer jolts to life. His fingers do all the work as he pulls up spreadsheets. I'm entranced by his hands. They aren't large, but not small either, somewhere in between. There's a little bit of dark hair too. Are they calloused or smooth? His nails are neatly clipped. Some veins pop as he does his thing. Am I attracted to this? No. Okay maybe a little. I'm a sucker for nice hands.

"This is my client list."

I jump back into reality at the sound of his rough voice. He catches me and it's so hard to hold in my laughter. He has to know I was checking him out. With one last narrowed look, he turns back to the screen.

"I have bookings up until fall next year. I color coded everything. Purple is weddings, yellow is baby showers, engagements are blue..." He drones on for several minutes about which colors are for what kind of photos, including the miscellaneous ones.

"All the social media accounts are already logged in and stored on the computer. If you need a password for some reason, let me know."

"You got it, boss man."

He rubs at the bridge of his nose. There's got to be a way to break the ice between us. "I may need help with some events. There's a sweet sixteen this weekend and I could use some assistance."

"My availability is completely open."

"Great."

"So, I just sit here all day and wait for the phone to ring?"

He nods. "Pretty much."

"Awesome. Is there anything else?" I ask.

"No, I think that just about covers it. I may need you to add my fall promo to social media later. I'm trying to create the perfect image for it, but I can't be bothered with it right now. I have to edit a family photo session. Do you think you'll be okay out here?"

I smile. "I'll be just fine."

"Great. Thanks again for uh ... helping. Any questions I'll be in the back room."

"Aye-aye, captain!"

Luke sighs and rolls his eyes. I watch him walk away. He's decent looking from behind too. I wait for him to disappear then pull out my phone and start a new Google Docs document. I figure it doesn't hurt to get some writing done for my blog, even if it's just some ideas for new entries. I'll do anything to prove I belong back in the journalism field, and if blogging about sex is what sells, then I'm going to keep on writing about it.

CHAPTER 5

*I*t's been two hours and Luke hasn't emerged from the back room. The blank screen on my phone is a reminder of how my creative juices have vanished, as the black cursor mocks me with every blink.

With each passing hour I'm plagued with various migraine symptoms. I've worked through it before plenty of times but dealing with a grumpy boss is taking its toll on my head.

I try to occupy my time and ignore the throb behind my temples. I search the desk for something to do. The phones have been quiet, and I'm not sure what else there is to accomplish. Did he really need someone to sit here and twiddle their thumbs all day waiting for someone to call? There must be something else.

Scanning the area, I see a sketch of something drawn out on white computer paper. A rough draft of a promo sits submerged amongst the pile. A pink Post-it note on top reads—

Luke, the pictures you took for the fall ad are perfect. Can you please do a mock-up for me.

Thanks—Dad.

Below it is a list of discounts for back-to-school, fall family photos, and one for holiday pictures. On the bottom of the page are notes about the usable images in the promo folder.

I roll the chair towards the desk and log in with the password, then search the desktop for the folder. It's titled *Luke's Pictures (Fall Images)*. He's got hundreds of photos in there, from adorable families to pictures of kids with their back-to-school signs. I chuckle at the one with the parents drinking at the bus stop, their arms stretched out in a high five, while the kids pile onto the bus. There are some cute couples too, two females dressed as witches, then one witch down on her knee proposing. I love the Halloween vibe with the setting golden sun, the red and orange leaves, and the trees blurred in the background, and a cauldron with steam coming out for effect.

Before coming here, I didn't have a sense of who Luke Parker was as a photographer. I knew nerdy Luke from high school and his Night Elf costume from junior year, but this Luke, he has an eye for images. I kind of remember his yearbook shots, but they were nothing like these.

I take it upon myself to create a promo for him. It can't hurt. After an hour and a half more of fooling around the back door finally opens.

"Absolutely not, Gretchen. You can't just pretend like we're good. No, I'm at work. I can't. I'm uh—I just can't, okay?"

The desire to turn around at the sound of Luke's tense, wobbly voice is strong, but I decide against it. I try to put my full attention on the promo I made. He's mumbling, keeping his voice at a dull roar, probably so I can't hear.

A red squiggly line catches my attention under one of the words on the screen. I go in to fix it and sit back looking at my work. Crossing my arms at my chest I smile. At least I'm good at something. I really think he might—

"What are you doing?"

I spin. It was a bad idea. I'm nauseous now but carry on. "You told me you wanted me to help with social media so I—"

"I never asked you to go through my photos."

"Luke, I was just trying to help."

He runs a frustrated hand through his thick dark hair and grabs at his scalp. "Today you were supposed to take phone calls."

"There were zero phone calls. I got bored. Come on, look at it. I think this looks great."

He takes a deep breath. There's a bit of redness in his eyes and I can't tell if he'd been crying back there or if the red was out of anger. His cell is clenched in his fist at his side. I wonder who Gretchen is and why she's got him all riled up.

"You can go home for the day. I'll see you tomorrow."

"But Luke, I'm supposed to—"

"I have to close up early for a personal matter. Thank you for your help today." His eyelids look heavy and tired.

I want to reach out. He snapped at me, but the stress is rolling off him like an early morning fog.

"Okay. I'm sorry." I save my progress, because hell, I worked hard on it. I grab my bag from under the desk and stand. A wave of vertigo hits and I pause for a second.

"Are you—"

I hold up a hand. "I'm fine!"

His eyes are focused somewhere over my shoulder. I don't think he's looking at anything particular.

"I'll see you tomorrow," I say, quietly.

Luke doesn't respond. Before I reach the door, I crane my neck. He's holding on to the desk, his focus on the computer screen. There are words on the tip of my tongue, but I decide its best to leave him be.

What's your story, Luke Parker?

IT'S ONLY three by the time I get home, and I'm starving. Although I'm an adult, Mom is very serious about dinner. The day I moved back in I tried to have a snack while her sausage and peppers simmered in the crock pot. She shot that idea down as if I were a kid again. Today there's nothing on the stove or in the crock pot yet, so I think I'm safe.

I found relief with my migraine meds. I'm grateful the episode wasn't debilitating like some. It varies and I haven't had a bad one in a while, but I always try to be prepared.

Craving something sweet, I grab the tub of Friendly's ice cream from the old white freezer. This fridge has been in our kitchen since I was a teenager. It has sprung a small leak and occasionally spills out onto the floor. Dad insists he's getting a new one, but I don't see that happening.

Mom was always a bit old-fashioned when it came to interior decorating. Our kitchen still has the same yellow tile backsplash it came with when we moved before I started kindergarten. The cabinets never changed either. They've been painted several times over the years from all the scratches and indents Ezra and I made.

To the left of the sink is the drawer for spoons, and as I open it Mom clears her throat behind me, the entire container of ice cream almost slips from my hand.

"Hey, Mom!"

"Dinner will be here soon. Your brother is bringing over a pizza. You're going to spoil your appetite."

Because I'm not ten anymore, I rip open the top of the container, place it on the counter, and dip my entire spoon into it, then eat it.

Mom's brow rises. "Want to talk about it?" she asks.

"Luke's fun," I say, digging in, getting a pile larger than the spoon itself.

She pulls out a chair at the small round table in the center of the room and sits. Then she moves the one next to hers and pats the seat. I grab the top of the container and stalk over. Plopping down into the chair, I take another huge bite.

"What happened? You were nice? Please tell me you were nice."

"Of course, I was nice, Mom. I'm an adult, I know how to play fair."

Mom purses her lips.

"The guy hardly smiles, it's like he has a stick up his—"

"Who's got a stick up their ass?" Ezra comes strolling into the house, his boyfriend Jake in tow. Everyone always assumed Ezra and I were twins by our similar facial features and matching almond-shaped eyes.

"Jake!" I shout.

"I don't have a stick up my ass." Jake's smoky brown eyes meet mine, and he grins. He's like a second brother to me. He was also part of their little *Dungeons and Dragons* crew back in the day.

"Not you, your old buddy, Luke."

"You saw Luke?" Jake asks.

After high school Luke went off and did his own thing. He went to school in California and lost touch.

"Uh-huh. I'm working with him at his dad's photography studio. Well, it will all soon be his."

Ezra places the pizzas down on the counter between the stove and sink. He turns and leans back. "Oh, that's right, I forgot he worked there. We're Facebook friends," he says.

Ezra pushes a strand of his wavy blond hair from his eyes. I can't help laughing to myself at Ezra's shirt. It's almost the exact same one as Luke's, but instead his shirt says Rogue.

"Apparently you all must be on the same wavelength with your apparel too."

"Don't knock some good nerd gear. I wonder if he still plays *D&D*. We could use an extra guy. Matt up and left, he had one fight with Tracy about how she doesn't know how to DM and all hell broke loose and they both quit." Ezra taps his lip.

"You lost me at DM. Like a direct message?"

"Dungeon master," Jake says, making himself at home by grabbing some plates for the pizza.

"Right. I knew that. I could ask him if you want."

"Could you? We play Thursday nights at our house."

Ezra and Jake have been friends forever, but their relationship bloomed into more about three years ago. They moved in together last fall. I'm beyond happy for my brother.

Jake walks back over to Ezra and shoves him playfully away from the pizza so he can start serving.

"Ice cream and pizza would kill my stomach."

Ezra watches me with an amused grin on his face while I shove the heaped scoop of ice cream into my mouth.

"This sucker can handle anything." I smile, patting my belly.

Dinner with Ezra and Jake is always nice. Dad unfortunately had to work late tonight, so it was just us. Living in the city I didn't get a chance to have these dinners often and, in a way, it felt a little lonely. I had Cheryl and co-worker friends, but nothing compares to dinner with your family. There's a small part of me that wants to drag out this unemployed status and stick around for a little longer, no matter how miserable it might be working with Luke. I like home, it's safe. But I wish I didn't feel as if I'd failed Adulting 101.

CHAPTER 6

$\mathcal{I}$t took me three alarms before I wanted to move this morning. Now I'm sitting in my car outside the studio, because I'm not sure I want to go in. Luke has always been kind of grumpy and stand-offish. I don't know why, but it seems more so now that we're older.

I'm scrolling through Twitter when the hairs on my neck stand. As I lift my chin, my eyes meet his through the window of the storefront. There's no hiding now. I slip my phone into my tan bag, swing it over my shoulder, and exit the car.

The door opens before I reach it. Today we've moved from a *World of Warcraft* shirt to *Critical Role*. I only know the web series, in which pro voice actors play *Dungeons and Dragons*, because of Ezra and Jake. I had gone to their house for dinner one Sunday and they decided it would be the perfect day to rewatch both the first and second campaigns starting from season one.

Luke's eyes remain focused on the ground, his cheeks a slight shade of crimson.

"Good morning," I say, trying to sound a bit cheerful. I pause in the doorway.

He mumbles something that sounds like *good morning*, but I can't be sure.

Instead of nagging him I head to my desk and take a seat, placing my bag underneath. "What's happening today, boss?"

He strolls over, rounding the right side of the desk, then leans against it, and shifts to face me.

"I know it's not my place," I say, "but uh— are you okay? Yesterday you were…"

His death glare says it all. I pinch my fingers together and pretend to zip my mouth closed. If I'm not mistaken, his lip might have very faintly twitched upwards. If I wasn't staring at him, I wouldn't have even noticed.

"I'm sorry," he says. "I looked over what you made yesterday, and it's really good."

"It's fine. If you're not going to use it—"

"I think I might want to. I mean if that's okay?"

"Really? That kind of makes me feel good." I huff a small laugh.

"Yeah. Really." He lowers his head and scratches at the back of his neck. "Did no one ever compliment your work at your last job?"

His words take me back to the day I got fired. How excited I was moments before my world came crashing down. The feeling of not being good enough has made me worry about my future in the industry and taken a toll on other aspects of my life.

Luke's eyes soften. "There's a lot you're not saying, huh?" He's reading me, better than most.

I try to look away to hide the emotion that I'm sure is plastered on my face. "Not really sure how to say it."

"Understandable." He runs a hand through his dark hair. He's still guarded. There's a mixture of uncertainty, sadness, and maybe a hint of forgiveness in his emerald eyes, but whatever it is never reaches the surface.

"Saturday, would you be able to help me with an event?" he

asks, changing the subject. "It would help me out a lot if I had someone to hold on to the extra camera and some equipment."

"Sure. No problem."

I expect him to move, but he doesn't. His attention is back on the ground. He's still the same awkward weird Luke from high school.

"Anything else?"

"No. I'll let you get to work." He pushes himself off the desk.

I swivel the chair to watch him. His shoulders are slumped forward like there's a heavy weight riding on them. "Hey, Luke." My voice catches in my throat.

He spins. "Yeah?"

"Ezra and Jake do Thursday night *D&D* games. They wanted me to ask if you'll join them."

"Oh. I uh… haven't played in years."

"Clearly you must still be into it if you're wearing that shirt." I lean back in my chair and cross my arms at my chest.

He squints, narrowing those piercing green eyes at me. "You know what this is?"

"I might have been forced to watch it one rainy Sunday."

A hidden grin surfaces, but barely reaches his eyes. "It's been a while since I've seen any of them. Are you sure they want me?"

"Yup! That's what they said. They are desperate: two of their players up and left. I mentioned you and I were buds and they begged me to ask you."

He scoffs. "Is it possible your sarcasm game has gotten better since high school?"

I purse my lips at him. It sounds like he's being playful, but I can't tell. "I've always been on point with my sarcasm. So, what should I tell Ezra and Jake?" I take my phone out and pull up the last text I sent to Ezra.

"I'll think about it."

"It's a yes or a no, man. They need a kickass Druid. And from what I'm told you're the man of wisdom."

Luke raises a brow, once again hiding a smile behind his eyes. Maybe he's easier to read than I thought. "You should play too."

A pig-like snort comes from me, and I cover my mouth. My cheeks burn. "I'm good. Are you in or not?" I hold up my phone and wait for him to answer.

He doesn't like my snippy remark. It's written all in his tight features. I almost want to take it back but decide against it. The stubborn side of me doesn't want to.

"Yeah. Tell him to text me the info. I've got to get some edits done. Can you try to behave today?"

"I'm always good. And I promise you won't regret your decision about D&D. My brother couldn't stop talking about how when you left for college, they lost their fiercest player."

"Get to work, Gibson," he says, in a jocular tone

CHAPTER 7

"So, are you ready to slay some dragons tonight? Ezra said you're joining them."

He puckers his lips, while staring down at the camera lenses in his hands. He's got a microfiber cloth and a bottle of some kind of cleaner and has been here in the back area of the main floor for the last half an hour. It was quiet so I came over to talk to him.

"We don't just slay dragons, just because it's in the title," he says dryly.

I shrug. "Ezra and Jake are really happy you'll be there. What happened with you guys anyway?" I ask, reaching out for one of the cameras.

Without looking up he shoos my hand away.

"So feisty."

He sighs. "Nothing happened. We just grew apart like most people do after high school. Do you still talk to Astra?"

Without thinking my hand connects with my chest. It's like I can still feel the open wound. She was in my life every day from the time we were in elementary school until the graduation party. We spoke and hung out after, but nothing was ever the same. It's been years, but the sting has never left.

"I— she—"

He finds my eyes briefly, then returns to wiping the outer edge of the lens.

"What's a Druid?" I ask, changing the subject, thinking back to what Jake and Ezra said the other night.

He laughs.

"What?"

"Nothing. Do you really want to know?"

"Distract me? Please?" I can hear the desperate plea for a subject change in my weary voice, and apparently so can he.

He finally looks at me, like really looks. His lip twitches into an almost smile as he dips his chin. "They—" He starts but gets interrupted by his phone vibrating on the table.

It's right on the edge where I'm standing. The name Gretchen appears. He was talking to her the other day. His demeanor goes from almost amicable back to hostile. He swipes the phone. Ignoring me he answers, "What?"

He stands, nearly knocking the folding chair behind him.

"The date is set. No, I'm not going back on my word. It's done. I wish you'd stop calling me when I'm at—" His voice fades as he slips into the back office.

I spin, leaning against the table and shut my eyes. I wonder what that's all about. Maybe I'll pull it out of him eventually, but we're not "friends" yet, so it's not my place to ask.

I take a seat back at the computer and answer a few incoming calls. I go through the motions of working, posting some photos Luke asked me to onto their Instagram page. I'm grateful I have a job again, happy to be with my family, I love where I grew up, but I never thought I'd come back. It's not that I wanted to run away and forget, it's that I wanted to move on from it. Maybe my dreams were too big. Too far out of reach. Whatever force brought me back here, I hope that it can figure out how to sling-shot me back out where I belong.

ॐ

SEXUAL TENSION IN THE WORKPLACE. Been done. Falling for an old rival, another overdone topic. Falling for the nerd—nope, nope, nope. I feel guilty when Luke's face pops into my mind. I wish my brain would work. Ever since I got laid-off my ideas have run dry. I used to be so good at spouting out ideas at meetings and my boss being like, *yes go for it, girl!* Now it's me, in my room and the same old blank page.

Instead of doing my work, I find myself scrolling through Facebook. I can't help wondering how *D&D* night is going. I was tempted to show up in one of my brother's old costumes, just to be an ass. Then I decided against it, because if I don't come up with something soon, my brain might turn to mush, and I'll never write a single article again.

I try to ignore the twist in my heart as my Facebook feed tortures me with pictures of Astra. Luke mentioning her set off emotions that I've suppressed. Her profile picture is only of her, but her latest status is rambling about an anniversary with her fiancée. Every time I think I've muted her profile, it pops up again, like it's mocking me.

Still in love with your best friend—the ten best ways to get over it. Ugh! I slam the laptop down. There's no way I can write an article about getting over someone, when my heart has never fully recovered. Although I did write about sex for years without having any, so maybe I could. I don't know. I need something groundbreaking, something to get me seen, but I have no idea what that is.

I lie back on my bed. It's so quiet here on Long Island. Compared to the chorus of ambulance sirens at all hours of the night, drunk people screaming outside my window, sometimes a car backfiring that sounded like a gunshot, and large rats raiding trash cans at three in the morning, wasn't exactly comforting, but it meant I'd made it in the world. At least to me it did. I close my eyes and try to imagine I'm back in my own apartment with my career still intact. As I do my phone goes off. It's almost out of reach, halfway down the bed. Grabbing it I check my messages.

> Ezra: You didn't tell me Luke got hot!

I chuckle quietly to myself.

> Me: Does Jake know you're drooling over Luke?

I wait a few minutes for my brother to finish typing.

> Ezra: He's the one who brought it up. I simply agreed. You should snatch him up, he's a good dude.

> Me: A good dude? You sound like Mom.

I close my eyes again. Even though adult Luke is scrumptious, his attitude irks me. Plus, I'm not looking to date right now. I'm more worried about my career than finding someone to settle down with.

> Ezra: He lights up when he talks about you.

I blink several times as I reread his message. I can't imagine Luke lighting up in any way.

> Me: Stop bullshitting me and go back to leading your people to victory. I don't need a partner. I need a real job.

Seconds later he types back.

> Ezra: I know, but it doesn't hurt to open yourself up to something.

I roll my eyes. Now he's being ridiculous.

CHAPTER 8

$\mathcal{T}$he scent of cherry envelops me as I step into Luke's SUV. The small fruit-shaped air freshener swings back and forth on the mirror.

"Afternoon, boss," I say, earning a scowl from Luke.

He's all decked out in his tux. It's hard to see the full view with him sitting down but Luke really has grown into himself. He throws his arm over the back of my seat, as he turns to look over his shoulder to ease out of the spot. I smirk when I see he's sporting a small red bow tie, instead of a regular one.

"What's with the grin?" he questions, as we move forward.

"Nothing. You look handsome, that's all."

He snorts. Aha! One point for Millicent. Maybe breaking the barrier between us is easier than I thought.

It's three o'clock on a Saturday and we're heading into the ritzy area of Nassau County for a sweet sixteen. The country club where the event is taking place is close to the border of Nassau and Queens. It's probably going to take us a bit to get there being that it's the weekend.

"So, how was *D&D*?" I ask.

Luke remains focused as we get onto the expressway. After a

few seconds of merging into traffic and safely navigating to the HOV lane, he finally answers. "It was good. I missed those guys."

He pauses for a second. "So, Ezra and Jake, huh? I'm glad those two finally stopped dancing around each other. I was rooting for them the whole time."

"Me too." I grin.

The small smile on his lips makes my heart jump. Lips that I almost kissed. Not sure why but my eyes zero in on them. He's not paying attention to me. His eyes are on the road. What would have happened if we had? It's a question I've been asking myself for years. Maybe it's the abstinence talking.

"Music?" he asks, pulling me from my ridiculous thoughts. *Thank you, Luke.*

"Depends. Is it a movie soundtrack or something normal?"

"Pshh, movie soundtracks are normal."

I'm surprised I remembered that about him. There was one time when Mom had to drive him home and drop me off at dance class. We rode in the backseat together and had a full-on debate about score soundtracks vs regular ones.

"Okay, so I'll admit the *Twilight* score actually helped me get through my first few nights in the city. It was loud and terrifying, and I threw that bad boy on with my headphones and—" I stop talking, because he's staring at me mouth agape.

In front of us is a clusterfuck of traffic, so we're not moving.

"What's with that look?" I ask.

Shaking his head, he grins, just slightly enough to throw in the Luke charm I used to see when he'd play games with Ezra.

"*Twilight*? Out of all the ones you could choose, you pick *Twilight*?"

I push his shoulder, playfully. The tension in the car slowly dissipates as our conversations become lighter and easier. As I predicted, the CD in his car is in fact a score soundtrack. It's not the worst thing we could be listening to—the techno beats are catchy—but it's not something I'd ever listen to on my own.

By the time we reach the venue, we have only fifteen minutes to prepare. Being that this is my first event I'm not sure what to expect. I anticipate Luke to be a little less cranky, but as we pull up his demeanor changes and in a strictly monotone voice runs through the plan for the night.

We enter the place and I'm immediately blown away by the atmosphere. I almost feel underdressed in my best tight red dress. Stunning chandeliers hang from the main lobby, shining bright. It's pristine, and there's not a single scuff mark on the cream-colored tile floor. I'm finding it hard to pull away from such a beautiful sight.

Not only the venue; but Luke really does look amazing. I've got a full view of him, and my eyes can't help combing over his entire body. Am I attracted to this? It's been a while since any guy has captured my attention. Again, I blame my dry spell for causing my hormones to rage.

He clears his throat, eyes meeting mine. "Hi." It comes out high-pitched.

I've been caught.

"Would you be okay to hold this backpack?" he asks.

"Sure."

He hands it to me, and his shoulders fall with relief. I grab it and realize it's much heavier than I imagined it would be. My shoulder aches just from the initial impact of the weight.

"Are you sure you're okay with that?"

He doesn't seem convinced I can handle it. I'll show him.

"Yup," I squeak, adjusting it to find a better position.

Luke is all business now as we reach the ballroom, and that's understandable. It doesn't stop me from wanting to chip away at his wall. Out of all of Ezra's friends. I always gravitated towards Luke. The other guys never held my attention the way he did. Not sure what it was about him.

"Come on. Let's get to work," he says.

THE PARTY IS in full swing, and I've been busy helping with lighting. This immaculate space makes me think about my sweet sixteen. The girl whose party we are photographing is stunning in her subtle yet unique makeup, and beautiful soft pink fluffy ball gown. She's got jewels in her hair, and a crown that probably costs more than my rent when I was living in the city. Her present table is also overflowing with gifts, and her friendship circle, and family takes up the entire room.

My party was small and in the backyard. I got a dress from Macy's on clearance, and Mom catered the party through a local deli. I had my closest friends, and a few family. I do remember a photographer, though, and he took this one photo that is still hanging on the wall in my parents' house. An idea strikes.

Luke's got his camera up taking pictures of the cake. I tap him on the shoulder, he spins, and stares with a questioning raise of his eyebrow.

"Can I make a suggestion for a picture?"

His brows now knit together, like he's contemplating it. "What did you have in mind?"

I have no control over my body as I pull him into a hug and grin. He steps back, nearly knocking into the table with the cake. I grab his arm to hold him steady, and his eyes flash to mine in an instant.

"I uh— I." I lost myself for a moment, I'd almost forgotten how under all the hardness how kind his eyes really are. They soften and wait for me to talk.

"Well, my mom has this photo of me in the grass..." I look around. "There's no grass here, but anyway, the photographer had me sit and my dress was sprawled out around me, he stood above pointing the camera down, then he asked my friends to join. They fanned out around me. The picture looks amazing, and it's one of my favorites. Maybe we could try it."

He's quiet for a moment, but even over the loud music it's like I can hear his thoughts just through his wandering eyes.

"Okay. Show me what you mean then."

I squeal and I'm almost ready to hug him again, but step back.

"Thank you!"

Rushing over I tap the birthday girl on her arm. Her raven black hair sits on her shoulders, it curls and twirls all the way down to her stomach. Something else to be jealous about, her hair is gorgeous, while mine is flat, straight, brown, and boring.

"Can you gather your friends for a shot?"

"Sure," she says, grinning wide.

Once she has everyone, I place her and her friends in the circle. Luke stands behind me observing my chaotic movements. She and I carefully pull out her dress so that it surrounds her in its beauty. Once I've gotten everyone to my liking, Luke takes a few practice shots and adjusts a couple of kids. He grabs a chair and takes the picture from higher up.

When he's satisfied, I extend my hand to help him down. As our hands touch, a warming sensation skitters up my arm heating me up to the core. He jumps to the ground, and I pull my hand away.

"It came out really great," he says, handing me the camera.

We lean in together, our heads almost touching. I pull back slightly.

He's right: standing up higher made the photo so much more beautiful. I lift my head and was unaware of how close our faces are. He's still staring at the picture, so I take the time to study his features, and the stubble on his face.

"It's amazing."

He lowers the camera and his hand brushes mine. There's only a sliver of space between us. The jolt of electricity that surges through makes me retreat.

"Say cheese." He steps back, puts the camera to his face, and snaps a picture of me when I'm not even ready.

"Oh my God, Luke Parker, how dare you catch me off guard." I laugh.

There's no mistaking the miniscule smile on his face. I'm not sure why but the thought of being the one to bring out the playful side of him fills me with a strange sense of joy. Maybe I'm looking for his forgiveness for all the times that I wasn't so kind. At first this job was just a way for me to work, keep busy, and not lose my sanity while being at home. A steppingstone. It's somehow turning into more, like it's a way to feel better about who I was before *Forever Twenty*. Whatever it is, I think I like the change.

"I'm going to use the restroom. Is that okay?" I need to step out for a moment and catch my breath, figure out what the hell is going on and why I'm wanting him to accidentally touch me again.

"Yeah, take a little break. Grab some food."

I jerk my chin in his direction. "What about you?"

"I have a few power bars to get me through. I'll probably pick at a few things, but usually I grab something on the way home."

"Oh. Care to share a bar with me? Fancy food isn't really my thing."

He smirks. "You mean you don't like caviar?"

Chuckling, I say, "I'd rather eat a McDonald's hamburger."

"Micky D's it is." Luke's smile doesn't reach his eyes, but it's progress.

CHAPTER 9

"Mmm, now this is good stuff," I say, my mouth filled with a Big Mac.

I choke a little, and he hands me a napkin. An amused look passes in his eyes but vanishes quickly. We've made some progress tonight and I don't want to destroy that.

We decided to sit in the parking lot at McDonald's and eat before driving back to the studio.

"What have you been doing since I last saw you?" I ask.

It's his turn to choke on his burger. The last time we really had any interaction was in the closet. I lift his drink, towards him.

"Thanks." He takes a sip. "I went to California State for photography. What about you? You stayed in New York, um... NYU, was it?"

My laughter comes out breathy. "Y-you remembered?"

"You talked about it non-stop. There's no forgetting that."

My cheeks feel warm with his confession. I look away, concentrating on eating. He's not wrong. I had been obsessed with NYU since I could remember. I was scared I wouldn't get in because it's such a well-known, top-notch school, but I somehow managed. This side of Luke is nice. We've had okay conversations before, but this feels a little different.

"Are you still friends with Astra?"

My heart freefalls into my stomach, I grab hold of the *holy shit* handle to keep myself steady. My burger almost tumbles off my lap. I count backwards in my head as I take deep inhales. Best friend break-ups are much worse than relationship break-ups. When you spend most of your life with a person and then they walk away, it's painful. I think what hurts the most is knowing that was the person you confided in.

"We uh... we still talk." It's kind of a lie, but he doesn't have to know that.

"Are you still uh... you date women, right?"

I cough like I've come down with the flu, my chest aches, and I smack myself hard to make it stop.

"Well, that doesn't sound good."

I chuckle through my coughing fit. "Are you asking for you or research purposes?" I grin.

He scratches the back of his neck with his free hand. His cheeks flush a deep pink, the color spreading to his neck. "I uh— I—" He stammers, and I instantly feel guilty for throwing him under the bus with that one.

"I'm bisexual. I date both. But if you must know, I'm going through a dry spell."

He's quiet for a few moments. "I'm sorry, Millicent."

"Don't be, Luke. It's fine." Another long pause falls between us. I toss a few fries in my mouth, and he sips on his drink, biting down on the straw. His leg shakes, vibrating the car. "What about you, are you dating anyone?"

"Nope. Are you ready to go?" He shoots back quickly, as he crumbles the wrapper in his hands with such a force that I almost think the paper will disintegrate in his hands. He doesn't even wait for me to say that I'm done before starting up the car. We sit idle in the lot. The light from the lamp post illuminates the inside of the car. His jaw clenches and a muscle in his cheek twitches with agitation.

"I'm good to go." I stop for a moment, watching him clutch the wheel in his hand and taking deep breaths. "You okay?"

"Fine. Just, perfectly fine," he says, before putting the car into reverse and backing out of the spot.

Well, there goes progress, I guess. I find it irritating that he can ask me things, but when I do the same to him, he panics. I'm not going to give up though. Luke and I have a strained relationship and while I'm here, fixing it will be one of my goals, especially if he's going to be hanging around Ezra again. No need to make things awkward.

I EXPECTED to have a relaxing Sunday. Luke and I didn't get back to the studio until almost one in the morning. I've been trying to nap, but Ezra, Jake, and my parents are way too loud.

Downstairs I find them all sitting in front of the TV watching football. Ezra hates football, but Dad and Jake have a team rivalry going on. Jake's all decked out in his Giants jersey, while Dad is in a Jets one. Ezra looks bored out of his mind, he's scrolling through his phone most likely reading, while Mom sits quietly in the corner knitting.

All eyes are on me.

"Did you just wake up?" Ezra asks.

"I was out late," I say, shoving him so that he makes room for me on the old brown sofa.

Dad shouts at the TV and gets to his feet. Unlike Mom, Ezra, and me, Dad's tall, nearing six foot. How Ezra and I never got the tall gene is unknown. Mom's around four eleven, and Ezra and I are just over five feet.

"Out late with whom?" Jake wiggles his brows.

"She was with Luke at a party." Leave it to my mother to make it more than it was. She says it in this sultry voice as if he and I were out having sex all night.

"Working, Mom!" I shout. "I was working."

Dad's dark brown eyes meet mine. "Luke?"

"Ugh. We were working a sweet sixteen and then..."

"She didn't come back until almost one in the morning."

"Mom," I growl at her.

Ezra is laughing beside me. I nudge him with my elbow. He chuckles. "Ow."

"We were at some ritzy place near Queens, don't start with me. We grabbed McDonald's on the way back and ate it in the car. That's why I was late," I say, poking Ezra's arm.

I'm still a bit confused over Luke's reaction to my question last night. After overthinking it on the ride home I think it might have to do with some of those phone calls he's been getting from that Gretchen girl. I'd ask Ezra, but then he'd accuse me of crushing on Luke and I'm not. I'm only trying to make things right.

"Ow. Mom." He whines like a child. "She poked me."

"Millicent dear, don't poke your brother."

I sigh.

"How is it going with Luke?" Ezra asks.

"It's fine. Nothing to report."

"He is handsome though, isn't he?" Mom teases, hiding behind the large blanket she's knitting.

"Oh my God!"

"She's not lying," Jake says, his attention more on the TV than me.

"What do you want me to say, he's hot?" I ask. My cheeks heat up saying the words out loud.

"She's blushing," Ezra teases.

"Okay, I'm done here. If you want me to join you for dinner, please let me know." I start to stand, and Ezra pulls me back down.

"We're just joking, relax, but when's the wedding?"

I leap sideways and tackle him onto the couch. He drops his phone on the floor. Jake's beside him and Dad at the very end, but I'm ignoring them. Ezra is crying from laughing so hard, and Mom is just watching us shaking her head. My brother and I never had any kind of real fight, only play-fighting like this. I could never be truly mad as he was my strongest supporter and the first person I told when I came out.

Ezra fixes his shirt as I lay off him.

"Stop being a jerk," I say.

"Just looking out for you."

"And I appreciate that, but like I said, I'm happy being single."

"That's my girl," Dad shouts.

Ezra and I stick our tongues out at each other then go back to watching the game. I find football to be boring, but I don't mind, because I'm here with my family and it feels good to not have to rush out of here to go to an empty apartment, alone.

CHAPTER 10

*T*he weather is changing faster than I expected, and my Toyota doesn't like it. She groans and skitters to a halt as I turn the key in the ignition. A burgundy red leaf flitters from the tree above, landing on my windshield. As I open the car door, a breeze flows through. The studio is only a short distance, but I'm not walking. This Manhattan girl who could walk in any weather has reverted to the "I'm cold and need the heater girl." Plus, it's a completely different type of walk. An empty narrowed sidewalk with traffic whizzing by does not compare to a city block in Manhattan.

I pull up Luke's name on the phone. We have been somewhat amicable since the sweet sixteen a few weeks ago. He picks up on the first ring, but the connection is muffled. He's already driving.

"Hey, it's Millicent. I know we have that gender reveal today, but my car decided to crap out. Could be the battery; it's always giving me issues. Mom and Dad left to do some fall activities together out east, and I can't bug Ez or Jake because they are at a friend's wedding. So, I'm stuck home."

"I'm a few blocks away; I'll come get you."

"You don't have to…"

"It's fine. You guys haven't moved, have you?"

"Nope, same house."

I shiver from the wind whipping around. My hair has a mind of its own and keeps falling into my line of sight. Today's event is outdoors. The cloudless vibrant sky doesn't look to be changing any time soon, and hopefully it warms up for the mom-to-be.

"Alright. No problem. I'll be there in a minute."

"Thanks, Luke."

I close the car door, lock it up, and shove my keys in my purse. By the time I walk up the driveway Luke's SUV is pulling up at the curb. He rolls down the window. "I can look at your car after work if you want?"

"Oh, so you're a mechanic too?" I ask, stepping up to the opened window.

"My uncle's a mechanic. He taught me a few basic things. Actually, if you need somewhere to go, I can make a phone call." His fingers dance on the steering wheel.

"That would be great."

"Door's open, hop in." His head leans in the direction of the passenger seat.

The moment I'm settled in the car he pulls away from the curb. His hands grasp the wheel, knuckles white as a sheet. A thick silence falls around us; not even the radio is on. Does he always drive to work without music? Why isn't he playing his favorite soundtrack?

His phone is attached to one of those devices on the dashboard. It's still lit up and on the call log. Gretchen occupies almost every space, minus a few random numbers, and then mine at the top. This Gretchen woman has no chill, my goodness. And just this morning she called him three times in ten minutes.

Luke reaches out, turning the screen off. I clear my throat. He's well aware that I was staring. I should ask about it, but not now, not when we have a whole day together.

"So, a photographer, and handy with cars. Anything else I should know about you?"

"Not really," he says, his eyes never leaving the road.

We inch forward through a small intersection that leads to the main road. He's driving like my grandma, but I won't say it out loud. He was less on edge when we went to the sweet sixteen. Something has gotten into him today. My guess is Gretchen.

Over the past couple of weeks working with Luke I've gotten to know some of his mannerisms, and his ticks right before he's about to have a mini meltdown. Usually those are the moments when he retreats to the back room and stays there.

"What made you fall in love with photography?"

His free leg bounces as we wait for the lights to change. "What's with the twenty questions?"

The car zooms to life as we follow the car in front of us. Flipping the blinker on Luke glances in my direction then back to the minor traffic jam near the heart of town.

"It's better than awkward silence."

"I prefer the latter."

"Writing, even if it's an article about something real; it helps me lose myself and creates a barrier between what's happening to me in real life, and what I'm writing about."

If silence had a voice, it would be screaming. He concentrates on merging into the left lane, his lips taut, and body rigid. "There's something about the beauty of capturing a single moment that I love."

His words catch me off guard, and I turn my attention to him to figure out if I imagined him talking.

"My favorite thing to shoot is people having a good time, or nature in motion. You never know what you'll capture. I've had brides and grooms tell me that their favorite photos are those when they weren't paying attention. There was this one…"

He pauses for a moment and checks my reaction. I'm hooked on him unable to turn away.

"It was a newborn shot, and the parents were trying to position the baby in their arms when the little sucker peed straight up nailing the dad in the forehead. I captured it, and the photo is on their wall."

Our laughter swirls together, the tension from a few moments ago is slowly dissipating.

"Now that's a shot worth saving," I say.

"Totally is. I've never laughed so hard during a session."

I find myself watching Luke and admiring the way his cheekbones lift as he smiles. It's one of the first genuine smiles I've caught. His lips turn down as we pull into a spot in front of the studio. It's too bad the moment couldn't have lasted longer.

"I have to run inside really quick to get the stuff."

"I packed everything before we left yesterday. Do you want me to run in and get it?"

"Thanks, but I got it. I'll be back in a jiff."

I snort. He glares at me, but the edge of his lip lifts ever so slightly, and I know I've chipped a teeny tiny piece of his wall.

"I wish I had funny stories about work like a peeing baby," I say.

We've been on the road for twenty minutes. We're heading out east, to the north fork, and from the studio will take at least another twenty minutes. The eastern end of Long Island is popular on weekends, even in the fall. There's pumpkin and apple picking, and people from all the way west near the city trek out here for their country-like activities.

"There's got to be something."

"Nope. Unless you count the time that my friend was researching an article about which tampon was best, and then lost the string to take it out. I had to read out loud how to remove it while she attempted to dislodge it."

Luke chokes.

"TMI?" I ask.

"Women's magazines, I'll never understand them."

I chuckle. "I'll admit it wasn't my first choice, but they offered good benefits and it got my name out there."

"What did you write about?"

"I— uh— relationships," I squeak.

I don't know why I'm having trouble talking to him. I can do this.

"Oh, so you're an expert on that?"

"Well—" I pause for a moment to figure out how to explain. "My articles have been based mostly on other people's experiences. Some of my own."

"What are some of the things you've written about?"

I know I shouldn't push but the temptation is there. Teasing him is like second nature to me.

"You want to hear the dirty stories or—" I grin.

The blush spreading all over his face and neck, stirs up something in me. I think I might like it but won't ever admit that out loud. "Sorry. It was hard to resist."

He scowls, but the corner of his lip twitches and I think I can give myself a half a point for that one.

"I wrote one about the best sexual position for uh— for— women." I clear my throat.

The article was based off my experience as a bisexual woman and focused on those relationships.

Luke shifts in his seat and clenches his jaw. I'd rather not go into the full details of the article. Joking about it is easy but discussing it for real. No. I can read the room—or the car.

"Well, we're almost there," he says, changing the subject. His blush deepens.

"I made you uncomfortable, didn't I?"

"No. I uh... I've had sex. It's not uncomfortable. Did you write a lot of sex articles?"

I lower my head so he can't see the ridiculous grin on my face.

"I had my fair share," I say.

"Oh." Luke scratches at his throat hard enough to leave marks against his skin. "About the gender reveal." His voice is high-pitched like a young boy. "I'm gonna give you one of the small Polaroid cameras. I want you to take some shots with it for me."

"Sounds like fun."

And that's it, the conversation ceases as we drive the rest of the way in silence.

CHAPTER 11

I can't help my wandering eyes, apparently neither can he. He looks away first, as he makes a turn onto a small narrow road. Cars are lined up along the road making it a little hard to pass by. There's a beautiful one-floor home a few houses down. A wooden archway covered in purple and pink flowers sits in front of their white fence.

Luke finds a spot down the road. We grab the equipment, and once again I know I'll wake up with a sore shoulder in the morning.

Before we get inside, he's already taking photos of the archway, and the beautiful wooden sign that welcomes everyone to The Bakers' gender reveal party. As we enter a stunning woman with a blonde braid that reaches down to her tiny baby bump smiles at her incoming guests. Her smile widens when it lands on us. Her flowing periwinkle dress sways in the soft fall breeze as she walks towards us.

"Luke, you made it." She leans in and kisses his cheek.

She's awfully friendly for a client, there's got to be some story there.

He smiles. "Yes. Sorry the traffic was a little bit of a mess on the expressway. Um, Julie, this is my assistant Millicent."

Julie's brown eyes glow as she takes me in. "Hi. Millicent, that's a beautiful name. It's lovely to meet you."

Luke looks at me. "Julie and I went to college together. Her husband and I worked in the IT department together."

"Ah. Got it."

"Those two could geek out for hours about computer parts. Come on in, Darin will be thrilled to see you."

She throws me a sweet smile, and my attention lands on the beautiful crown that reminds me of my favorite Disney princess.

"Your crown is beautiful," I say, as we follow Luke into the yard.

A soft melody plays through speakers hanging off the side of the simple white colonial home. As we enter the backyard, I'm enthralled by the beauty of the landscaping and decor set up around the yard.

"This is a *Tangled* party?" I ask, my eyes wandering the entire stretch of land. It's not an oversized property, but it's the perfect space for the number of guests that are here.

There's a cobblestone banner that hangs along the entire perimeter of the back fence. In front of one of the stretches of fencing is a blue and pink backdrop with different sized balloons in different colors as a border. This is picture-perfect, I'm in awe.

"She's my favorite princess. That's cheesy, isn't it?" she asks.

I shake my head. "Not at all, she's my favorite too."

"Ah, there's Darin."

Underneath a large white canopy tent is a man dressed exactly like Flynn Ryder. Brown and green fabric fits his well-endowed muscular body.

Julie skips towards her man, and I lean forward grabbing Luke's arm for a quick moment. His head lowers to study the hand I've placed on his arm.

"He's in IT?"

"Funny, Millicent."

"What? Seriously, those two are like a picture-perfect couple. If Disney ever did a live action version of the movie those two could play the part."

Darin's hair even matches Flynn's. I'm enthralled by this whole thing, and even more so when my eyes land on the in-ground pool decorated with an array of floating lanterns sitting poolside.

"Luke, what's up, man." Darin's deep baritone voice takes his attention away from my hand, and I finally remove it, almost forgetting it was there.

"Hey. Congrats. This is amazing."

"Thanks."

Darin winks at him, then switches his focus on me. "Who's your lady friend?"

"Lady... oh."

I roll my eyes, a playful smile tugging at my lips. I slip forward, keeping myself flush against Luke, his body stiffens from my touch.

"Millicent. It's a pleasure," I say, reaching out to shake the real-life Flynn Ryder's hand. "I'm Luke's assistant."

Darin's white teeth sparkle. I'm still enamored by how gorgeous they both are, and how perfect their little life together is, and with a baby on the way, that kid has won the gene pool lottery.

"Please make yourselves at home. Luke, don't stay behind the camera all day. Enjoy yourself a little." Darin turns his attention back to me. "This guy always had his head in his camera at school. I kept telling him to enjoy the little things. Even at graduation it was like permanently glued to his hand."

All of us laugh, Luke does too, but it's easy to tell he's not entirely amused.

The two go off to mingle with their guests, and Luke leaves my side to go and do his thing, while I take the Polaroid around and get strangers to group together for photos. There are a few times I take my phone out and snap a shot or two of the floating lights.

The party goes well into the late afternoon and early evening. As the day winds down, the sun begins to set, and after a hearty meal, everyone turns their attention to the lanterns and the pool.

I find Luke; he's been in his own world today. We ate together, but he wasn't that talkative. We're standing side by side at the front to capture the moment. There's not much space between us since everyone wants in on the action. Each guest is handed a lantern to place in the water. The lantern that the couple has is special. The light inside changes color when it hits the water. It's safer than sending one off into the air.

"This is the most extravagant gender reveal I've ever seen. Not to mention this is my all-time favorite movie. The best part of it all was when they're singing in the boat and all the lights go up around them. What I wouldn't give to see the actual flying lanterns in person."

"I watched that movie with my cousin Ronnie. She made me watch it like fifty times a day while I was babysitting."

I chuckle. "Admit it, it's the best movie."

"It's not bad."

"I can't be seen with you."

I step aside and throw a Cheshire cat grin in his direction. Tilting his head, he glares at me, but the perfect smile is peeking through.

"Smile, Luke, you're celebrating your friends' special day."

I poke at his sides, attempting to be friendly. Soft laughter that he's trying so hard to hold back tumbles out.

"Say it's the best movie or I'll quit."

"Hush, it's starting," he says, but there's a teasing tone to his usual edgy voice.

Julie rushes up to us. "Here." She hands us both a lantern. "You guys go first since you're taking pictures."

Luke lets go of the camera around his neck, and grabs hold of the lit lantern. We step forward together and kneel.

"If you didn't have that expensive camera on your neck, I might have contemplated pushing you in," I whisper. Really, I'm trying to get a smile from him. I find him a lot more tolerable when he's less uptight. What my brother had said about him being good-looking isn't far from the truth, and when he smiles, there's this glow that I'm suddenly determined to make happen more often.

"You better watch it, because I've got another one of those Polaroid cameras so pushing you in wouldn't be so bad."

We let our lanterns go and get to our feet.

"Did I get a glimpse into your playful side again?" I grin.

"Maybe I'm not the guy you thought I was." He picks his camera back up and starts photographing the guests placing their lanterns in the water.

"Maybe you're not."

He half-smiles, then disappears in the crowd to get some shots.

Everyone follows our lead, and before long there's a beautiful display of lanterns floating along the fancy in-ground pool.

"Alright, guys, here we go," Darin gleams.

Julie and Darin bend together at the pool's edge, and with ease drop the lantern in. It takes a minute, but the light slowly flickers a light shade of blue. *It's a boy.* He lifts her from the ground as the music from the lantern scene of the movie plays. I find myself singing along.

Lost in the moment, my arms fill with goosebumps. I'm aware that it's not from the cool fall night surrounding us. I scan the crowd. Across the pool, with his camera slightly pulled from his eyes, Luke is watching me, his dark eyes ablaze with something I've never seen. He's not undressing me with his stare, it's too soft for that, but it's like he's taking me in and seeing me for the first time. The adult version of me, not the girl he once knew. I almost don't want to pull away, but he does first, so he can capture a kiss between the happy couple.

§♣

AS THE CROWD THINS OUT, and the night comes to an end, Luke and I pack up his things. We sought out Julie and Darin before leaving.

"Hey, we're going to head out," Luke says.

"This was the most beautiful gender reveal I've ever seen." I couldn't not say something. It truly was an amazing event.

Julie looks at her love with this admiration I've only ever read about in books. "It was perfect, wasn't it?"

The two nuzzle noses before returning their attention to us.

"Hey, man, we really appreciate everything," Darin says.

"I'll call you both when the images are ready. I can either come drop them off or you can come pick them up."

"Yeah, either way is good. Oh, are you going to the meet-up next weekend? You should bring your assistant." Darin wiggles his dark brows.

Luke's body freezes again.

"As lovely as that sounds, I'm going out with some old co-workers," I lie, and Luke's shoulders fall. From my angle I'm convinced he's relieved that I declined.

"I'm just his assistant," I say.

"You two seem closer than that," Julie says. "I see the way you—"

"Jules, this isn't one of your rom-com books," Darin pleads with her.

It's the most ridiculous thing I've ever heard, but not the worst.

"Sorry. Luke here deserves someone great after—"

"Well, we should really get going, we have a long drive." Luke interrupts her, but I wish he would have allowed her to finish that sentence. I'm getting even more curious about Gretchen. I wonder if he'd even answer me if I asked.

"It was nice to meet you," I say. We finish saying our goodbyes and head to the car. "Everything okay?" I ask, as he haphazardly puts his equipment in the trunk.

"Fine," he says through gritted teeth, slamming the trunk a bit too hard.

As we drive away Luke's quiet again. By this time of night, the temperature has dropped drastically, and I shiver. Luke must notice, because a second later he's reaching for the knob and the warmth of the heater kicks in.

His phone lights up, the name popping up again. He briefly closes his eyes and sighs before turning onto the expressway. I don't ask if he's going to get that, nor do I make a comment. If he doesn't stop clenching his jaw, he's going to end up with severe jaw pain.

"It was a beautiful party." I want to break the silence, but all he does is shrug. Whatever Julie was going to say has him reeling. I decide it's best to ignore it and keep quiet.

It doesn't take as long to get back home, which I'm grateful for. The silence tonight slices through me, and I'm ready for it to end. That, and as we pull up to the house, I'm reminded that my car needs to be serviced.

"I'll call my uncle tomorrow," Luke says. "If you want, I can stop by and check out—"

"Hey, don't worry about it. I'm sure my dad has a mechanic. Thank you though."

"Fine. Do you need a ride on Monday?" he asks.

It's dark inside the car, but the streetlamp above shines in. Luke's forehead wrinkles. I hate that I can't form the words to ask him what's wrong. Seeing him this torn up irks me for some reason. But I'm also pissed that he's always taking it out on me, like I have something to do with it.

"That won't be necessary. Goodnight, Luke." I reach for the door handle, but his hand wraps around my other one.

His expression has softened. "I'm... I'm sorry." He's fixated on how our hands fit, like they belong together.

"No worries. Goodnight."

I tug my hand back and get out of the car without looking back. His hot and cold attitude is irritating, and I'm not in the mood to deal with it right now. Things were looking up and now it's back to him being closed off, because of our immaturity as teens.

Inside the house, I'm greeted by Ezra and Jake who are scarfing down Mom's homemade apple pie in the kitchen.

"Join us!" Ezra says, as I grab a cold water from the fridge.

I take a few long swigs before replacing the cap.

"It's been a long day, my car died, and I had to deal with Luke's grumpy side. Pie will have to wait. I need a hot shower first."

I stalk past but Ezra stops me by holding out his arm. "You can bring it to the mechanic I go to."

Ezra's phone chimes. He hides it from my view. I would question it, but the spot behind my eyes is throbbing. An early bedtime is in my near future. I'll worry about the car tomorrow. I give a sad wave to Jake, and he blows me a kiss as I exit the room, giving me a small reason to smile.

CHAPTER 12

*M*ale voices chatter below my window. A strand of light beams through the partially parted curtain. My stomach gurgles with hunger pangs. After my shower last night, my head was throbbing enough that the thought of food made me nauseous. Now it's making up for that by sending a different type of nausea through me.

I throw the blanket off and look out. Down below in my driveway are Luke and Dad. Beside Luke is a car battery. They aren't even paying attention to the task at hand, they're just standing there chatting like old pals catching up. Their laughter seeps through even with the closed window.

There's a deep urge to be angry at Luke for ignoring my request to not help, but then watching him down there with my dad lights a whole different spark that I've been pushing down. I don't want to face him, but I'm not going to let him believe that I'm the bitch he remembers from high school.

Downstairs Mom is putting away some groceries. "Good morning," she says, her voice more chipper than usual. "Luke came over early this morning to tell us your car didn't start yesterday."

"I told him I'd take care of it." At my side my hands curl into tight fists. I'm grateful for his help, but I didn't appreciate the way he spoke to me. I won't get into detail with Mom about it; she'd only tell me that it's because he likes me, and I should give him a chance. I'm not interested in dating, not right now anyway, and not Luke. No matter how much I might find him attractive.

"Oh, honey, if a boy wants to fix your car you let him."

"Mom, I can handle it myself. I've lived on my own so I can take care of my car."

She crosses the room to stand in front of me and places a hand on my shoulder. "Sweetie, I know. Maybe you need a little love in your life…"

"I don't," I say sharply. I know her heart is in the right place, but I'm not actively wanting to be with anyone.

"Suit yourself." She backs away. "But you might want to thank the man."

She's right, of course she is. I'm not that evil. She hands me two bottles of water. "Go give these to them."

I open the door and Luke's eyes flicker towards me. He almost drops the battery. His eyes narrow but don't linger. Carefully, he lifts the heavy square block into the front of the car, and places it down.

"Now remember, son, the…" Dad stops and looks up. "Good morning, sweetheart."

"Hey, Dad. Can I talk to Luke for a moment?" I hand him one of the bottles of water.

"Oh, yeah of course. You got this, son?" he asks, a sparkle in his eye.

"Yes, of course, Mr. Gibson."

"Call me Jerry."

"Right. Jerry."

Dad walks up beside me and leans in. "You've got yourself a good one there, kiddo."

I want to correct him. Luke isn't mine, and never will be, but my entire family seems to have other plans. Luke is mumbling to himself while he points at the wires hanging. While he does, I pick at the wrapper on the bottle and wait for him to finish. I am aware of the dangers of replacing a car battery.

"This one here, and there we go. Here." He tosses me the keys, and somehow with the bottle in hand I'm still able to catch it. "Try it."

I hold my hand out to give him the water. He takes it, then nudges me towards the driver's side door that's already wide open. He shuts the trunk and I slip the key in and turn it. The car sputters to life.

Luke takes a swig of water. "All fixed. You gotta run the car for a bit to allow the alternator to fully charge it," he says.

Without another word he strides towards his SUV parked at the curb. I leave the car running and almost tumble out after him.

"Wait, Luke."

He refuses to stop, so I pick up the pace, and as he pulls open his car door, I grab hold of his arm. My hand accidentally slides down and I grasp his hand tugging him towards me. "Luke."

He doesn't fight to let go, neither do I.

"I told you not to come," I say, biting my bottom lip.

"I promised I'd look. I don't go back on my word. It's fixed, no big deal."

"But it is. It is a big deal. It's not even ten in the morning on a Sunday and you drove here to fix it. That's— did you pay for the battery?"

"I did. Like I said, no biggie."

His hand slips, but I hold on tighter and allow my thumb to slide against his smooth skin. He shudders at my touch.

"Let me pay you back, please. I can't just let you—" My thumb has a mind of its own as it continues to rub. With my pulse racing under his watchful stare, I'm almost as flustered as him. The funny thing is… I don't want to stop touching him. It feels nice. I take a step closer. "Please, let me pay you back."

"Millicent, I won't accept your money, just, it's fine, and you're welcome. I do have to get going though..." His attention focuses back to the spot between us. I'm fully aware of what I'm doing. *Don't make me stop*, I think. Each stroke of my finger only makes me want more.

"Sorry... I... Thank you."

Our eyes meet and I'm lost.

My heart plummets as Mom yells out from the steps. "Luke, darling, are you staying for breakfast?"

Before I can dive any further, I take my hand from his and place them at my side.

"I'm sorry, Mrs. Gibson, I have to run over to Mom's."

Luke takes note of our hands no longer touching and draws his back from between us.

"Next time?" she asks.

"Definitely."

"I'll see you tomorrow?"

"Yeah. Thank you."

As we're chatting, Dad comes back out and slides into the driver's seat of my car. Most likely to sit with it while it runs. I ignore both of my parents and pull my attention back to Luke.

"Maybe next time don't be so stubborn. I said I'd help." The tension in his voice is replaced with a little friendliness.

Without another word I step away from his car and stand on the sidewalk. He gives a quick wave before taking off down the street. I don't know what I did to deserve his kindness, but for those few lingering moments when our hands were linked, I got a sense of home. Shaking the thoughts, I turn to find Mom leaning against the doorway.

"Don't start with me," I say, heading inside.

"I didn't say a thing." She grins.

As I make my way back to the kitchen, I swear I hear her say she's calling his mom, but I ignore it and head straight for her Sunday morning egg breakfast.

I sit at the table and take a bite of Mom's cooking. Suddenly, I'm a kid again, safe in the comfort of my childhood home. A feeling that I've only gotten rare glimpses of over the last few years with my few and far between visits. I put the fork on the plate. Closing my eyes, I take in everything around me, from the sound of Mom chatting in the next room to Dad singing along to the car radio outside.

Mom says something about how happy she is to have me here, and that she's proud of me for taking this job with Luke and not losing myself in the whirlwind of depression from job loss, even though it wasn't in my plans.

Tears prick along the edges of my eyes. I may have failed the eighteen-year-old girl who left this house by moving back here, but it's the sights and sounds of home that make me feel as if maybe I haven't failed at all. Maybe this is just the beginning and if I keep going and try this new thing then it'll all fall into place exactly the way it was meant to be.

CHAPTER 13

J'm finally getting the hang of everything at the photography studio. I haven't messed up scheduling in a week. That's got to be some kind of record, right? Also, I hope Luke appreciates the fall decorations in the window.

Luke has been in the back room doing his edits for the past three hours and there hasn't been much action up front. I probably should have asked, but we've been getting along this past week, and I think he's been happy with my assisting skills at events. Although the waters have settled, there's still a large wave of sexual tension brewing between us. I've felt it since I grabbed his hand outside my house.

In fact, two days ago, we were working on a promo together for Christmas. I deleted something during edits by accident and he was standing over me. Me, being me, I panicked, but Luke remained pleasantly calm. He reached over the chair, setting his two hands on either side of me. His breath tickled my ear as he grabbed the mouse and fixed what I had done.

"See," he said. His face turned slowly. "All fixed."

We were so close, that I could almost taste his soapy scent. I expected him to pull away, but he lingered. It was only for a moment, but still took me several seconds to get my brain to function again when he eventually did.

Finally! I'm like a kid at Christmas when the phone rings. At least I don't have to think about Luke and sex in the same sentence for the next few minutes.

"Thank you for calling Parker Photography, how can I help you?"

"Hello." A gruff female voice responds. "I want to get some photos done, but I'm not sure if your studio does the type of shoot, I'm looking for."

"What is it? I'm sure we could—"

"Do you do boudoir shoots?"

I choke on my own spit. "As in sexy lingerie and all that?"

The image of Luke taking pictures of women in their undergarments makes me snicker. I bite my bottom lip to keep from smirking.

"Yes." The confidence in her voice is amazing.

"Uh, well that is definitely something I'd have to find out. Could you please hold?"

"Of course. And I'm totally fine with a man doing the shoot."

Sure, you are, lady. I stare out the window a few feet in front of me and out into the street. "Right. Um, well let me go ask him."

"Ask me what?" Luke's simple, yet velvety tone makes me jump.

Don't laugh, don't laugh, don't laugh. Keeping it together is hard, so I continue to bite my lip. Luke crosses his arms. His foot taps on against the floor, as he waits for me to speak.

"Do you do boudoir?"

Luke's brows raise like The Rock when he smells something cooking. There's no hiding my grin now. Luke's entire body goes pale, minus a little redness that creeps on his cheeks. Has this guy ever seen a woman naked? The thought gives my lady bits a weird buzzing energy that I shut down right away.

"I— Is— Uh— that—"

"Spit it out, Luke." I giggle.

He scowls at me. "I don't think Dad would want that kind of shoot done here. I don't know," he says.

"What about you?" I ask. "I mean, it's going to be your studio soon, right?"

He's frozen. It's as if Elsa blew through and turned him into an ice cube. I don't know why this man has so much trouble expressing his sexual desires. Is it only because I'm his friend's sister?

My brain has decided to choose this very moment to cling to an idea that is beyond dumb. What if he took pictures of me and I used them for my blog? It could not only give him exposure for his beautiful work, but if this post does well, it could change things for me and maybe open new avenues for Luke with his photography.

I can't even fathom that Luke would agree to it. I can understand him not wanting to do it as the image of this studio is family oriented, but what if—I laugh to myself—well, here goes nothing.

"I could be a test subject."

Luke's cheeks are bright red like a raging fire ball. His eyes glaze over as he stares out into nowhere. I can't tell whether he's looking at me or lost in his own world.

I'm in deep shit after I get off this call. He presses his lips together. His Adam's apple dances in his throat with each swallow. I stand and walk a few inches towards him, then poke at his small bicep.

"Poke. Are you okay there?"

He narrows his eyes in response. It's probably a bad idea. Maybe not bad per se, because it could be great for my blog, but bad in that it would mean going through with being his test subject.

"She says she's okay with a man taking her photos." I pause

and twirl a strand of my hair around my finger. "Or you could always just take them for me."

I'm shocked at the flirtatious tone in my voice. Does he notice? He's going to fire me. I can feel it. I wait for the blow, cringing, but it never comes. After a few seconds I say, "I can tell her no. You can tell me no too. I won't be offended." I poke him again. This time he swats my finger. I chuckle.

"You want me to take pictures of you in your underwear?" he squeaks.

"Hey, maybe this could bring in a whole new clientele?"

"Yeah, until some macho boyfriend or husband comes strolling in to kick my ass for looking at their girl naked."

I tap my lip. "True. But technically they aren't naked, so—" I pause. "Just do one for me then. I don't have a partner who would go after you. It could be an experiment of sorts."

What am I even saying? Am I so desperate to find something to write that I'd stoop to this? Wait a minute. Another idea strikes. I could write a post on what people think about their partners (male or female) doing a boudoir shoot.

"I've been bone dry for an article for my blog. I'm trying to get seen again, and I think I have the perfect article. Who knows, maybe it would help your business. I could credit your photos. It could be a win–win for both of us."

Luke rubs at his neck. His eyes meet mine and there's a spark of something behind the soft emerald tones that I can't quite read.

"Think about it," I say. "In the meantime, what should I tell the woman on the phone?"

Even from my perspective I can see his brain moving a mile a minute trying to figure this whole thing out. I put my hands on his shoulders and get him to look at me again. He's zoning out like he's not totally into the idea. I pull away and get on the phone.

"Ma'am, I am so sorry. We don't really do that kind of

photoshoot. The owner is not entirely opposed, but I can't guarantee we'd be able to."

She's quiet for a few seconds. "Oh, no worries, sweetheart. If you decide to go ahead with it, I'd love to be informed. Is there a mailing list or anything?"

"No, but now that you bring it up, that's actually not a bad idea. Let me take down your info and email and we'll reach out if anything changes."

She accepts this. I promise again to reach out and thank her for the newsletter idea. I'll have to run it by Luke and his dad, but I think it would be a good way to keep customers informed of new things happening aside from social media.

I turn to Luke. He's shaking his head and rubbing his temples. "Okay, Millicent. I'll do this for you. But only you."

The way he says, *but only you*, makes my insides twitch with this fascinating desire over him seeing me in lingerie. "So, where should we do this? My mom is home like twenty-four seven and she already snoops in all my things. She'll probably want one herself, and I'm not sure that's something you're willing to shoot."

He cringes, and I should be offended but I'm not, because that would be weird. "Why not here?"

"We need a bedroom scene—what about yours?" I ask.

Eyes wide he stares at me, like it's the most ridiculous idea I've ever had. Oh, wait—it is. "You do have your own apartment, right?"

He nods. "True. I have my own place, yes."

"Okay. It's not like I'll be naked on your bed. My parts will be covered."

He chokes. "Uh."

"Be brave, Luke. Take chances, but if you're really uncomfortable we don't have to."

I expect smoke to shoot from his ears with how hard he's thinking. "Okay, my room. When am I free?"

I slide into the desk chair and log into the computer to check his schedule. He's mostly booked, but I notice one potential day. "Sunday. You have that small wedding; you said it ends early."

He blows out a breath. "Okay then. I'll give you my address and you can meet me there, like five?"

"Yup."

"And do you have what you need—"

"Plenty." I smirk.

I realize that he doesn't know about the insane amount of lingerie I've acquired working for *Forever Twenty*. "Maybe I didn't need to know that."

"Probably not, but we're doing this and there's no turning back now."

His eyes finally land on the decorations in the front window. I may have gone a little overboard with the fake leaves along the sill, a few ceramic jack-o'-lanterns, and some happy fall window clings.

"I'm not even going to ask about my storefront."

I smirk. "You know you like it."

His lips twitch. No matter how hard he tries to deny it, he likes the little touches I've given the place in the past few weeks.

"I have to get back to editing. Can you maybe not create any more chaos while I'm back there?"

I shrug. "I can't promise that."

His eyebrows rise.

"But I can try."

Without another word he turns and heads into the back room. I'm in a bit of shock I offered to do this, mostly because it will be on *his* bed. I can only hope in the end, it helps us out. I do need my hair and makeup done. There's a salon a few towns over that have rave reviews. Hopefully they can squeeze me in.

CHAPTER 14

Sitting in the car I stare up at the bright glass storefront. *Mia Bella* salon is a few towns over, about a ten-minute drive when there's no traffic. I don't have to be at the photography studio until nine thirty, and I need to book my hair and makeup for the boudoir shoot. *Mia Bella* is the most raved about salon.

As I move the shifter to park, something in the window catches my eye. Astra Sullivan? I knew she owned a salon but not this one. My heart is not cooperating. Not one bit. The pounding in my chest aches as I watch her through the window.

She moves like a ghost in the night across the sparkling crystal windows. The salon door opens, and she swaps the white sign on the door to open. For a moment she doesn't move, her dark eyes focusing on something across the street. I slink down in my seat, hoping she doesn't notice, only somehow my hand slips on the wheel and presses lightly on the horn. It comes out in a short staccato beat, but it's enough for her head to turn a little to the left in my direction.

At first, she ignores it, but after a second, she does a double take. Her jaw hangs open, and her long lean legs move towards me. I can't help my wandering eyes, she's even more gorgeous than she was in high school. A pink flush forms on her olive toned cheeks. Beautiful strands of dark hair swirl down her shoulders and bounce as she picks up the pace. My breath catches in my throat as I stare at the most perfect person I've ever seen.

I don't want to look ridiculous, so I lock the car, and with trembling hands open the door. I grip the keys tight, most likely making marks as the rough edges push into my skin.

"Millicent!" Her eyes glaze over, her voice breaking on the "t" in my name. She doesn't give me a chance to react as she throws her arms around me, as if we'd never lost touch. I breathe in her coconut scent and my whole body relaxes into hers, as I finally hold her too.

I swallow the knot building in my throat, saving it for when I'm alone. I can't let her know that my feelings for her have never changed, even after all these years. By the time she pulls away, I've somehow collected my thoughts.

"What are you doing here?" she asks, a bright smile tugging on her vibrant cherry painted lips.

"I— I have this thing and I needed hair and makeup done. It's not today; I just wanted to—"

"Oh my God, of course I'll do your hair and makeup. Come inside we can figure it out."

Her hand slips into mine naturally and I have to stop my heart from feeling any sort of happiness. She tugs me inside. The salon is as fancy on the inside as it is outside. A mixture of dyes and shampoos tingle my nose. We stop at a small counter at the front of the store.

"So, when is this event, and—" She gasps. "Are you getting married?"

"No, not married. Um, so I'm doing a boudoir photoshoot for a blog, and I would much rather have someone else do my hair and makeup than attempt it on my own."

"Oh, boudoir, you're gonna kill that photoshoot, I mean look at you—" She pauses as her eyes roam over me. I shudder. "Gorgeous as always." She winks.

I hate the way my whole body reacts to her voice, and her words. She's silent for a moment as she flips through some screens on the computer. Her fingers diligently work as she types something, then uses the mouse to navigate.

In the strange silence, a door in the back shuts, and a familiar woman walks forward. Her dark strands of curls are tossed up into a messy—yet—poised bun. Her black heels click along the solid tiled floor. As she reaches Astra, she comes up from behind and I catch her pink polished fingernails gliding up Astra's arm. Astra leans back and smiles up at the woman, who is a few inches taller than she is. It takes me a moment to grasp that she's the woman from Astra's Facebook page.

"Millicent, this is my fiancée, Katherine. Katherine, this is Millicent."

"From high school?" Katherine asks, wide-eyed.

"That's the one."

"She's just as beautiful as you said she was."

She opens her arms and hugs me. I awkwardly stand there unsure what to do. She steps back. "I've heard so many crazy stories about you."

I revel in what she just said. Astra has told her about me. Maybe not the kiss part, but she still thinks about me like I do her. The thought does not help my feelings, not in the slightest.

I give a soft chuckle. "All good, I hope?"

"Good in that you were the best friend a girl could ever ask for, but I might have told her some of our club stories," Astra says.

"You didn't?" I half-smile, attempting to mask my embarrassment.

"I did. But it's all in the past and we were young and stupid. Oh—I have some openings, when did you say this was?"

I give her the date, and she slips me into one of the time slots. After a few more minutes of reminiscing, I check the time on the small round clock above her head.

"I should get going. I have to get to work." I turn to find Katherine's twinkling brown eyes watching me. "It was really nice to meet you, Katherine."

"It was such a pleasure. I'm so glad I got to meet the famous Millicent." The front door opens, and she excuses herself to help the customer walking in.

"I'm glad you stopped by," Astra says. There's a tightness to her voice that confuses me.

"Yeah. Me too. I'll um, I'll see you soon." I start to walk away when she calls my name.

"Yeah?" I ask, peeking over my shoulder.

"I've missed you."

The only thing I can do is smile, because if I speak, I'll cry. I hurry out the door and don't let the tears fall until I'm halfway down the street.

𝄞

INSIDE THE STUDIO, Luke is sitting at my desk, his eyes glued to the screen. Other than the soft hum of the overhead lighting, the studio is dead silent. I walk around and find him browsing emails as I put my bag under the desk. My sniffle is the only thing that catches his attention. I've stopped crying, but now my nose won't stop running. His eyes soften, but he returns his attention to the computer. I almost think he's going to ignore me, but with a little shake in his hand he closes out the emails.

"Hey, are you okay?" He stands, then closes the gap between us.

"Mhmm," I say. My chin wobbles as if I'm going to cry again.

A single tear escapes, but it doesn't make it far, as Luke's thumb swipes it away. For a second, he holds it there. I tilt my head into his touch. Warmth radiates from where his thumb is and down to my toes. He tugs his hand away and fidgets like he's not sure what to do with it.

"So, I know I gave you tonight off, but I was wondering if you'd like to come with me to the event I'm photographing. It's different from the rest and it might take your mind off whatever is bothering you."

Confused by his worry over my feelings, I've lost my ability to form words. "I— yeah, I don't have any other plans."

His lips curl up into a real smile, one that lights up his eyes. And I can't help being drawn to him. The sting of my encounter with Astra is slowly fading.

"Okay, good. We are leaving at two, if you need anything at home, I can always swing by and pick you up."

My brows tighten. Having him pick me up at home would feel like a date, and this is far from that.

"No, I have everything I need."

"Okay," he says, unmoving. His phone beeps. He takes a moment to check, but then shakes his head. "Not today," he whispers, before slipping it back into his pocket.

"I'm sorry."

Neither of us move and for the first time he's not having any trouble meeting my eyes. The studio phone rings.

"I should— I should get that."

"Oh, yeah. Right."

Luke finally steps aside but lingers. It's not until I am browsing through the schedule do I hear the door close. I'm excited, and glad he invited me. I don't think I would have been able to go back to the house without moping over this old nagging feeling inside my chest. Even after all these years she still has this pull over my heart that I can't erase.

❦

IT'S ALMOST TWO, and Luke still hasn't emerged from the back room. I finish saving the updated schedule, then shut down the computer. Twiddling my thumbs I wait for a few more minutes, before checking the time. When he still hasn't come out, I head back to see if everything is okay.

There's no answer when I knock, and I'm wondering if he's fallen asleep. I try once more, and when that doesn't work, I walk in and pray he's not doing anything I shouldn't see.

I scan the room and as I do Luke turns, his shirt stuck on his head. I gasp, not out of horror—maybe embarrassment? I don't know, but my eyes are glued to the taut muscles of his back as he wiggles himself out of his shirt.

He spins as the shirt releases and his eyes meet mine. Luke's cheeks burn a dark crimson red, and I'm sure my face mirrors his.

"I'm sorry, I didn't... I knocked."

He's quiet. His mouth opens, and he's unsure of what to say. The image of him getting stuck in his shirt makes me smile because it's so Luke. I try to look at something else, anything else, but there's this tug trying to pull me in and look again.

Ooof, there's some chest hair. I try to stand my ground and focus on the low ceiling instead, but my deceiving eyes have wandered, and I capture him bending over to grab a second shirt. Before he can catch me, I pivot so I'm facing the wall to my right.

"Spilled the leftover coffee that I had all over my shirt."

"Oh. Okay. Um... are you ready?"

I keep my eyes trained at the small brown stain on the ceiling, but I'm still fully aware of his shirtless chest in front of me.

"Yeah, now I am."

He's gone from a white shirt to a black one. I'm enamored by how the dark shirt makes his eye color pop. I don't know where this sudden attraction has come from. The tiny zaps of electricity when we touch, and the long gazes, are drawing me in more than I care to admit.

"Are you sure everything is okay?" he asks.

Coming back to reality I jump at the realization of how close he is. His hand is outstretched like he was tempted to touch me, and as he pulls back. There's fear in his eyes.

"I'm perfect. I'll meet you at the car."

CHAPTER 15

*L*uke takes the expressway and heads west towards the city. I didn't get a chance to check and see what event was slated for tonight. He must have booked it long before I started because I don't remember penciling anything in.

Although we left at two the traffic heading towards Manhattan is building up. Rush hour doesn't start until around four, but now we are battling the after-school chaos, and with it being the end of the week, people are in a rush to get things done, or get to where they planned to be for the weekend.

His phone on the dashboard lights up over the map directions, her name appearing.

"She sure calls a lot," I say, finally speaking up.

He sighs. "She's my ex, but tonight I just want to forget."

I give a soft laugh. I get it. I want that too. "Can we both forget tonight? Let's just have fun. Be Luke and Millicent, two friends on an adventure who... kind of tolerate each other."

His laughter takes me by surprise. "I don't just tolerate you, Millicent. I put up with you."

"Are you— Are— Luke Parker, are you saying we're friends?"

I'm enjoying his perfectly flushed cheeks. I made that happen, and I fucking love it.

"I'm pretty sure you have powers and have somehow convinced me to like you."

"Ezra was right, the sunburst spell works well. I've blinded you. It's the only explanation for you thinking of me as your friend." I snort.

He does a double take, while trying to keep his eyes on the road. I think he's going to swerve but he stays steady.

The other night Ezra and Jake were over at the house, and they were talking strategy for their next game. I listened while I busied myself making lunches and when I finally sat down, I couldn't help glancing over their character sheets and asking a ton of questions. Not much of it stuck; it's a lot, but I wanted to try and understand it.

"How did you…? And that's not really how the spell works."

I chuckle. "Hey, I'm learning, okay? There's so much to understand. And to answer your question, I might have asked Ezra."

Luke sniffs a laugh then looks over at me. His smile is breathtaking, and I try and take a snapshot in my head to hold on to for later when he's busy scowling.

WE'VE REMAINED quiet for a bit, taking in the view as we pass through the island. Luke lightly drums along to the music on the radio—he's listening to a rock station. It keeps fading in and out, static interrupting the song every few minutes.

"What, no score soundtracks today?"

"I was in the mood for old-school rock this morning. I mean I do have…"

"Rock is fine, but we may have to change the station with all the static," I say.

"I can swap to my CD. I have Harry—"

"Nope."

We come to a stop amongst the traffic. When I peek over, I'm not expecting him to be watching me, but he is and I'm— I'm drawn in again. Without turning away, I reach over and fiddle with the dial. I hit a button and an entire orchestra fills the car.

"Shit."

His entire body shakes with amusement. "Serves you right for trying to touch a man's radio."

In my peripheral I catch the car ahead slowly ease up on the brakes.

"Better move up, buddy. New Yorkers are impatient people."

He grins. "Always so feisty."

"That's me."

He shakes his head and focuses all his attention on the slow-moving traffic ahead.

"So, where are we going? I don't like surprises," I say, glancing out the window as the city skyline comes into view.

My heart squeezes. Passing by the familiar buildings of Manhattan leaves a pang of longing for what once was. I spent such a long time nestled between the large skyscrapers, and now from a distance it all seems like a dream.

"We're going to a festival in Jersey."

"You're taking pictures at a festival?"

"Yeah, why not?"

"Was this on the schedule?"

"Nope, I read about it online and I thought you might like it, so I ordered us tickets."

My attention swerves back to him. "You what? I can't let you just pay for a ticket for me, how much did it—"

He places a hand over mine. I jump at the unexpected jolt from his soft touch. "Don't worry about it. The night is on me."

I try to argue, but before I can, he removes his hand to adjust the volume knob, then focuses on the road.

CHAPTER 16

*I*t's a long two-hour drive, but as we slow, I notice signs for a light festival. In the distance cars are slowly inching forward into a large field. A heavy bass pulses around us. From here my eyes land on a stage, and people gather around it, dancing to a band playing their hearts out.

"What is this?" I ask.

"Do you remember the gender reveal party? The *Rapunzel* themed one. You and Julie spoke about your favorite scenes, and you rambled on about how you would love to see the lanterns in real life."

"Wait this— this is..." I bite my bottom lip to keep my voice from squeaking.

It figures Luke would remember such a random detail. He's not wrong, *Rapunzel* is my favorite Disney movie, and the lantern scene always makes me tear up.

My nose tingles and I try not to release the building sob begging to crawl its way up my throat. I'm confused by his gesture. It's always felt like Luke didn't like me, but more recently things have changed.

"Why are you crying again?" The small smile behind his voice lets me know he's only asking out of concern, and not saying it to mock me. "You looked so distraught when you came into work, and I feel like it's half my fault. Maybe I've been too— maybe I've been an asshole, and I feel bad."

Tears slide down at a rapid rate and touch my lips. "It's perfect, but I... you're not an asshole, I deserve some of the shade you've thrown at me."

"You didn't deserve it at all. I had my head in high school mode and kept my defenses up. You're not the same girl who harped on us about how nerdy we were. I should have given you a chance."

"I'm guilty of stereotyping you, even now, but I'm sorry." I adjust in my seat to face him. "I'm an adult and there's no reason I should act that way. Today was hard; it has nothing to do with anything you did. I'm not ready to talk about it."

"And I won't poke around for answers. Maybe I'm just trying to say if you need an ear or a shoulder, I'm here."

I wipe my eyes. The memory of his thumb erasing my tears earlier sends a shiver down my spine.

"I appreciate that. And for you as well. I can see the hurt in your eyes when she calls."

"Thank you," he says, his voice barely above a whisper.

An understanding passes between us. One that has been building over the last few weeks.

He clears his throat. "We should go. The launch is in two hours, and there's food, music, and some personal fire pits. We can roast marshmallows and make s'mores." As he talks, his sparkling emerald eyes land on me.

"What?" he asks.

"Oh, nothing."

AT THE ENTRANCE we were given lanterns and markers to write a message on them. I'm in awe of the turnout of the event. As we find something to eat the crowd swells, creating a bit of a jam where the food trucks are sitting off to the side of the field.

We take up residence at an old picnic table with our pulled pork sandwiches and French fries. Luke sits across from me. Behind him the sky is lit in a violet-blue sunset illuminated by a pinkish glow.

"It's the blue hour," he says, looking over his shoulder where my attention is.

"I've never heard of that."

"It's a term us photographers use. It's the time just after sunset or just before sunrise. It doesn't even last a full hour, only about twenty minutes or so." He has a far-off look when he describes it. There's much more going on inside his head than just the blue hour.

"Hey, get over there so I can take a picture." He ignores his food and stands, taking out the camera he brought with him.

"Why me?"

He shrugs. "Thought maybe you'd want some pics to remember the night. I mean because you love the lanterns and…"

"Okay."

I stand and make my way to his side of the table, and I swear when he passes me our hands brush. His soft touch is light enough to make me think I could be imagining things, but it's enough to make my pulse throb and vibrate my skin.

After a quick picture, we pass again, and I reach out for his camera. I'm not sure how to use it, but he offers it up to me anyway. Spinning the camera around I grab his shoulder and attempt to take a selfie. In my head the moment was much smoother because the camera refuses to click.

"You can't do that." He chuckles, grabbing his cell from his pocket, then carefully taking the camera from my grip.

With a click of his phone, he takes the photo then turns it to show me. My arm is still around his shoulder. He's close enough where his warm breath dances along my lips.

"Awe we're cute," I say.

He scoffs, but the tone is more playful.

I pull away first, and he clears his throat. "We should finish up so we can get a good spot."

After our stomachs are satisfied, and Luke has eaten every crumb from his French fries, we head to the expansive field and find a spot. Couples dance, and kiss around us, families linger over small fire pits, kids get their faces painted, and all around us there's laughter and joy.

We lay out the blankets, and afterwards Luke snaps a ton of pictures of everything around us. The countdown is on, and when he's done, he sits with me, and we open our lanterns.

"I don't know what to write," I say, glancing over at him. He's scribbling away, while mine remains blank. I lie on my stomach. The tip of the pink felt pen leaves a small dot on the fabric.

"The lanterns are supposed to represent the releasing of one's deepest fears and desires. What do you desire most?" he asks, only looking up for a second, before writing something else.

My mind feels like an empty space. If I shouted loud enough there would be an echo of my own voice. I have plenty of fears, like, a fear of never finding job security again, and losing the ability to write a good article that someone wants to publish. I love the idea of blogging, but let's face it, a blog can't get me health insurance or my own place. Then I comb over my disaster of a morning. Astra had moved on. She looked truly happy and I'm happy for her, but seeing her brought up everything I once felt.

A hand on my shoulder startles me. "Hey." Luke's tone is different today, it's softer. "Hey, we're supposed to be forgetting, remember? I lost you there for a second."

I chuckle and bounce my shoulder into his. His laughter fills the wide-open space around us. It's real and raw and it warms my entire body and shields it from the cool fall night.

"I wrote that I'm grateful for being able to share this moment with someone, even if we don't always get along," he says.

I like this side of him; it's playful, which is the opposite of who he's been the past few weeks, and much different from the boy who shied away from me in high school.

It won't be long now, but I think I know what I'll write. I cover it with one hand, while writing with the other. *Grateful for people who take a chance on me, even if I wasn't so kind in the past.*

Within minutes the first lantern takes flight. I scramble to my feet, Luke helping me with his free hand. He retrieves the lighter and gets ours set to go. We stand close, but don't touch, and watch each other, nodding to count down. I reread the pink words, and finally let go. Luke picks up the camera strapped around his neck and snaps a shot. I'd grab my phone, but I'm in awe, as little by little the sky fills with glowing lights.

Inside Luke's pocket a familiar song softly plays. He lets go of the camera and pulls out the phone. The moment the words start I hear it loud and clear. He's playing my favorite song from the movie.

My lips twitch, and in seconds they form a smile. One I normally reserved for only certain people. I'm not sure when Luke became one of them, but I can't help thinking maybe he always was, I just was too blind to see it.

He takes a few more pictures before letting the camera fall to his chest. He looks up mesmerized by the lanterns. While he may not have meant for this night to be romantic, it's in the air. I feel it in the way my heart flutters. A calmness hovers over me, over us. I kind of wish we could stay here forever.

"Hey, can I borrow some of your pictures for my blog? I have an idea."

"Of course you can. Monday we can go through them all and you can tell me which ones you like. I was only planning on keeping them for myself, and maybe for the website or some promos, but other than that they are all yours."

"I'll credit you, promise."

His hip gently bumps into mine, and for a moment my eyes jet to the side to observe how close our bodies are.

"No worries," he whispers, and I note his eyes doing the same. Standing together like this my hands have a mind of their own. The side of his pinky slides into mine, and without hesitation our hands link, like they belong together. A soft gasp escapes my lips.

"I'm sorry for how I've behaved," he apologizes again. "I hope you can forgive me." His palm becomes sweaty, and there's a light tremble in his hand.

I don't know what makes me do it, but I rest my head on his shoulder and tilt my chin to take in the beauty of the moment. It's just like the movie, only better. "I'm sorry too. I guess we both have some things to work on."

We're both quiet for several minutes as we watch the lanterns fly further away. There's a calming silence, even over the muffled chatter; it's like we're in our own bubble.

"Thank you for tonight," I whisper and am met with a simple squeeze of his hand.

❦

BY THE TIME we pull up to the studio, it's well past midnight. We hit some late-night traffic on the Verrazano bridge, but afterwards it was a quick ride back to town. I'm so tired but had a hard time dozing off in the car, because my mind refused to shut off, as I replay the moment in my head where he held my hand.

It's been a while since a man—or anyone—has made me feel something. We sit in the car in silence for a few minutes. "Tonight was wonderful. How can I ever repay you for—"

"I don't need you to repay me. I did it because I wanted to."

A minute passes, but neither of us make a move to exit the car.

"I should go," I finally say.

"Yeah."

"I'll see you on Monday."

He scratches at the back of his neck. "Goodnight, Millicent."

He doesn't pull away until I'm safe inside and have the car running. I need a few moments to collect my thoughts and figure out what happened tonight. He was only being friendly, there's no reason I should read into this. Taking a deep breath, I put the car into reverse, and back out of the space. It felt nice with Luke, like we were friends with a spark of something more. I'm glad I have all weekend to clear my head, because even if there was a spark, I don't think my heart is ready, not now, and maybe not ever.

CHAPTER 17

I stand tall as I enter the studio. It's Monday morning. The weekend didn't help clear my mind. My room became the dumping ground of my collection of sexual toys, lingerie, and whatever other samples the magazine had given during my time there. I wanted inspiration, and I also needed to find some lingerie to wear during our session. The only thing I found relaxing was when I opened one of the vibrators and my God did it release some tension, but I digress...

As I tug at the door, my heart gives an intense jolt as emerald eyes meet mine from behind the computer.

He leans over and smiles. "Good morning."

I stop walking. "Wait! Who are you, and where is the grumpy dude that works here?" I say, hoping my tone conveys teasing rather than snark.

He ignores me, but lets out an amused huff.

"What are you up to, imposter Luke?" I ask.

"You're a comedian, Millicent."

"And you're sus, Luke."

He rests his elbow on the desk, covers his eyes, and slowly shakes his head, but even so I can see his cheeks wrinkle.

There's a shift in the tension between us and I plan to take full advantage of this side of him. Not going to lie, I might have a slight crush on Luke version 2.0. I skip around to stand beside him and gasp at the images on screen. It's an article about boudoir shoots but also has pictures to go with it.

"Searching for some ideas for our shoot."

"Are you sure that's all you're doing?" I push my shoulder into his. I can't believe my own ears as my voice comes out sultry and sexy, a tone I've never used around him before. Come to think of it, I've never heard such a low growl come from me, ever.

"Yes." He nudges me back. Then looks at the screen to x all the tabs out. When he stands our bodies are so close I can feel his heat. I slide to my right, towards him, like I'm not in control of my own body. We are facing opposite directions, but that doesn't stop him from observing me. My arm tingles with goosebumps. This seems to be our new routine, getting caught up in what we want to say, neither of us moving.

"After I'm done working on some edits, I'll comb through those pictures for you from the other night."

"Sounds good. Oh, you have an engagement shoot this afternoon. Do you want me to prep your cameras for you? Let me know which one and I can make sure everything is loaded into your SUV."

Luke's eyes find mine. His lips part as if he's about to speak, but nothing comes out. A soft smile forms on his lips. "I made a list. You can come get it when you're ready. Thank you."

"Of course."

He finally steps aside. We don't touch as he passes, but the anticipation of wanting it kicks my pulse into gear. On trembling legs, I take my seat, and open this week's schedule.

I answer a few phone calls and call clients to set up a time to come and get their photos. Once I'm done, I head to the back to get the list of the camera and lenses he's asked for. He has them stored in the back room where he is currently.

Before I enter, I knock out of courtesy because of what happened the last time. There are other voices behind the door, some have thick accents, and I'm hearing music as if I were transported to a renaissance fair.

When he doesn't answer, I cup my hand over the door and yell, "Luke, I am your—" I don't get to finish my—amazing—-Darth Vader voice, as the door swings open.

"Really?" he asks, but there's a hint of a grin sitting behind his pressed lips.

"Master Luke, I have come for your cameras. List, please."

"Funny."

He steps aside, allowing me in. In the corner of the room, just a few inches over from the door sits a flat screen TV perched on the wall. A familiar group of people are sitting at tables while talking in accents. This is the show Ezra and Jake made me watch.

"How long does it take to create a character?" I lean against his desk turning my attention back on the TV.

"There's a character sheet, kind of like writing. I know you don't write fiction but—"

"I've dabbled," I say, keeping my eyes focused on the people playing D&D on TV. "But it never really stuck. Okay, so there's a sheet. Is it computer generated, or do I have to do this on my own?"

He's stunned for a few seconds. I want to make a promise that me doing research on the game isn't to poke fun. It's my fault he doesn't entirely trust me. I'm starting to understand how it must have felt for him all those years ago when I judged him. This is him judging me right now. He's hesitant to let me in, to talk to me about it. We made progress, but then again, he still feels like he has to protect himself from my jabs.

"You can make one online too. It's kind of complicated for the amount of time we have…"

"Maybe another day then," I say, pushing off the desk.

He looks away, then back up at the TV, zoning out as if he's lost in another world. It's not until I clear my throat that he finally snaps to.

"I have to finish the photo I'm working on. Uh, while I do that, get the cameras ready and then you're good to go."

I get a flash of a smile before he frowns again.

"Great. Luke, I..." There's more I want to say. If I could, I'd scream at the top of my lungs that I'm trying my hardest to make things better between us. "N-never mind," I say. "The list, please."

He walks around to his seat and rummages through a few papers before handing it to me. Without another word I head to the closet to retrieve the cameras.

"Nikon D850. Check. Nikon 85mm F1.8 lens. Check. Sb700. Check. Alright," I mumble to no one. "All set."

IT'S GETTING COLD, but the couple insisted they wanted a fall themed shoot. As I place the last bag in his trunk, I close the door, and jump at the sight of him. My heart skips several beats.

"Sorry, didn't mean to scare you." He laughs.

"It's okay. You're all ready to go. I'll shut down the computer and then you'll be good to lock up."

"I shut everything down already. Um—" He scratches the back of his neck. "Do you want to come with me today? It's an easy shoot but having an extra hand wouldn't be so bad."

I don't want to read too far into it. He's only asking because it's part of my job. "Yeah, sure, let me get my..."

He lifts his other hand. In it are my jacket and bag. Luke may have his grumpy moments, but when he does things like this, and like the lantern festival surprise, I see a true gentleman. Any lady would be lucky to be on the receiving end of this side of him.

"How'd you know I'd say yes?" I ask.

He shrugs. "Wild guess?"

CHAPTER 18

*T*he park is gorgeous. Even amongst the stubborn green leaves that haven't changed, it still feels like fall. We walk through the grassy knoll, kicking leaves along our path. A bright orange-gold one snatches my attention, and I stop to bend down and retrieve it.

"I'm going to set up over here," he says, glancing over his shoulder.

"Oh, okay do you need any help?"

"No, I just have to fidget with some settings. You're good for now."

We've arrived an hour early. Luke is very cautious about time and wanted to make a plan of where he wants the couple to stand for the pictures.

I go back to gathering leaves with long stems. Fall is my favorite season, and leaves are my weakness. If we weren't in public and there were piles, I'd probably jump in them.

While he fiddles with his camera on the step of a small white and blue gazebo, I settle down next to him with my leaves. He checks on me occasionally, his eyes peering over the camera. I pick off the stems then fold the colorful gems over one another.

It's a slow process, but within a half an hour I've completed my crown.

Luke went to the car a few moments ago but is heading back in my direction with a grin on his face. I like when he's at ease around me. There's something about him I've always been drawn to. Too bad it took me so long to realize it.

I stand and twirl; my knee-length red plaid skirt lifts a little as I spin. I come to a stop and curtsey.

"I was wondering what you were doing over there," he says.

"I was making a crown. Here, try it." He steps within range, and I extend my arms up, and place it on his head.

"Hold on, don't move." I slip my phone from the convenient pocket sewn into the skirt and tap the camera. "Smile."

Luke frowns, but underneath his lips turn upward. I flip the screen into selfie mode and adjust the crown to sit on top of both of our heads, then snap a selfie, and steal my creation back.

"As good as it looks on you, this baby is mine."

He chuckles. "Looks better on you anyway."

"So, did you find some good spots for the shoot?"

"I think so."

"Can I suggest something, if you haven't already thought of it."

"I did bring you along for some help, so suggest away."

I bring my hands close to my chest and clap them together. Skipping towards a tree with more leaves shed than the rest, I push them together in a pile.

Luke hesitantly walks over, arms crossed as he watches me with curiosity. "You're not gonna jump in those are you?"

"It's not like I haven't thought about it, but no. Now get your ass over here." I wave for him to come over.

His nose wrinkles in this cute way I've never seen before, and the ridiculous look on his face causes my heart to flutter several uneven beats.

"Ready?"

He holds out his hand as if to say, proceed. I take the hand and force him to stand closer.

"First throw the leaves." Leaning down I grab a handful of leaves and toss it up into the air, letting them cascade down around us. "Then the woman wraps her arms around her man's neck." I demonstrate by doing it to him, then lift my right leg, and throw my head back.

His hands hold my hips steadying me. A leaf lands on his head, and I snort. His shoulders fall, and I expect a grumpy face or a snide remark, instead I find amusement dancing over his lips.

"Our couple should be here soon. Can you try to act normal?"

"I'm not really sure I know how to do that," I say, lowering my leg, but leaving my arms around him. I tip my chin up, and my eyes roam over his smooth jawline and the five o'clock shadow grazing his cheeks. I fight the urge to unwrap my arms and touch his face with my hand. "Did you like my idea though?"

He shifts like he's uncomfortable. It's not my intention to make him feel that way, at all. The mixed signals are driving me crazy. "It could work," he says, face taut.

"Can we ask them if they like it?" I bite my bottom lip, and tilt my head, batting my eyelashes flirtatiously.

"Sure."

For the tiniest second, I imagined his face is moving closer, but it's over before it starts, and his eyes are focused over my shoulder.

"They're here." He pulls away, and with the absence of his body my hands finally fall to my sides. I release a shaky breath, and count to five before turning around to greet the couple.

❧

IT TURNS out they absolutely love the leaf idea—although it needs several takes until Luke is satisfied, but they don't mind. I even give the bride-to-be my leaf crown for a few shots, and she happily poses with it. Her fiancé smiles at her, even with the ridiculous crown, like she is his world. It stings to watch them, and there's a few moments I look away to gain composure, but I'd say in the end the photoshoot was flawless, and the pictures will turn out beautiful.

"That went well," I say, once they are out of earshot.

"They really loved your idea. Thank you," he says, while stuffing his camera back inside the bag.

"See, even my weird ideas can turn into something great."

He straightens and turns to me. "I never doubted you, Millicent." His sincerity is what sends a shiver through my body.

"We should head back. I have a lot of work to do."

"Aye, aye captain," I say.

A grin lights up his face.

"What?" I ask.

He shakes his head. "Nothing. Come on," he says, his hand finding the small of my back as he pushes me along, and doesn't let go until we reach the car.

When I finally get home, I have a hard time settling down. I can't get the image out of my brain of us standing in the middle of the leaf pile with my arms around his neck. The moment felt so natural, and something inside me wanted to get closer to him, even though I shouldn't.

I wasn't expecting to rekindle old friendships or make good with the people I hurt while I was home. I know I've hurt Luke. It's still there lingering between us. Like bait hanging over my head waiting for me to take it and strike again. I won't though, I've made a promise to myself.

Liking Luke or wanting Luke feels wrong because he's my younger brother's friend. If something were to happen between us and it was a bad split, I would hate for Ezra to be stuck in the middle. I half blame myself for him and Ezra drifting apart the first time. Even if it was just because of distance, I still feel like a tiny part was due to our seven minutes in heaven debacle.

I'm also not really sure I want to date. Dating leads to heartache and I'm better off without it. I've been happily single for four years, it never bothered me. So how can someone waltz into my life and suddenly make me question everything?

CHAPTER 19

The door to the studio jars open, jolting me from my work. Tony, Luke's dad, looks up at the same time as me. I've been showing him the social media pages and what I've done. Luke's been letting me pick images to display—with the client's permission of course. We've had several new followers since I've taken over and his dad was curious.

Tony's face pales. The woman strutting towards us has fire in her brown eyes. Her hair is tossed into a "mom bun" and her makeup is a little smudged. "Where is he?" There's not an ounce of kindness in her tone.

She registers me right away, but her glare is at Tony. He stares at her, eyes wide, not sure what to think. She looks around my age, maybe a few years younger like Luke. It dawns on me who this is, and I get to my feet immediately.

Tony engages her. "Gretchen, I didn't know you were in town. Can you reach out after work? This is not the time or place for these conversations. He's busy."

This gives me the perfect opportunity to slip away and warn Luke of the storm coming his way. I don't bother to knock: if he's naked in here he's naked.

He's behind his desk working diligently and watching another episode of the *D&D* show, *Critical Role*. His laughter over whatever was just said ceases to exist the moment he looks at me. Fear grips him. He stands and the chair rolls out from behind him, slamming into a metal filing cabinet. He winces at the bang.

"Millicent, are you okay?" He's around the desk and to me in a single moment. I don't know what my face looks like but the way his eyes roam over me makes me believe he sees worry there.

"I am—but you might not be. Your dad and Gretchen are squaring off out there and she looks kind of pissed."

He gasps, and with rough hands rubs the back of his neck. "Fuck!" He stomps. He moves past me, but when he reaches the door, he grips the knob and turns back. "Thank you for the heads up," he says, sincerely.

"Sure."

Without another word he pulls open the door with a force so strong, I almost expect it to fly off the hinges. I stand in his office listening to the sounds of laughter on the TV and a man's deep voice pretending to be an innkeeper, talking to the other characters about staying the night.

I shouldn't intrude, but I go back out into the main space anyway. Staying back, I listen to the chaos that's ensued.

"Fuck that, Gretchen. I'm not discussing things now. Everything is set, I'm not going back on my word. This is over. Please leave."

"Luke, you can't just leave me like this. I need— we need you."

We.

"You don't, Gretchen. You only think you do. You liked the idea of us, the idea of a family, but that's all it was. I don't have a place with you and him. We are going through with this, and I told you this shit does not come into my workplace. It can't."

Someone clears their throat next to me. It's Tony. I was wrapped up in their convo I didn't realize he was there.

"Is Luke okay?" I ask.

Tony sighs, shaking his head and doing the same neck rubbing gesture as Luke. The similarities between them are uncanny. His familiar eyes meet mine.

"She's a piece of work. Luke didn't tell me she was in town. I thought she was still in California and had stopped harassing him. I can't wait until this shit is over. It's not my place to talk about it. I just hope once it is she leaves my son alone."

The bells on the door sound like they'll break the glass as they ring. The studio grows quiet once the door shuts.

"Hey." Tony's hand grazes my shoulder. "Luke's strong. He'll deal with it. I know he can be a bit angry at times, he doesn't mean to take it out on others, but I think once all the shit with Gretchen is done, he'll be fine."

My eyes find Luke. He's sitting in my seat, his head resting on the desk.

"I see the worry in your eyes," says Tony. "Luke's been a little less irritable since you started working here. Hell, even I am."

I smile at that. It's nice to hear that I've made some kind of impact on their business.

"He'll be okay. I have to go call Jennifer and let her know. Oh, and thanks for that tutorial on social media. I think you guys will do great here. I can see this becoming a budding business in both your hands."

Guilt tries to force its way out. This isn't permanent, but Tony complimenting me, and the fact that I'm helping, is going to make it much harder to leave when I find a new job.

He gives my shoulder one last squeeze before retreating to the back room. I stare over at the hunched defeated figure. I have to decide if it's worth going over there to check on him. I'm not expecting an explanation and I still have no idea what that was all about, but maybe he just needs someone.

I take a deep breath and make my way over to stand beside him. He doesn't move. *Just break the ice, Mill.* Without a word I touch his back. His body jerks but he doesn't lift his head.

"Ezra said a good starting character would be a Barbarian. If I want to hit shit. Tell me about your Druid."

He freezes under my touch. I almost think he's about to retreat to his grumpy self and I wouldn't blame him, but when he lifts his weary gaze, I see a hint of smile in the corner of his eyes.

"He said that, huh? You want to learn about my class?"

I remove my hand from him as he sits back in the chair and crosses his arms at his chest.

"Yeah, Luke. I genuinely am curious. Oh and he mentioned a Warlock might work for me too and I'm intrigued. He said their spells hit faster. I'm not quite sure what that entails but I'd love a kickass spell."

Luke's smile finally shines through all the sadness. The best part is that I did that for him. I brought him back out of the slump he was feeling from whatever that woman did to him. I'm not going to ask or intrude because that's not who I am. I can only hope that this moment will let him know that I'm serious about fixing everything I did wrong. I don't want him to hate me anymore; I like him too much for that. I want him to trust me so maybe eventually he'll tell me what's going on with Gretchen.

"So, you think I'm ready to slay some dragons?" I ask.

He shakes his head, but his grin never fades. His soft chuckle fills me to the point where a bubbling happiness descends from my heart.

"I think you should slay some work first," he says, standing.

I snort.

He starts to walk past me. I know he has a ton of work to get done as is, but as he goes, he stops and his hand slides up my arm, and holds steady on my elbow. "Thank you. I'm sorry about all of that."

"Are you okay? Or—will you be okay?"

He nods. "I will be. Maybe if you finish early, I'll let you in on some *D&D* secrets."

I like the comfort of his hand and the way he's watching me

with that hopeful gleam in his eyes. He's going to be okay. For the first time since being home, I don't want to leave. The dream of Manhattan is slowly fading and that frightens me more than anything in the world.

"Tell me all your secrets, Luke." The words that come out were meant for *D&D*, but I think they have a deeper meaning. One I'm not going to admit—at least not yet.

CHAPTER 20

onight, my goal is to get started on my latest blog idea. Luke loaded some images on a drive, and I've got them downloaded onto my laptop. I'm combing through trying to find the perfect ones to add. Instead of sex, I've chosen to write about the festival, the romantic side of it, and new and exciting date night ideas. I had no idea that the lantern festival was even a thing.

I was thrilled to see Luke had taken a few shadow-like photos of couples with their backs turned to us. Their arms outstretched over each other. One couple is kissing, another holding hands. None of their faces are there, only the darkness of their shadows. To me it's the little things that show love and affection. You don't need to say I love you. It's there hidden sometimes. Like tiny gestures.

A thought grasps me, taking hold of my heart and squeezing it enough to cause a pinch. Everything that Luke has done for me the last few weeks suddenly comes to mind. The car battery, the ticket to the festival. While those things could be just a friendly gesture because that's who he is, there's a nagging feeling that tells me it's more.

Creating this article is helping the anxiety over this weekend's boudoir shoot, and my appointment with Astra. I'm spiraling out of control, but then Luke pulls me from the wreckage and I'm okay. Seeing her again after all these years should not affect me, but when you're friends with someone for more than half your life, it makes it harder to let them go.

My phone rings beside me, as I type out the third paragraph. Ezra's smiling face pops up on my screen, so it feels like I have to answer.

"Hey," I say.

"Hi. Look I know you're probably busy, but I left a set of dice at Mom's. My D20 is in there, and I'm going crazy trying to set up for tonight's D&D game. Would you be able to drop them off?"

That's right, it's Thursday, D&D night, which means Luke will be there. It's not that I'm trying to avoid him; we've been together all week, but even so, there's this weird mixture of feelings that have been silently floating between us.

"Mil?" Ezra's calm voice pulls me from my thoughts.

"Yeah?" It comes out softer than I mean it to.

"Everything okay?"

"I'll be okay, nothing I can't handle. Where are your dice?"

"In my old room, top draw of the wooden desk. You're a lifesaver."

"It's no problem; can you give me like half an hour? I want to finish up the project I'm working on."

"Oh, yeah, that's cool. The guys aren't coming for another hour. I'm trying to make dinner now." In the background cabinets slam shut, pots and pans clink together, and I can tell he's a bit overwhelmed.

"Why not just order Chinese?" I ask.

"You know me, always trying to go big." He chuckles.

"Right. I'll see you soon."

❧

EZRA AND JAKE rent a house on the other side of town. It's not a far drive, but by the time I pull up there's already cars, including Luke's. Their loud, rambunctious voices and laughter leak through the open windows along the front porch. The floorboards creak with each step. My hand raises to knock as the door yanks open. I'm greeted by Jake's bright smile.

"Your dice are here!" he yells behind him.

The scent of Ezra's homemade pizza wafts out the open door, and like a monster hungry for food, my stomach makes note of the smell, and growls loud enough to hear.

"Join us, we're about to have some dinner."

It's so tempting to take him up on his offer. Ezra is a better cook than Mom with some things. Will Luke be okay with me being here? I don't want to make it too awkward.

"I'll take a to-go box. I have to get back and do some writing."

"Oh, come on, it's just dinner. Plus, you know your brother and his Tupperware."

I chuckle. Ezra won't lend out his Tupperware, because he claims that's how lids end up without bottoms, and he's got a system in his cabinets.

"Only for dinner," I say.

He moves and swiftly motions for me to step inside. Their house is one of the older colonial homes in the neighborhood, built in the mid-1940s. It has a certain antique charm about it that I love.

Jake takes my jacket, while I make my way down a small narrow hallway towards the kitchen. The guys all sit around a round table in the center of everything. The yellow glow of the chandelier light above their head brightens up the kitchen.

Familiar faces turn in my direction.

"Hey, Mil." Ezra waves with his oven mitt from the other side of the room.

Sitting on top of the stove is a large pizza pan with steam rising from the finished product. The scent of tomato mixed with onions, peppers, and meat swirl together making my stomach yell out for a second time.

"Hey, Luke, can you get my sister a chair?" he asks.

Luke stands. Without hesitation he grabs one of the folding chairs leaning against the wall near the backdoor. I expect him to put it on the opposite side of the table, but instead he makes one of the other players, Patrick, scoot over and sets the chair beside him.

"Thanks, and what am I doing with these?" I hold up the bag of dice.

"Oh, give it to Sean. He's our Dungeon Master. Tracy quit on us," he says.

"Dungeon Master," I bow, in front of Sean. I've known him for years, so I don't feel awkward around him.

"Why thank you," he says, flashing me a devilish grin.

I walk around the table to the seat that Luke has gotten. Scooting myself and the chair forward, I bump into him. His neck flushes a deep shade of red.

"Sorry," I mumble.

"S'okay," he says. He clears his throat and shifts his chair, but there's only an inch or two difference.

Ezra comes over with the pizza and sets it down in the center. As if they were animals, every man reaches in and claws for the pizza, Luke included. He takes the slice and instead of putting it in front of him, he slides it over to me.

My face warms, and all I can do is nod. When did things become this weird?

"Are you joining us for our campaign tonight?" Patrick asks, running a hand through his long blond locks.

"Nah, I got some writing to do. Trying to get back out there."

"Oh, right. Ezra told us about your job, I'm sorry," he says, sincerely.

Like Sean I've known Patrick a long time too. They were both part of the original crew from high school.

"It is what it is." I shrug. "But Luke here took me under his wing," I say, with a smile.

Luke bumps into me. "You're getting better," he says in a teasing voice. I expect there to be snark, but it's all playful.

"Hey, I'm the best assistant you've ever had." I return the bump and we stay like that, shoulder to shoulder, for an extra few seconds. My heart drums harder, skipping around in weird beats.

The guys are all eyeing us, especially Ezra, who's got a ridiculous smirk on his face. I move away from Luke, not wanting it to seem like we're flirting, because we're not, are we?

"You should stay," Sean chimes in. "You don't have to play."

"Yeah, Mill, I mean you have been asking me all these questions about the game. Why not see it in action?" Ezra says.

I feel Luke's eyes on me. The hairs on my neck stand on end, and goosebumps prick at my sensitive skin. I peek over at him. There's a softness to his eyes. "You should," he says. "Your brother is right. Seeing the real thing will help piece together all the questions you've been asking."

Around the table each one of them nods in agreement. Maybe this is part of my redemption arc. I stay and watch them play, then Luke won't look at me with such hesitancy and he'll let me in more. Is that what I want? My stomach flutters.

"Okay. I'm in. I can't stay the whole night, but I'll watch."

❧

THE REST of dinner Luke's a bit more reserved, but still occasionally, there's a new level of banter between us that not even I can figure out. While the guys scatter and prepare for their game in the living room, I decide to help Ezra clean up.

"So, are you ready to admit something is happening between the two of you?"

I nearly choke. "Me and Luke? Why would you think anything is going on?"

"Oh, I don't know," he says, placing a dish in the drying rack, as I wipe down the table. "Maybe it's the way he gave you a slice first instead of himself, then he asked if you wanted seconds, and don't get me started with how as the dinner went on his chair and body sat leaning in your direction."

"Are you going to give me some kind of brotherly lecture?" I ask, slipping the sponge under the water to rinse.

"No, I'm just simply observing."

A snort escapes me. "Observing, but clearly you have an opinion, so spit it out."

"Nothing, I— I worry about you, that's all. And I think you should go for it."

"I'm a big girl now. I can make these decisions all on my own."

He laughs. "Yeah, I know."

I toss the dish rag at him, but it falls short. His laughter grows louder into a cackling frenzy as he points to the rag. I cross the room, unable to hold in a grin, and swipe it from the floor. Then I smack him with it.

"Stop acting like Mom."

"I swear," he says, holding his hands up in surrender.

I pull back to playfully hit him again when the doorbell rings.

"Saved by the bell."

"Funny." I grin, getting him as he turns to head for the front door.

"There's our new player. One of Jake's co-workers, Nora, is joining tonight. You'll like her, Mill; she's cool."

"What class does she play?"

He raises his brow. "She's a Bard."

"Oh—they seem like an interesting class. I read that their magic comes from artistic expressions. I love that. If I were a Bard, I'd play the flute because—"

He pauses his retreat as mirth dances across his features. "Not into Luke, huh?"

I jerk at him as if I'm going into attack, and as I do Luke appears in the entryway of the kitchen. If he heard what was said, he doesn't act it. Ezra whistles as he walks past Luke and throws me a shit-eating grin over his shoulder at me, before disappearing.

Luke points in the direction Ezra went. "Should I be worried?"

Growling softly, I shake my head. "Nah. Just Ezra being Ezra."

"Right… so you're staying?"

"Mhmm. Can I sit next to you?" I ask.

His lips curl in the most beautiful, charming smile ever. Ezra's onto me big time. I hate admitting it but there's something there. Even if it's small.

"Already has your name on it," he says, in an almost seductive tone, one I don't think he even catches as it passes through his lips.

Am I turned on by this? No. Nope. *C'mon, Millicent, time for some D&D.*

CHAPTER 21

*I*n the living room, the couches are spread far apart, and a folding table is in the center. I take my spot beside Luke. Our chairs are close, not more than an inch apart.

Nora floats in like some kind of beautiful garden fairy. Her thick black mane of hair sits heavy on her shoulders. She's dressed the part for sure in her flowy pink floral cami dress and a crown kind of like the one I made in the park with Luke.

I nudge him. "See, crowns are cool."

He shakes his head, amusement dancing in his eyes.

"I love your crown. Nora, right?"

She settles down next to Sean. "Yeah. So, you're the famous Millicent Jake hasn't shut up about." She eyes him across the table, he shrugs.

"Oh God, what did he tell you?"

She chuckles. "Nothing bad. Pinky swear. Little did I know that my favorite writer from *Forever Twenty* would be sitting in the same room as me. I'm sorry about what happened; Ez and Jake told me, but you were seriously my favorite."

Her words mean a lot to me. I wait for the sting I usually get when someone brings up the magazine, but it never comes.

"See, Mill, told you you'd be okay," Ezra says.

"Thank you, Nora. I've got a blog and some cool ideas on the horizon. I can give you the info later, so you guys can start your game."

Her grin is spectacular, with dimples forming on her pale cheeks. "Love that. I'm stoked."

Luke nudges me as Sean talks about the game. We give each other a quick grin, before turning our attention to Sean. He sits behind what looks like a wooden box that opens in several different locations. He's got his attention on whatever is in front of him, and he and Jake are quietly discussing something as he works.

Luke pulls out a folder from a bag beside his chair. It holds textbooks and papers curled up over other folders. He puts a pencil between his teeth and scours over a sheet.

I lean over. We aren't that far apart, and our chairs are touching. "Is that the character sheet?" I whisper. "Hm... Kyus. Interesting name."

He bites down on the center of the pencil, grinning as he gives me a once-over, before reading something on his sheet. I'm trying so hard to understand all the numbers and words I'm unfamiliar with. There's so much to learn and I can see it taking me a while to grasp.

"What's that?" I ask, pointing to a square on the lower left-hand corner that has a bunch of random things written on it. "DRU-I-DIC?"

He pulls the pencil from his mouth. "It's the secret language of the Druids." He doesn't seem annoyed that I'm asking questions. Bringing the sheet between us he rambles off the different things on it. While he does, I can't help sneaking a peek at him when he's not paying attention. I wish my brain would focus on the character sheet, but I can't. My heart is humming in my chest, speeding away like a race car.

"These are their abilities. Like their strength and how smart they are." He points to each one on the paper.

"How do you get these numbers?"

"I rolled them up," he says, jutting his chin towards the dice on the table.

"And the higher the better?"

"Yup."

I open my mouth to ask more, curiosity at its best, when Sean clears his throat. "Alright, is everyone ready to jump back in? I think we were heading into town?" Sean speaks up behind his little box.

"Sean, what are you hiding behind?"

"It's called a DM screen." He chuckles.

I nod, not wanting to delay them any longer. I stare down at the large grid mat with a hand-drawn map on the table. Miniature figures are placed in strategic spots. Whoever drew that map has some serious skills. Everything is so precise and drawn perfectly to scale.

Sean's powerful long drawl catches my attention. It's a lot deeper than his usual voice as he starts the game. Listening intently, I reach down and grab the water bottle I left at my feet. I uncap it while Sean sets the scene.

"You entered Willowdale Village at nightfall and have just woken with the sun. Zarad—" He turns to Jake. "You are exploring the village and come across The Gold Digger Tavern."

My snort is loud enough to wake up the next-door neighbors. And the water I was drinking dribbles down my chin and out my nose. It burns and stings but I'm okay. Everyone looks at me, no one serious at all, grins on each face as I scan the table.

"Sorry. S-sorry, guys. Keep going."

Nora gives me a knowing smirk, and then turns her attention to the guys.

To my left, Ezra hands me a napkin. I look across the table at

Sean whose grin is bright enough to light up the room. I clean up my dribble, then set the water back down.

"And Maridanna," Sean says to Nora. "You are seated on the far end when Zarad enters. You're intrigued by the Goliath, maybe a bit smitten as he sits down at the bar. You lock eyes but turn away in time to see the bartender slipping some kind of concoction into one of the drinks."

I lean into Luke and whisper, "Does Sean have a character as a DM?"

He puts his arm behind me, the warmth of his skin brushing against my neck causing me to shiver. "No. He's like the narrator of the story. He tells players what to do, and also plays the role of any NPCs—that's non-player-characters."

"Ah. Okay. Is it hard to be a DM?" I ask, softly.

I expect him to remove his arm, but he doesn't. I'm heated like molten lava but find myself sinking into Luke's touch a little further.

"You create everything, so yeah. You've gotta think on the fly and be ready for changes. Right now, it's Sean's world and we're just living in it."

I snicker. "I hope he's not planning on poisoning you."

Luke dips his head, as mine lifts to meet his stare. "And why's that?" We're both lost in each other. The game around us continues. The sound of dice hitting the table, their voices, but everything sounds distant like a wind tunnel.

"Because... I kind of fancy you, Luke Parker. Now go be my Druid in shining— no that's not right... in dull... brown hide... leather? They uh, can't wear metal, right?"

His lips part, green eyes sparkling. My breathing is labored, and I find myself placing my hand on his chest.

"That is correct," he says softly.

"Back off, ya big lug! The lady is under my protection!" Patrick's loud booming voice shakes us from our trance, but

Luke keeps his arm around me as he jumps into the game as if what happened seconds before never did.

❧

AN HOUR and a half into the game I'm fully invested in the story line. They have already had a brawl in the tavern and Luke's character Kyus saved the day. The role-playing part seems easy, and I love how it flows between them so naturally as if I were listening to someone read me a book.

Nora's character is so intriguing. Her backstory is she's a violinist that travels with an orchestra. They have stopped in town for a few days, and as much as she loves the traveling life, she's starting to feel drained and stopped for a drink to think about her life choices.

I stay quiet taking it all in. Luke sits up when he has something to say or when he has to roll the dice (which is the most confusing part. I'll have to ask Luke about that later, so I don't interrupt them). When he's finished or when he's just talking in his character's voice, using a slight old-fashioned accent, he leaves his arm around the back of my chair. I don't hate the feeling. In fact, I never want to leave this spot.

It's so late and I'm exhausted. From what Ezra told me sometimes these games could go on for hours. I find myself drifting and getting closer to Luke.

While Jake and Sean are in a heated fictional argument Luke's breath tickles my ears. "You're quiet."

I look over at him. "Tired. Just observing and taking in everything. This looks like a ton of fun. I'd love to join and try it out, but this seems way advanced for me."

He chuckles. "Maybe we can do a one-shot campaign. Pick a night and I'll help you learn how to play."

"Would you really consider that?"

His eyes search mine, like maybe he's looking for me to jump out and say, *gotcha!* *D&D is for nerds, I'd never want to play that game.* I guess I brought it on myself for my behavior all those years ago. Guilt sucks.

"If you really want to learn."

I don't look away. I have to show him that I'm serious about wanting in. Into what, though? Being his friend? To maybe be more involved in not just his interests but my brother's too. Me and Ezra are close, but I never really cared about his hobbies. Or maybe I want Luke to let me into his heart. There's this tug like gravity reeling me in.

"I— I..."

"I need a piss break," Patrick says, yawning and stretching his long legs out under the table on the other side of Luke.

I avert my eyes from Luke and stare down at the almost empty water bottle at my feet.

"Same," Jake says, standing to stretch as well.

Luke's arms retreat from the back of my chair as he stands. He looks away and I hate that I hesitated to answer. It almost feels like maybe he really does think I'm lying.

"I think I'm going to call it a night," I say, following everyone's lead. "I loved watching the game. I'd love to maybe—" I watch Luke closely. He's taking a swig of his own water bottle and staring out the front window. "Maybe do a one-shot. Luke said it's a good way to learn the basics."

My question pulls Luke from his trance, and he looks at me. Not just a simple once-over, he REALLY looks at me, like he's seeing me for the first time. His eyes get all lit up, and although his lips aren't curved into a smile, it feels like he's no longer questioning the reasoning behind me staying tonight. I grab at the fabric of my shirt right over my rapidly beating heart.

"I think that would be great," Ezra says, bringing my attention back to the group.

"I don't want to intrude on your gaming time."

"Intrude?" Sean clears his throat. "No way. I love that you're coming around to the idea of playing. Although it seems your interest may have been piqued by a certain sexy-ass Druid."

Now it's Luke's turn to spit out water. The guys laugh and when I look up to check on Luke, his neck and cheeks are rosy red.

Nora's bubbly laughter fills the room. "Yes! Please intrude," she pleads, pressing her hands together.

"I'm kind of invested in your Bard. Maybe you can teach me a thing or two, although it doesn't sound like a beginner class."

Nora chuckles. "It's not the worst, but there are lots of moving pieces. I'm down to talk with you about it anytime."

I search the guys' faces for any indication that they are against it, even though they are saying they aren't. They all pass the vibe check, and I'm greeted with a smile from all.

"How can I say no to that. Between sexy Druids and a beautiful new friend, I'm game. Just go easy on me. K?"

Ezra grins. "Ha. You're only asking for trouble now."

"Ugh. Ez. Well, thank you for letting me watch." I say a quick goodbye, giving Ezra and Jake hugs as I leave. Nora too. She's excited to see another girl in the group.

Jake helps me find my jacket, and Luke just gives a casual goodbye nod as I walk out the front door. Outside the late fall wind picks up. I jog down the steps towards my car lit up by the glowing streetlamp above it.

"Hey, hold up." It's Luke.

I stop halfway down the walkway and turn. Luke shivers from the cold. He rubs his arms, my eyes wandering, I'm an arm girl and I can't help myself. Knowing they were around me for half the night gets me all hot and bothered and I ALMOST think about using one of the toys inside that big black bag of magic when I get home.

"What's up?"

Shy Luke returns, scratching the back of his neck, and having a hard time keeping eye contact. I kind of want to shake him to snap him out of it.

"Um, are you all set, have everything you need? If not, we can totally postpone…"

"You mean the boudoir shoot? Do you want to postpone?" I'm kind of relieved that I have tomorrow off to put myself at ease. I think that's why he gave me that day off. He needs to prepare and so do I for what we're about to do on Sunday. We still have to be together on Saturday, but there'll be not much time to chit-chat and make small talk since we are shooting a wedding. And his dad will be at this one as a buffer.

"If you're uncomfortable about this we don't have to do it," I say, staring at Luke. Even in the darkness it's easy to see he's nervous.

He fidgets with the belt loop on his jeans. "No, no. I promised you we'd do this for your blog. I don't like to break promises. I'm making sure you're cool with it and everything." He removes his hand from his neck.

"Hey." I reach out and touch his hand. His breath hitches as I do, either that or the gust of wind that passes through knocked the wind out of him. "I'm still good. I have everything."

Silence surrounds us for a few moments.

"I'm getting my hair and makeup done around three, since we said five was good."

"Oh, you're not doing that yourself?"

"I want to look good, and although I've been given tons of makeup samples working for a magazine, I'm not the best at putting it on," I say, releasing a strangled laugh. "Astra, she's uh— she's doing my— doing my makeup."

I stare at the small space on the empty concrete between us. My nose tingles as if I'm about to sneeze, but instead it leaves a sting in my eyes.

"Are you okay?"

"It's fine. I'm fine. Honestly, we haven't spoken in years and seeing her… it was hard. You don't have to worry about me though. It's a long story." I push out a tense smile.

His brows narrow. "You don't look okay."

My eyes meet his, and there's this weird understanding that silently passes through us. Like he gets that I don't want to talk, but he's also here if I need to vent.

"I will be. Love is complicated, right?" I shrug.

He nods. "I get that one hundred percent. It's not the end of the world if you skip the makeup; I think you'd look great without it too."

His words make my skin heat up. I avert my gaze and realize it's not only his words heating me up, but also our hands that are still connected. Neither of us try to pull away first.

"Thanks."

"Okay. So, Sunday evening," he says, curtly.

"Yeah, Sunday. And I'll see you Saturday, nine at the studio?"

"Mhmm."

For a few lingering moments I keep his hand in mine, and he doesn't bother to pull back either.

"Okay, I should uh— go." I point over my shoulder and reclaim my hand.

"Yeah. Have a good night. I'll see you Saturday."

I wave goodbye, and by the time I get into the car I'm thankful he's already gone inside, because I have to sit there and give myself a moment to go over everything that happened tonight. The hand holding, the flirting, the spark. I'm questioning if what I'm feeling is real or am I just desperate for affection after being single for so long. I haven't felt anything for a man in years, but maybe there is something there; I just need to figure out what it is.

CHAPTER 22

*W*ith all the confidence I can muster I tug the salon door open and walk inside. A floral scent tickles my nose as I enter. Glancing around, there's no sign of Astra. I check the time to make sure that I'm not late. I'm twenty minutes early.

Luke sent me a text a little while ago to let me know that he's on his way home and will have everything set up by the time I get there. Underneath my clothes, the lingerie burns into my skin, reminding me that in a few short hours I'll be half naked in front of him. The idea scares me, but at the same time, it's Luke, and I don't mind. Something has changed in the past week or so, and there's almost like this electric current ready to explode between us.

"Millicent. Hi. How are you?" Katherine, Astra's fiancée, smiles wide. She looks genuinely happy to see me. I wonder if Astra gave her the full story about us. From the looks of it I highly doubt it.

"Hi. I'm here for my appointment."

"Yes, I'll get you set up. Astra is running behind."

"Yeah, that's perfect."

I'm still in awe at how fancy this salon is. On a normal occasion I'd deem it out of my price range, but for this I want to feel and look my best. My blog and getting myself noticed is important to me.

I settle down in one of the salon chairs. While I wait for Katherine, I stare in the mirror and play with strands of hair. This shoot couldn't have come at a better time. I need a trim badly. The plan for the boudoir shoot is to curl my hair so that the ringlets cascade over my shoulder. I don't get a chance to make myself up often, and with the loss of my job, I think I deserve a little something for me.

Katherine is prepping the shampoo as the front door opens and Astra comes rushing through. "I am so sorry," she says. "The line at the smoothie place was insane."

In her hand is a tray with three cups. Her eyes find mine and she smiles.

"Oh, you're just in time. I haven't started yet," Katherine says, tossing a loving glance over her shoulder.

"Perfect." Astra rests the container down on the counter up front.

She grabs two drinks, and heads towards us. I expect her to take a sip from one, but instead she hands Katherine one, and me the other. "There's extra strawberries," she says as she puts the cup in my view.

I take the cold plastic into my hands. Her grin has fallen into a soft smile, like the drink is an apology. Even after all these years, reading Astra comes naturally.

"Thank you." I take a sip releasing a small moan as the cool drink coats my throat. "This is amazing."

"Joe's has the best smoothies in town," she says, wrapping a black cape around me.

I set the drink between my legs and lean my head back into the sink. My neck aches from the angle, but the moment Astra's long, thin fingers comb through my hair, any discomfort vanishes.

I close my eyes and attempt to keep my breathing steady. Even with them closed her stare burns through me. When she runs the shampoo through my hair, I never want her to stop. In high school I was always her practice dummy. I didn't mind allowing her to do my hair because she had the softest touch. I shiver.

"I'm sorry, it's a bit chilly here. I can turn up the heat," she says, as she wraps my hair in a towel.

"I'm okay," I manage to say, but it comes out in a rasp.

She leads me over to a chair in the center of the row. Katherine is greeting another customer as we walk up.

"So, tell me more about this photoshoot," she says as she brushes.

Her eyes meet mine in the mirror, and for a moment I spiral back in time, and it feels like we are in her mom's basement playing beauty salon. To push down the knot forming in my throat, I take a hearty sip of my drink before I answer. "I've been trying to come up with an idea for a blog, and I was having a conversation about it with someone, and the idea struck me. How do significant others feel about their spouse doing a boudoir shoot for them? I have a few couples who are willing to give me their takes."

"You always had such great ideas. Are you still at the magazine?" she asks, snipping away at my hair. "Oh, how much off the length did you want?"

"Thanks, and no. I was let go. Not much off the length, a trim, and tighten up the layers."

She nods to me in the mirror and continues cutting.

"I'm sorry about the job. It's great that you have such a good outlook though. Starting a blog and branching out on your own. You always were determined to get your writing out there."

It's funny how she says that I have a great outlook. It's been one battle in my head after another. Sure, I haven't given up hope, but at the same time my brain keeps telling me that I'll never be enough for this career. I'll always fail. Shaking those thoughts is hard.

"What about you? Huh? I mean this place is... wow."

I attempt to persuade my eyes to focus on anything but her, but it's hard to concentrate on anything else.

She stands in front of me brushing my long bangs forward with a comb. Through the tendrils of wet hair, I watch her body. I've always loved everything about her, including her curves.

"Ah. Well Katherine was the big brains behind it. The business aspect was a lot and she just swooped right in like it was nothing."

"How'd you meet?" I ask, and suddenly regret it. Listening to this story might be enough to destroy my heart.

"Cosmetology school."

Her eyes come level with mine as she goes into full detail about their "meet cute". I avert my attention down to the plastic cup on my lap. Her eyes are not mine to get lost in. A stray unwanted tear falls down the far side of my cheek.

She brushes my hair aside, her face in line with mine. She didn't even notice. Good.

"So then, she left the dye in too long, and it totally fried my hair," she says, then stands straight, brushing the hair in another direction.

"And you still fell in love?"

"It took some convincing, but eventually she kind of just swept me off my feet."

Her eyes wander the large space, and she grins when they meet Katherine's. Watching their goo-goo eyes for each other in the mirror slices right through me.

I finish off my drink in between the haircut and curl. She doesn't stop talking my ear off as she works. It's okay because it's distracting me from the little touches that make my heart flutter. With my hands free I can grip the chair to calm my nerves.

"So, what have you been up to? How's Ezra?"

"He's good. He and Jake are living together."

"Jacob? I knew that they would be endgame!" She dances around, like it's the best news she's heard all day. It's not unusual, she and Ezra got along when we were growing up. He treated her as another sister.

"So, what do you think?" She touches a strand of hair and the curl bounces back up.

Turning my head, I check and I'm in awe by how the ringlets spiral in a perfect curl against my shoulder. It's exactly what I imagined. "It's perfect. For makeup, can we do a more natural look? Something a little dark around the eyes."

"Sexy eyes, got it." She grins.

She lowers her head, her lips nearly grazing my right ear. "But you don't need makeup for that." My eyes catch hers in the mirror. For a fleeting moment I'm transported back to the night I kissed her.

It was mostly quiet out in the backyard with the party raging inside. Astra and I sat on a porch swing that was placed in the back of the yard against a wooden fence. The night was beautiful, the stars clearly visible. We always sat close to each other, we were best friends, always whispering secrets in each other's ears.

"I can't believe we are off to college in a few short months. I don't know if that makes me happy or sad," she said.

"A little bit of both, maybe."

"You're going to be a Manhattan girl. You get to live your dream. When you're famous, I can tell everyone that you were my best friend."

I choked. "Were?"

"I mean you're going to be famous and all..." She gave a smile, but there's something hiding behind it.

She made it feel as if it were our last summer together. It

wasn't the first time she used us in the past tense, especially as the school year wound down. I had to tell her. My feelings were not fake. I hurt when she hurt. I cared for her so deeply I thought that if I kissed her, it would banish the doubt in her mind that we would end up being those friends who slowly phased each other out of their lives.

"Astra."

"Mmm," she hummed, her beautiful light airy voice did things to me. My stomach filled with intense fluttering that only happened around her. I'd felt it for years but thought it was just some weird friendship thing.

Without saying another word, I pressed my lips to hers and my whole world exploded like fireworks on the Fourth of July. She kissed me back too. Opened her mouth, let me in, let me think that maybe—just maybe she felt something.

Her lips were soft and smooth, her Bath and Bodyworks Juniper Breeze lotion surrounded me. I loved that smell so much. She even reached up, held my face in her hands, ran her red-tipped nails through my hair. It was a kiss that I felt all the way through to my core. I'd been questioning my sexuality for so long at that point but kissing her solidified my love for both male and female.

When she pulled away her hungry eyes were on mine. I know they were. I saw it in the way they softened and looked into my soul instead of past it.

"I'm sorry, Mill. I-I-I don't feel that way about you."

"But you kissed me back," I said. My heart raced and tears burned my eyes. I couldn't breathe, I remember how hard it was to just take one breath.

"Of course, I did. You're beautiful, Millicent. Inside and out. But I don't feel anything like that towards you. You're my best friend and that's all it can ever be."

I blinked but the tears were relentless. She reached out trying to get me to understand. Her words, even now, are all still a blur.

On a small vanity on the salon wall my phone vibrates pulling us both away from the emotional moment. It goes off a second time. Briefly, my attention falls on Astra's lips, there's a small itch to press mine to hers, because if I do, everything will be right in the world; but that's not the reality here. She's taken and has only platonic feelings.

"Want me to grab that for you?" She sets the makeup down.

"Yeah. Thanks."

Her eyes flicker to the screen and then back up, like she's curious as to who it is.

Once the phone is in my hand, she continues to lightly powder my face with some blush.

> Luke: Hey, are you hungry? Maybe we can get something in between...

> Luke: Did you have anything specific you wanted? Any shots? I did look stuff up, but I don't know what you're comfortable with. I can show you some of my ideas or we could just go with the flow. It's up to you. Let me know. Either way.

I snicker. Funnily enough I can imagine him stuttering as if he were asking me these things out loud. His face pops into my head, and my entire body ignites in a hot flash.

"You're blushing under your blush. Who's got Millicent Gibson all flustered?" she asks.

"It's— it's nothing," I say, biting my lip. I hide the phone under the cape, and try to bite back the smile, but I can't help it.

"That's not nothing, but if it's new I totally understand not wanting to jinx it. When I met Katherine, I kept it from Mom, because I wanted to make sure she was the one."

"Oh, no— this isn't— he isn't. It's not anything."

"Okay, whatever you say." Astra wiggles her brows at me. As she finishes up, we talk about other things, like her schooling, my life in the city, and everything we've missed out on over the years.

Our goodbye is quick and easy. While her soft touches sparked some emotion behind them, her hug did not. I'm not sure what that means; maybe I'm over her or maybe there is something there with Luke.

"Please don't be a stranger, okay? I miss you, Mill." She sniffles, and when I pull back her eyes sparkle with moisture.

The only thing I manage is a nod, and a squeak of a goodbye. There's still that missing piece in my heart that broke off when Astra and I drifted, but as I head out the door there's another text from Luke, and my heart somehow swells with joy again. I never responded to his previous messages. I was too wrapped up in my conversation with Astra that I'd forgotten.

> Luke: Hey, everything okay? You haven't responded.

I step out onto the sidewalk. Staring at the text, I'm taken aback by his genuine concern. The tears that threatened my eyes a few minutes ago have vanished like they were never there. A completely different feeling takes over in its place.

> Me: Sorry. I got caught up at the salon. I'll be there in a few minutes. I'm between okay and not.

> Luke: If you're more comfortable you can wear my wizard costume instead.

A mixture of a snort and a sob tumble from my lips.

> Me: Nice try! I'm not going to dress up like all the women in your fantasies.

Maybe that was a little forward, but the three dancing bubbles pop up almost immediately in the chat.

Luke: Woman. There's only one...

I'm hot enough that I'm contemplating calling 911 to put out the fire. The thought takes me back to what Astra had said. I can't help wondering how flushed I was, and what everyone sees on my face when Luke comes up in conversation. She's not the first to say that I've had a reaction to Luke's presence. Sure, I've felt the zing between us, but I figure it was nothing more than me being sexually frustrated. There's a twitch in my lower half thinking about tonight's photoshoot, and his most recent text. It may have started out innocent, but now... now I'm not too sure.

CHAPTER 23

$\mathscr{I}$ pull up to a high ranch with sky-blue siding, and double check the house number to be sure. He told me his apartment sits on the lower level. I'll have to go around back to get to it, so I park on the street, not far from the house.

Cutting the engine, I begin to gather my things, but something stops me. Am I really doing this? My mind is reeling from my makeup session with Astra. There was still unresolved tension between us, I felt it with every fiber of my being. At least I thought I did. Then Luke came out of nowhere with that text and I— He makes me want to open my heart again.

It's like there's an angel on one shoulder and a devil on the other and they are both vying for my attention, tempting me to feel things that I shouldn't.

Shrugging it off, I grab the gray duffel bag from the passenger seat. I pulled a few different choices of lingerie from the samples I'd gotten to have more options.

My breath catches in the mirror as I stare at the woman looking back at me. Sure, I had to doll myself up every morning for my job to pretend to be someone I wasn't, but this was different. The woman staring back at me is sexy, determined, and nervous.

I shiver as I step out of the car, a frosty chill blasting me with a wall of cold air. I throw the bag over my shoulder and attempt to look as confident as I was the day I asked him to do this.

Following the property line, I open the gate on the hefty white fencing. One large tree in the yard sways and its leaves scatter all over, floating along with the breeze.

Gray clouds roll in and tiny droplets of cold water splatter against my head. With trembling hands, I press the doorbell. I don't know why I'm nervous. I've been naked in front of two guys my entire existence and now Luke would be my third. But it's not like this is anything sexual; it's work related and that's it. I'm about to close my eyes when the freshly painted white door swings open.

Luke's cheeks are already a light shade of pink, and we haven't even started yet. His eyes immediately flick down to my body, like he's imagining what's underneath. He won't have to imagine for long.

"Hi." His voice is raspy, so he clears his throat. "You can come in."

Inside the apartment the gray walls match all the black and gray pieces of furniture around the room. Dark wooden photo frames are strategically placed. They are filled with pictures that have a similar style to his own.

"Should I leave my shoes at the door?"

"If you'd like." With tight shoulders he stands beside one of two doors along the right side of the apartment.

"Do you want to change in the bathroom or—" I slip my shoes off and place them next to his black and white checkered vans. Goosebumps rise on my arms and neck. I can feel him watching me.

"If that makes you feel more comfortable." He pauses, observing me as I walk through his apartment. "I'll be waiting in

my room. I have some lighting to set up. Bathroom is next door."
He points to the second door, then vanishes into his room.

His space is so neat I feel like I'm on one of those HGTV
makeover shows. My idea of how he lived is completely opposite
of what is in front of me. I expect to find a display of fictional
beasts, and magic cards, but I don't even see an Xbox. Maybe it's
hidden in the cabinet under the mounted TV.

The scent of pine makes my nostrils tingle as I enter the
bathroom. It's strong like one of those scented sprays that Mom
keeps in ours. If he would have come to my apartment when I
lived on my own, he probably would have walked out from the
disaster that it was. I'm not neat, I'm a mess, and my bathroom
has never smelled this fresh.

I slip off my clothes and let them drop to the floor. For a few
moments I stand in the center of his bathroom in my black lace
two-piece, and a silky matching thong, but instead of shocking
him right away I cover it with a sheer black robe. Getting the
stilettos on is the hardest part. I'm not the kind of person who
wears tall, thin heels, so this is a huge step for me. I let go of the
white porcelain counter and come close to breaking my ankle.

Taking several huge breaths, I give myself some time to
process this whole thing. This is for business and business only.
Luke is my boss and that is all, he won't be staring at me with
those beautiful green eyes wanting a piece of me, he's doing this
to add more to his portfolio as I am doing it for work. Plus, I'm
clearly not his fantasy woman; he said there was one; there's no
way it's me.

I place all my belongings in a neat pile and head to his room.
Before entering I linger in the doorway. His walls are dark
enough to almost be a midnight black. To make it a bit brighter,
he's lit up the room with some of his lights from the studio, but
they aren't super bright. I love the deep rich tone it gives the vibe
of the room.

Luke stands by the foot of the bed. He's contemplating

something, while pointing his finger into thin air. I clear my throat and thank God he's got his camera on a strap around his neck, because as he faces me his hands slip and his camera falls. I take a step forward and my amateur heel-walking self nearly goes down. Thankfully, it goes unnoticed.

His bedroom is spotless too. On the far wall there's a wooden shelf with video game guides, miniatures, *Magic the Gathering* cards, *D&D* guides, and other similar items. It's like the nerd's guide to life. If this was high school, I probably would have made a comment, but now seeing his place and being in the comfort of his room, I'm realizing how attracted I am to every part of him.

I take note of the different lenses he has on the table. I recognize them now: there's a 35mm and an 85mm, and the one he's got on the camera is the 50mm. I've shocked myself with how much I've learned over the last month or so.

"So, where do you want me first? I was thinking maybe we can do a few shots with the robe on?"

He's stuck for a moment. His eyes dart around the room, like he's trying not to look at me. "Yeah. The robe on would be good. I did a lot of research on this and when it's off I want to try something with the heel of your stiletto."

"Holy shit, you know your women's shoes."

An amused look crosses his face, but still hidden under his serious demeanor. I stumble over to his bed and sit. His navy-blue comforter is tucked perfectly into the frame like it's never been slept on.

"So should I maybe cross my legs?"

He steps in front of me, his piercing emerald gaze holds mine as he sucks on his bottom lip.

"Move forward, sit on the edge. Knees together, toes pointed in." He observes my every movement. "Don't slouch, Mill. Back arched, shoulders like... perfect."

I adjust to his liking. God, I love how it feels when his eyes roam over my body. It's like I'm on fire, but it doesn't hurt, it's filled with pleasure and—shit, tingles in places I shouldn't feel them. He's not meaning to do it—or at least I'm sure it's just because he's making sure I'm seated right.

"I'm going to take a few practice shots, get a feel of the lighting. Hold it." Behind the camera the man is a menace. He's shooting like he was born to do this. Every few seconds he lowers the camera to check on me.

"Let's try with your legs crossed. Back arched. Bring the robe down just a tad off your shoulder." He points to his own shoulder. Then lifts his camera and buries his focus on the settings.

When he reroutes his attention back to me, he does a double take at the black rose tattoo on my left shoulder. He clears his throat again and lifts the camera. I stare at the tattoo, then at the ground while he presses the button several times. The shutter clicks and clicks as I adjust myself.

He gives me several directions, and after a few minutes of sitting up he asks me to lie down and open the robe a little. I lift my knee as he instructs and open the robe so that it spreads out under me.

"Do you mind if I straighten the robe a little?" He's trying so hard not to look at my body through his own eyes, only the camera's. Like that makes a difference. It's weird, he's a different person when the camera is up to his eyes and he's looking through a lens. Like he's more confident.

He adjusts the robe and I'm very conscious of the soft flab that sits loose around my gut. I try to suck it in.

"Don't do that," he says softly.

"Do what?"

He lifts the camera again, talking behind it. "Hide your real self."

My lips part as I fix my eyes on Luke. He's not paying attention to me. His camera holds his interest.

After a few quiet seconds, he lifts his gaze and cocks his head. "You alright?"

I look back down at my stomach, then at him again and swallow hard. With his face behind the lens, he says, "You're perfect the way you are, don't hide it. Okay?"

The only thing I can do is nod. There's a lump threatening to make me cry. I'd love to tell him that he is too, and I wish I would have noticed it sooner.

He keeps himself hidden, but occasionally, when he peers out from behind the lens, he regards me in such a way that gets me a little hot and bothered. In fact, I hate to admit it but this whole thing is making me want to see what it would be like to have him. It's hunger and lust and everything in between but I shouldn't act on it... or should I?

He reaches for the robe, but his hand slips and he grazes the skin near my hip. I try to hide the gasp that escapes my lips, but it's blatantly obvious. I'm not sure what came over me at that moment, but the soft touch of his fingertips sends a jolt through my body. "Maybe you should get me that wizard robe," I say, attempting to lighten the mood.

"I... uh, lift— lift your knee and tilt your head this way." A splotch of pink settles on his scruffy cheek.

Instead of acknowledging my comment, he motions for me to look at him and takes a few shots, then we reposition. "Take off the robe," he says, looking into his camera again.

I sit up slightly and shimmy it off my shoulders and throw it off to the side. It catches his arm and drapes over him. He jumps and looks over. I wait for a smile, or anything, but there's nothing there. He turns his attention back on the camera, and with trembling hands adjusts some settings.

"Put your hand low near your— your— your panty line."

"Panty line?" I snicker.

His face is permanently pink by this point. Blowing out a breath he takes a few long strides towards the bed. "Keep your hands moving up your body, don't stop when I stop clicking. Okay? Move them like it feels good."

I arch a brow at him, but he ignores it. Doing what he says, I start at my waistline just about the underwear and slowly inch up, eventually touching my shoulders. He pulls the camera down.

"May I, uh, take your hand?"

"Yeah." My voice jumps.

The tips of his fingers glide along the top of my hand. He takes it and gently settles it against my lower stomach right above the lacy underwear.

"Tuck it under here." He moves his fingers with mine and my lower half twitches with anticipation as our hands get caught up in each other.

A soft hum leaves my lips while his hand lingers for what feels like an eternity, but really, it's maybe seconds. He takes a few shots like that, the camera in his hand shakes a little. His nerves are shot.

"Let's take a break," I suggest. "See what we have so far."

He blows out another long staggered breath, and his entire body relaxes. "Okay."

His head remains buried in his camera for a few minutes. I stand from the bed and cross the room to him. Leaning down I scoop up the robe off the floor and put it back on.

"Do you have any of that food you promised?" I ask, attempting to get him to relax.

"Oh, um, yeah. I got a bunch of cold cuts from the deli near the studio. I know how much you love their roast beef."

I'm once again in awe, by how much he remembers. First with the lanterns and now with my food choice. I've never had someone other than my family and Astra remember silly mundane things about me.

"Tell me you got the poppy seed rolls."

Placing the camera down on his desk, he urges me into the

kitchen. I slide onto one of the stools at the counter dividing the living room and kitchen.

"You think I'd get roast beef without it? I know how picky you are."

Crossing my arms at my chest I huff. His lips twitch as he shakes his head at me.

"Hey! I'm not that picky. I did eat without complaints when they gave me rye instead."

He narrows his eyes, lips partially pulling into a smile, but falters quickly. As he dips behind the door of the fridge.

"Okay, okay. Maybe I complained a little."

His head peeks out over the top of the door.

"Okay, a lot."

"Honey mustard?" he asks.

"You're nasty."

He shrugs and pulls out everything, including the bread, and a bottle of my favorite brand of apple cider.

"You found it? I have been having such a hard time, it seems no one had it in stock."

"It was the last one, I recalled you complaining a few weeks ago about that too."

"I sure complain a lot, don't I?"

He chuckles. "Yeah, maybe a little."

"So rude! Anyways, thank you. For dinner. For putting up with my pickiness, and for doing this photoshoot for me. I'm sorry if you're uncomfortable."

"I'm not, it's fine. I'm not." He sits beside me.

With trembling hands, he attempts to undo the package of lunch meat, but his fingers keep slipping. In a brave gesture I reach out, touching my fingertips to his soft skin. He pauses and removes his hand. I take over and start preparing the sandwich myself. I reach for the rolls too. While I do the sandwiches, he pours the drinks.

I attempt to make small conversation during the meal, he's

giving one-word answers, and is having a hard time making eye contact. I don't want to push him, so I lay off, and we finish our meal in silence.

Once we're back inside the bedroom, I slip off the robe again and wait for his instructions.

"Stand by the window." His voice is taut as he points towards it.

The sun has already set now, but there's a soft light from the night sky peeking in through his horizontal blinds. I lean against the window, and he takes a few shots. I stare out into the darkened sky and my mind wanders to Astra. This day has been weird and I'm still trying to process everything. I don't know why the thought of her finding happiness bothers me so much. I hate that she was the first girl I loved and the only one who never loved me back. Mostly, I miss our friendship, the one we had before the kiss.

"May I?" I jump at the sound of his voice. I hadn't realized he'd crossed the room.

"Hmm?" I turn my neck and he's literally right there.

He narrows his eyes.

"Okay. You, okay?"

"Yeah," I whisper.

My attention falls on his lips as he carefully observes me. I never realized before how perfect they are. They form a straight line, like they always do when he's concentrating, but it's like they were perfectly drawn on his face, slightly plump on the bottom a little thinner on top. Perfect for— Oh jeez, I'm so sex deprived that I'm thinking about all the things Luke Parker's lips could do to me, or what I can do to them.

Lifting his hand, he brushes the soft ringlets of hair that have fallen against my shoulders, behind me. He takes a few small steps backwards and lifts the camera to his face. Shaking his head, he releases the camera, closes the gap between us, and moves my hair again. This time his fingers tickle my jawline.

"I— I'm sorry. Is this okay?" He pauses. "T-touching you? That's okay, right?"

He's so close that the soft scent of his floral bar soap swirls around me. Ah, so he's a Dove guy.

"I don't mind."

He parts his lips. *Oh God! Stop looking, Millicent!* I look back in time to catch his tongue dart out and wet them. He backs away like he can sense all the hormones rolling off me. I glance down at the edges of my tattoo and hear him clicking some more pictures.

He moves forward and adjusts my body to turn inwards towards him. I feel him behind me. If he takes another step, we'd be flush against each other. His warm breath dances across my shoulder. I'm shaken by the shiver that radiates through me.

For the first time with the camera down, he's not scared. His hand commands my attention as it slowly slides down my arm. There are a few silent beats as we both watch our bodies reacting to each other. Our eyes meet and I do see a confidence building in him, like he's not going to back down. He continues to stroke my arm with his fingertips, and I feel myself about ready to lose control.

He must notice because he pulls away. The lingering tickle of his touch stays with me.

"Can we try a few more positions? I'd like to get you back on the bed." The rasp of his voice has me wanting to cross my legs to fight the flutter in my lower half. "Lie on your stomach," he instructs, but his face is buried in the camera again.

"Okay." I walk towards the bed and the stupid stiletto wobbles. That roller coaster dropping feeling hits my stomach. I think I'm going to go down but instead fall into his warm touch. At this angle my lips graze his collarbone. I right myself and begin to stand, but I'm unsteady on my feet, and my unbalanced body brings me within kissing distance of his lips.

A loud quiet passes through the room. The thumping of my

heart echoing in my ear is intense enough for both of us to hear. There are two things I could do at this moment. I could back away and finish this photo shoot or lean in for a taste of him. Luke is a mystery to me. I love how he confidently controls the room when he's behind a camera, but I'm also kind of into his shy side too.

It's been a long time since I've wanted to kiss someone, male or female. What would he do if I just went for it?

I allow myself to lean in, and carefully move his camera to the side, so that I can close the gap between us. I place my hand on his chest, and his heart thumps hard against it.

I'm so caught up in the moment I hardly realize that his hand is lingering on the small of my bare back, until he adjusts it slightly and I whimper at the softness of his touch.

"Millicent, I—"

I cut him off with my lips. There's definitely something brewing inside his jeans and it's not the battery pack for the camera. My tongue dances along his lower lip, and they part for me as if he's been waiting for it too. His entire body goes almost limp with the release of a content sigh.

I let go and lean into him, enjoying how his tongue massages mine. He tugs the camera off and lays it on the bed as we shift over to it. Lowering me carefully he places a hand behind my head and back.

I'm strewn across the bed with him on top. He's pressed against me, and I let out a moan in response. His hands are roaming my stomach like he knows exactly what to do. Maybe he's not as inexperienced as I thought. Our heavy breathing syncs as he rolls off me but stays close. He rests his arm lazily over my stomach, then with the tip of his pointer grazes my panty line. My hips buck upwards into him, and he releases a low guttural groan.

"It's okay. I want— I want you to touch me, Luke," I urge,

trying to catch my breath. "Please," I beg, desperate for him. I can already feel my insides pulsing with need.

It's not like me to be the first to initiate dirty talk, but while his tongue seems to know what it's doing, he's way too quiet. His fingers slip lower below my underwear and over the smooth surface. He finds my center and hisses at the moisture pooled there.

"Fuck," he whispers. "Did I— did— is that...?" He can't finish his thought, but his throaty voice intensifies what's already happening down there.

"Hmmm... what do you think?" My hips thrust in response to his tender touch. His kisses become more passionate. He takes his free hand and rests it on the side of my face while using the other to touch me. The muscles in my lower half squeal with pleasure, and I bite back a scream. I'm already half naked and this could go so much further.

"I've wanted to touch you for so long," he admits, his voice cracking.

His confession doesn't throw me off, although I am curious as to what he means by "for so long."

"Invitation accepted. You can touch me anytime you want. Any fu— Luke," I moan into his mouth.

He's on expert level with how his fingers dance around putting more pressure on my center. His eyes meet mine. My body convulses and I'm almost certain I never want this to end.

"Are you getting close?" he asks in a growl. Holy shit, Luke Parker just growled and it's the sexiest thing I've ever heard in my life.

"Yes, Luke. Oh my God. Yes! Keep—" My breaths are short yet heavy as I shake with the impending orgasm. "Keep going," I cry out.

His chest rises and falls as his fingers pick up their pace. Magic fingers. Probably from hours of video gaming. I laugh at myself but keep it inside.

I'm so close, and when I say his name again, I think I'm about to burst, but then something crosses his features. He blinks several times, and when he does look at me, he's staring right through. This isn't good. Just as I teeter on the edge, he pulls his hand out.

"We should finish the shoot. It's getting late. I'll uh— I'll be right back."

I'm zapped back into the night with Astra. The look in her eyes when she pulled away. The sting of rejection hits me like a damn slap in the face. I blink to rid my eyes of tears because I can't cry in front of him.

"What the hell?" Instead of weak, my voice comes out in a rage of unforgiving anger.

"I— I'm sorry, I just—"

"Damn it, Luke. Spit it out, what the hell was that? You can't just get me close to an orgasm and then flake out."

He winces. His mind is clearly in other places as he zones out. Maybe he's thinking about Gretchen, or maybe he realizes how big of a mistake touching me or even liking me and taking me in as his assistant was.

"Luke! What are you so afraid of?" My lip quivers, giving away the pain.

For a flash I swear I see the hurt in his own eyes and the longing to reach out. The look vanishes and I shy away from him. Rejection. What am I doing wrong?

I've lost him. Even when I lightly push at his chest trying to get him to snap out of it, he does nothing. After a few seconds of zoning out, he gets off the bed and rushes out of the room almost tripping over his own two feet on the way out.

"You're not getting off that easy, Luke Parker!" I don't chase him though. I'll give him time to mull over what he did to me. I'm humiliated.

I sink back into his bed. I'm left with the disappointment of an unfinished orgasm and the overwhelming urge to sob on his bed. A few tears manage to sneak past, but I wipe them away quick enough to not ruin my makeup.

When he returns, he silently grabs his camera and starts fooling around with the settings.

"Lay on your stomach, stick the stiletto inside the thong from behind."

"Are we going to talk about it?" I ask, hating the anger in my voice.

"Can we just do this one last shot and be done with it?" he deadpans.

He's not looking at me when he says it. He's too busy fidgeting with the other lens he's put on.

"Fine." I pause. "At least something will be able to finish today," I mumble.

I try to get back into the mood, but I've lost all my drive. I saw the position he was talking about online and it was sexy as hell. Hopefully I can pull it off. Instead of touching me, he just directs me from his spot across the room, and only looks up briefly to make sure I'm positioned right. The sting is all too powerful, and I can't wait to go home.

CHAPTER 24

"*Y*ou look like you've seen a ghost." Ezra stands in his doorway, shirtless, with tousled wet hair.

I was not expecting him to be half naked, but I mean it is late and I didn't call first, so I blame myself. After I left Luke's, I drove around aimlessly. My brain was trying to make sense of what happened, how far we had gone, and what that means for us working together. While I could probably drive for hours stuck in my own head, Ezra is and has always been my go-to person, aside from Astra. I have Cheryl too, but we haven't talked much since I moved out here.

"I'm sorry, I know it's late—"

"Who's at the door?" Jake, also shirtless, strolls over to the open door.

I cover my eyes with my arm. "Maybe I should come back."

"Don't be ridiculous, Mill. Come inside, we'll get dressed."

"I didn't, uh, interrupt any sexy time or anything like that, did I?"

Ezra and Jake chuckle at my embarrassment. It's partially their fault for answering the door half naked... I mean who does that? I could have been a complete stranger or a murderer.

"No. We were getting ready for bed. Come on in," Ezra says.

"Thanks," I say, keeping my eyes on the old floor beneath my feet.

"Make yourself at home, we'll be right back."

I slip into their living room, and crash onto the hand-me-down tan sofa Mom gave him from our basement. Taking one of the gray square throw pillows I hold it to my chest and bury my face in it, taking deep calming breaths.

The sofa sinks as Ezra sits beside me, finally wearing a shirt. He adjusts the hem of the dark tee, and then turns to me. "Spill it," he says.

"Luke and I kissed tonight. Well—maybe there were some touchy-feely moments too—but it was mostly kissing." I stare off at the D&D miniatures on the tall, thin wooden shelf across the room.

"I can't tell if that's bad or good."

I shrug. "It was more than just a peck on the lips, it was filled with—" I pause. "I can't believe I'm coming to you about this. I should have girl friends like a normal girl, but here I am talking to my brother about almost having sex with one of his friends."

I run a hand through my hair. Slipping my shoes off onto the deep, brown rug at my feet, I curl my legs under me, and rest my forehead against the pillow.

"And how does that make you feel?"

I smack his shoulder, and he lets out a deep roar.

"Not funny. You are not my therapist. And it makes me feel... I don't know. I guess I just never imagined things would go in this direction."

"Is he a good kisser?" Jake comes strolling in, a wide grin on his face.

"Ugh," I moan, tossing the pillow at Jake, who comes to sit criss-cross in front of me on the floor.

He chuckles. "But your brother is right, how did it make you feel?"

Warmth floods my cheeks at the thought of how Luke took charge, and somehow knew the right way to touch me with his hands... But how can I explain that to my brother and his boyfriend?

"So, he was a good kisser. And how did that make you—"

"Oh my God, can you be serious for once, Ez, jeez. I come to you for advice, and you give me shit. Maybe I should just go."

Ezra chuckles. I start to stand, but he pulls me back. "I'm sorry, I didn't mean to tease you. It's obvious by the look in your eyes that you like him."

"What look?" Immediately, I check for a mirror, even though I know there isn't one.

"Millicent, there's nothing wrong with kissing Luke. If you're worried about it being because he's your boss, it won't be for long anyway, right? You're planning on finding a job in journalism. And even so, it's his company, and you guys have known each other for years, so it's not like it's going to ruin your or his career."

I swallow the lump in my throat. "H-he pulled away and when he did..." My eyes sting with impending tears. "The look reminded me of Astra. It was the same damn one. The oh, you kissed me first, so I'll just go with it type of look. Does this make me... Am I still—"

Ezra knows exactly where my brain is going. I'm worried about how others will look at me, think of me. "Mill, sometimes we can't help who we're attracted to. Just because you fall for someone, doesn't make you any less valid with your sexuality."

The one person who stuck by me through all my sobbing phone calls was Ezra. He knows my heart isn't strong, and I'm not even sure I want to put myself out there. I haven't dated, or had sex in four years, because every time I'd get close to someone the fear of rejection sank in. Being vulnerable for Luke and then getting slammed on was my worst fear come true.

"You know how Luke is. He's always been a closed-off kind of guy. Did he kiss you back?"

"He was turned on. Very turned on. And I— I thought— I swore he wanted it just as much as I did."

"Give him some time to process. I think you should take some time and do the same. I know you're scared to open your heart, Mill. And I'm not taking his side, but I don't think Luke would play you."

I sniffle and wipe at my traitorous eyes.

"Are you in love with him?" Jake asks.

"I don't love him," I say. "That would be crazy. The kiss was good, and I enjoyed what we did, but I hardly know him. Sure, he spent weekends LARPING with you, and then spent some nights in our basement while I teased all of you, but love can't be a thing, not yet. Can it?"

"It can," Jake says, reaching out and touching my leg. "I said I'd never fall for your brother and look where that got me."

Our laughter fills the room. It's true. Ezra and Jake were friends first, and Jake needed some convincing, but Ezra did everything in his power to get him to say yes, and when he finally did everything fell into place.

"I think there's more there than you're letting on. I saw it the night we played D&D. The whole room saw and felt it. Seriously, it's okay to fall in love," Ezra says, eyeing Jake with so much passion I almost feel as if I should step out of the room.

"But then why did he pull away? People keep doing that to me." I clutch my chest, holding on to the sob. "I feel terrible for what I did back in high school. Maybe he's still sour about that. I dunno. I do like him and kind of a lot…"

Ezra sighs. "My best advice would be to allow each other some space and when you're both calm and rational then talk."

I close my eyes trying to keep myself together. "Okay." It comes out as barely a whisper.

"I like you two together, so don't pull away because you're

worried about what I'll think. I'm not going to be upset that you're dating my friend."

"We were supposed to kiss the night of graduation during seven—"

"Minutes in heaven. I know."

I stare blankly at him. "Y-you know?"

He chuckles lightly. "Yeah. He confessed that summer."

"And you've just been going around keeping this to yourself, that you knew?"

"It's fine, Mill." He touches my arm to comfort me.

"I don't even know why this is bothering me so much. People have bigger problems and I'm over here upset because I had an amazing kiss that I don't regret."

"We all have things that bother us, or make us anxious; just because it's not life or death doesn't mean it shouldn't be discussed," Ezra says. "It's your life; you had a bad first love experience. Sometimes that's all it takes to throw up some walls. Small problems should be worked out, because if they aren't they'll grow and grow, and before you know it, it piles up so high that you crumble."

"Ezra is right. Don't be afraid to come and talk even if it's something minor."

Closing my eyes, I take in a few deep breaths. "Thank you both for listening to me."

"Anytime."

Talking with Ezra and Jake eased my mind about Luke. I'm not going to deny the kiss was hot, and amazing, but there's nothing wrong with being cautious to protect my heart from breaking again.

CHAPTER 25

*H*alloween is one of my all-time favorite days, and it seems to be Luke's too. There's been no mention of the kiss since it happened last week, but it's been weighing on both our minds. Luke has been tiptoeing around me, and trying not to come too close, and I've been keeping myself at a distance as well. I liked the place we were at as friends, and maybe the kiss was too much for either of us to handle.

Three days this week he was out of the office while Tony was there instead. I hate this dance we're doing. I wish he would just talk to me about it.

I'm using today as a distraction from all the thoughts inside my head. I'm excited to join in the fun town festivities by setting up a small table outside the studio with decorations and candy. Since Halloween is a Sunday this year the town decided to have their safe trick-or-treat on the day of. Luke volunteered to take photos, and I immediately jumped on board volunteering to hand out candy to the cute trick-or-treaters.

Across the street I catch a glimpse of the man that has somehow captivated me. My gaze lingers for a heartbeat too long and his eyes find mine. I wait for him to turn away, but instead he smiles, a big one only reserved for rare moments, and my heart jumps. Seeing it again after a week of cold gestures makes some of the stress fade away.

I never imagined I'd find a man in gray chain mail, black leather gloves, and a sword in his pocket sexy, but damn Luke Parker has me smitten. Now if only he'd stop avoiding the subject of us.

"Trick or treat."

I'm torn away from the man in armor to a small superhero standing before me. I grin, and reach into the orange bucket filled with treats, and place the goodies into the small boy's bag.

"Thank you!" he says. He glances up at his mom, as she urges him down the sidewalk to the Lottery store to our left.

My eyes lift again, only Luke's not there this time. I've lost him in the crowd.

"Let me guess, you're…."

The familiar voice is Ezra. He's standing beside Jake and Jake's little cousin Jerry. He's seven and is all decked out as one of my favorite anime characters in an orange onesie. Jake's bright pink wig catches my attention, and Ezra with his blue one. Both are wearing white shirts with a red-letter R in the center.

"The evil queen from *Once Upon a Time*," I say, crossing my arms against the soft fabric of my gothic-black dress.

"See, I told you she wasn't a vampire," Jake says.

Ignoring them I focus on Jerry. "Hey, buddy, I love your costume by the way." I place two bags of candy into his jack-o-lantern bucket. There are no other kids around, and not to be biased, but Jerry's the best kid.

"Well, we have to make our rounds," Ezra says. "Where's lover boy?"

I reach over the table tempted to give him a piece of my mind, but pull back, because of Jerry, and the children now running across the street towards us.

"He's taking photos. And no, nothing has happened since the

kiss. You guys didn't bombard him with questions during *D&D* on Thursday, did you?"

Jake shakes his head. "I made sure to keep Ezra in line that night. He didn't mention a thing, but when your name was brought up during a random conversation, Luke's face lit up like a jack-o-lantern."

"It didn't."

"Oh, he's not lying," Ezra says, sneaking a hand into our bowl.

I grab his hand. "Kids only."

Ezra scowls. "We should probably get some more trick or treating done before the storm blows in."

The sky is growing dark faster than I expected. It's not supposed to rain until after five, it's only a little past two, but the wind has picked up, and the gray skies have brought a chill.

Once they've moved on to the next table, I concentrate on the crowd of kids who are now staring up at me with their candy-hungry eyes. As I'm handing out the candy I can't help searching for Luke. I'm dropping a treat into the bag belonging to the last kid of the large group when I finally find Luke again.

Only, he's not taking pictures, his hands are balled into fists at his side while he talks with a woman dressed as a vampire. I can't see her that well from here, but she's wearing a long black wig, and so much makeup that it's impossible to see her real self, but there's only one person who makes him angry and that's Gretchen.

His body language is no longer fluid like it was while he was snapping shots of the crowd. Even from a distance it's easy to see he's in defensive mode, but he seems to be allowing her to do all the talking. Her hands are waving all over the place.

I decide to go and save him while there's a lull. I'll make up an excuse that I need him for something. As I cross the street my heart begins to race. I'm only inches from them. What if he told her about us and our kiss? If I turn around now, he'll never know I was here.

"You're not making this easy." Luke's half-trembling voice catches me off guard. I pull my attention to them, and decide he needs to be rescued. Clearing my throat, I straighten myself and strut in their direction. As I tap him on the shoulder, she glares at me. Yup, it's definitely her; she's just all made up for Halloween.

"Luke, I'm sorry to bother you."

"What?" he asks through gritted teeth.

My heart sinks low as I try my hardest to get my words out. They are both eyeing me with displeasure like I interrupted the most important conversation of their lives. I take several steps backwards bumping into one of the tables.

"Um, forget it." I shake my head, and glance down at the littered sidewalk.

I turn towards the street when his hand grabs mine. Does she notice how my entire body stilled at his touch, or how my mouth defied me and let out a gasp. It's loud enough for the couple standing on street level a few inches away both turn and gawk.

"Hold on," Luke says, his voice barely above a whisper.

He turns back to Gretchen, his hand never leaving mine. I want to pull away, but at the same time I can't as his thumb gently rubs over my skin.

"We can discuss this another time. I have work to do."

She protests, her lips jet out in a pout, but Luke completely ignores it. He lets go of my hand and places his on the small of my back. In silence we retreat to the other side of the street where our table remains untouched.

"Everything okay over here?"

"Yeah, I just— Is there more candy?"

"More?" He points to the contents of the bowl. It's almost half full.

I'm burning up from the heat of his stare. Why is this so awkward? I bite hard on my bottom lip as he gently places a hand beside mine on the table.

"Thank you," he says, staring at the closeness of our hands, and our bodies.

Being brave I rest my hand over his, and for a moment his eyes close, and he sucks in a long-drawn-out breath.

"You're welcome."

An unspoken understanding floats between us. I should ask more, but we're treading thin ice and I don't want to make the tension worse. Tiny raindrops fall on the table, leaving spots. The crowd on the streets is dispersing as the drops become heavier.

"We should get this stuff inside."

"Yeah, it seems the rain has come early."

The two of us work in silence, bringing the candy and decorations inside. While he folds the table I scavenge through the leftover candy, searching for something yummy. Unwrapping a KitKat, I pull the lining down and chomp down into both sticks. Luke gasps.

"What?" I ask, a mouthful of chocolate.

"That's just wrong. How can you eat a KitKat like that?" He reaches for one in another bag, rips the package, and breaks it in half. "It's against the law to eat them both at the same time."

I hold his stare and take another bite of both sticks.

"That's blasphemy!" Reaching behind me into the bucket his hand grazes my side, and I shiver. He pulls another KitKat from the bunch, breaks it off and hands me a stick.

In a playful gesture I grab for the other one in his hand as he's about to take a bite. Swiping it from his grasp I hold the two together and eat it the way I had the last one. His smile returns, and I'm glad he's forgotten all about whatever Gretchen had said.

"You ate my candy."

I shrug and start to walk away, only to be pulled back by his arms snaking around my body. I fall into him, while he leans against the desk. His fingers find my most ticklish spots and my bladder tenses as he does.

"I'm gonna pee myself." I chuckle.

"Serves you right."

For a few minutes we engage in the playful act. I spin in his arms and almost crash into his lips from losing balance. We're so close I can almost taste the warmth of his perfect mouth.

"Thank you again, for what you did back there."

"I won't ask what happened, but you didn't look very happy, so I— I intervened." I can't help my wandering eyes as they flitter across his lips.

"I'm not ready to talk about it but thank you."

"Mmm," I say, my voice trailing off as we move towards each other like magnets.

The world around me stills, there's no one here on this earth, but Luke and me. His breath tangles with mine, and I can almost feel his lips when there's a banging on the locked door. We bolt away from one another fast enough where Luke loses his balance and nearly crashes into the desk.

Glancing up at the door, I sigh. Leave it to Ezra to ruin a moment. Him, Jake, and Jerry stand in the rain with pleading looks on their faces. Luke clears his throat and lets them in, locking the door behind them.

"Sorry, Jerry has to pee, and the sky opened up before we could reach the car."

"He can use the bathroom, it's right this way."

Jake and Jerry follow Luke towards the back, while Ezra hangs back a grin a mile wide on his face.

"Don't start."

"We interrupted something, didn't we?" he asks. "You are both flustered."

"Okay, so if you want to know, if you hadn't had barged in, I would have…"

"Woah. La-la, too much information," he says, covering his ears.

I laugh. "Hey, you're the one who brought it up."

Luke and I don't have any more chances to be alone. We end

up playing four very intense rounds of Battleship, and teaching Jerry how to play. By the time the darkness falls, we are all leaving in separate cars, and the only thing Luke has a chance to say is goodnight. Maybe if my brother hadn't interrupted, Luke and I would have gone further. The big old question is, did I want that to happen? The answer should be no or maybe, but my heart, it has other plans, and says it definitely would have.

CHAPTER 26

$\mathcal{T}$he sexual tension inside this studio is enough to make anyone crazy. I think it's rubbed off on our customers. The couple in front of me are here to pick up their wedding photos. They are making goo-goo eyes at each other and haven't stopped touching since they arrived.

I try not to stare for too long, so I put my attention on the photo in front of me. Luke was going through pictures from my boudoir session and gave me a few samples this morning to look over. He, of course, gave me the stiletto one. My entire life I've been mildly confident in my appearance, but seeing these photos, especially this one, made me see myself in a whole new light. I didn't grimace at the extra skin on my stomach or ass, and my love handles curve in such a way that rounded out my body in all the right places.

Luke comes out of the back office with the couple's wedding pictures. I stand to help him with the large, framed portrait of their wedding day.

"Let me get that," I say.

Reaching out I accidentally let my hand touch his, and he lets go of the portrait too soon. Thankfully, I grab it before it can crash to the ground. Luke clenches his jaw and sucks in a harsh breath. He glares at me with his wide green eyes. If he was a cartoon, I'd probably be shot to death by the lasers jetting from his angry eyes.

The couple stands, large grins on their newly married faces.

"Hi, hope you had a great honeymoon," Luke says, as we approach. His demeanor changes immediately, as he puts on his customer service voice.

"Oh, it was so amazing."

The young bride looks maybe a few years younger than us. She gleams and stares up in admiration at her husband.

He leans down and plants a sensual kiss on her lips. Luke and I stand in awkward silence, with half grins on both our faces. The husband brushes his wife's raven black locks behind her ear, before facing us.

"Well, these are the digital prints." Luke hands them a USB drive. "In this envelope are the eight by tens you asked me to print, and that—" He points to the large golden frame. "Is the one you both picked out."

I turn the frame so that they can see. They gasp at the sight and touch each other again like they can't get enough. I give them both a tight smile as the burly husband looks at me.

"These came out amazing. Seriously, you are getting a rave review from us. Luke, your photos are unbelievable."

Luke is beaming. He deserves it with all the effort he puts into his shoots and edits. I've never seen anyone's photos turn out as amazing as his. While he's talking to them, I find myself wrapped up in his gorgeous smile. Back in high school, I thought he was cute, but not enough for me to be attracted to him. Getting to know him these past few months has given me more insight on him as a person, and I think part of it is that I'm falling for the guy he is underneath all the nerdy exterior.

"Excuse me, I don't mean to pry, but is that you in those photos?" The young bride's eyes land on the boudoir pictures on the desk. The husband glances over, but then turns away, his heavily bearded cheeks turn rosy when he realizes what they are.

"May I have a peek?" she asks.

I look up at Luke. He's gone pale. "Sure," he manages.

I grab them from the desk, then hand them to her. She grins as she flips through the three images. There's one of me standing against the window, one lying down, and when she gets to the stiletto photo she gasps. Her husband stiffens beside her, like he's afraid to look. She elbows him anyway, and he checks it quickly before his eyes meet hers.

"I want to do this," she practically begs.

Luke stands still as a statue, probably waiting for the guy to knock his lights out.

"You took these photos?" she asks him.

Luke nods, a tight smile on his pressed lips.

"And you. You are absolutely stunning. Isn't she, Paul?"

I can't tell who she's more in love with, me in the photos or her husband. Her eyes gleam with excitement, and she can't stop staring at them.

"They are lovely," he says.

I almost snicker, but I hold back.

"How much are you charging?"

"Uh-uh."

Luke looks as if he's having a stroke. *May-day, May-day.*

"Oh, I'm sorry. I don't think we are going to offer boudoir shoots." I swallow. "These were an experiment of sorts, but um, you could always check back." I turn to Luke. "Oh, that reminds me your dad said the other day I could start a newsletter for the studio. Maybe I could take their info?"

"Y-yeah, sure. That's a really great idea."

I smile at him, then turn back to the clients.

"Yes, please can you add me," she shouts, causing her husband to jump. "I wish I could have done these for the wedding—or maybe..." She turns to her husband. "We could do a couples one. Would you do that?"

Luke is slowly dying beside me. He's stuttering. I kind of hate how uncomfortable this is for him. Maybe it's best that he doesn't do these for anyone else; but I'll wait for him to decide.

"Not sure. We'd have to discuss it. I can put you on that list and you'll be the first to know."

Once we get their information, she happily skips out of the studio, while her husband carefully carries the large portrait out the door. The room goes silent when they leave, and beside me Luke is taking deep breaths and staring off at the door. I reach for his hand, and he retreats with a trembling jump.

"If doing those photos makes you uncomfortable you don't have to do it. I appreciate you taking them for my blog, but it can just be for that. I can disguise your name if you want me to."

He doesn't say a word. I know this look well enough to realize I've been there. His anxiety has finally reached its peak and it's partially my fault.

"Hey," I say, softly.

With a long stroking motion, I rub his arm. Tiny goosebumps pop up along the surface of his skin. He gasps, then spins me around pushing me up against the desk. In one swift movement I'm lifted off the ground and onto the top of it with him between my legs. I wrap my legs around his waist as he leans down and kisses me. Reaching up, I cover his scruffy face, and open my mouth for him. He moans the minute my tongue hits his and the overwhelming surge of electricity powers through me like I've been struck again.

He pulls back, taking my face in his hands. "I am so, so sorry for hurting you, Millicent. I panicked. I never meant..."

Resting my head against his I close my eyes and sigh. "It stung, badly, Luke. But I guess I deserve—"

"No!" I jump at the volume of his voice. "You didn't. You didn't deserve that at all. Fuck. I don't want to mess this up.

Okay? And I know there's nothing I can say or do to make it up—"

I press a soft kiss to his lips to stop him from talking. We both have done awful things to each other. It's time we try to fix it. Be better. Do better. I know we can. It's a matter of how much we both want it.

"Lock the door," I whisper, leaving some space between our lips.

He starts to let go but presses his mouth back to mine. A second later he rushes across the studio, locks the front, then takes me back in his arms. Lifting me off the desk he starts for the back room. We kiss at a frantic pace the entire way. When we reach his desk. He sets me down on top of some papers. I tug on his bottom lip with my teeth, then suck hard, receiving a low moan from him.

"What, you're not going to clear off the desk first?" I ask between kisses.

He grins under my lips. "It's fine."

Our laughter gets buried in the kiss as he deepens it. He lets go of another moan, and it's enough to make my body twitch in an almost orgasm just from the vibration. His mouth trails down my chin to my neck and I roll my head to the side to give him more space. I'm feverish, hot, and sweaty. Reaching for the hem of my wool sweater, I pull it up over my head breaking his kiss for only a few seconds.

At the sight of my breasts pushed up in the white silky bra, he hardens against me, and I thrust my body forward to feel him.

"Ah you're a chest man," I say with a grin.

With a swift shake of his head, he reaches out and cups my breasts in both his hands, crushing them beneath his palms. I toss my head back and yell out his name. Meeting his gaze I tear at his plaid button-down, opening it with such force that two buttons fly off.

He starts laughing, my own laughter soon follows. His hearty voice fills the entire room and me with pleasure. He takes over, finishing the rest of his shirt without tearing anymore buttons off. Underneath he's wearing a black T-shirt. Nope we can't have that, I need to see his chest.

"Take it off," I tell him.

Without looking away, he grabs the back of his shirt and pulls it up and off his body.

He's not packing a six pack, but damn if he's not beautiful under there, even with the hair, I'm more turned on than I've ever been with any man.

I touch him all over his chest and it's his turn to lean back and moan. We undress each other. The delicate touch he had the other day has turned into something eager and rough. I like it. A lot. Where did he learn all of this?

"It was you," he says, voice all airy and staggered.

"What was me?" I ask, pausing for a second.

"The text I sent before the boudoir shoot. There's only one woman. It's you, Millicent."

Neither of us move or say a word. Our eyes are the only parts doing the talking and it's a showdown between them. He's undressing me with them and as much as I love how he looks at me; I want him to be inside of me.

"Luke, I'm going to need you to decide what we're doing. I am so fucking wet right now…"

I don't have to say another word. He shimmies my pants down and tosses it to the side. His own jeans fall to the ground, and he kicks them off, but his eyes remain focused on me. He's seen me stripped down before, but for some reason his soft emerald eyes sparkle like it's the first time all over again.

"God you're beautiful," he says, in a raspy tone.

There's something about the way he says it that brings tears to my eyes. No one I've dated has ever called me beautiful and meant it. His lips meet the top of my breasts as he reaches around to try and unclip the bra. Only… he can't. I giggle a little and help him.

I observe his every move, and note the expressions on his face, and the one thing I notice is when he's touching me, he's as confident as he is behind a camera. The thought makes my stomach flutter with dancing butterflies.

His eyes go right to my hard nipples, standing at attention, waiting for him. He takes the right one in his hand and the left one in his mouth. His tongue flicks over every sensitive part and I moan so loud it echoes.

Glancing down, I realize he's still in his underwear. I love that he's a "boxer man." Plaid too. So him, so sexy, I love it. Although I was hoping for something funny like maybe a cartoon character. I reach my hand inside while he continues to devour my nipples. The size of him in my hand is just right.

"Mmm… Millicent," he moans.

His lips make a trail down the center of my body, over my belly button, and finally he peels off my matching underwear. I wasn't expecting to be ravished on his desk, so shaving was the last thing on my mind. There's definitely a bush there, only he doesn't care. His fingers gently rub against my center, and it doesn't take more than a few seconds for the wetness to drip out. He moves in, lowering his head and using his mouth to finish the rest of the job. I grip the edge of the desk the best I can, my hips unable to control their movements. His tongue is doing things, so many things, and once again I'm screaming out his name as I come undone.

"Hold on," he says roughly.

He bends down and reaches into his pant pocket, leaving me panting over the edge. He pulls out a condom.

"You just keep condoms inside your pants?" I ask.

"Uh, I—" he stutters. "After our kiss last week, I wanted to be prepared."

I smirk. "Oh, is that so?"

He nods and rips the wrapper, then pauses. I almost expect him to shut down on me again, but instead his lips curl up. "Is this what you want, Millicent? I'll only do it if it's what you truly..."

Taking charge, I tip his chin in my direction. "I want you, Luke. All of you. Every fucking piece." I press my mouth to his and bite down on his luscious bottom lip again, needing more of him. "I've never had sex on a desk before," I say.

As I say it the wicked sex blogger in me comes out and I wonder if I should write about it. Once he gets the condom over him, his eyes find mine and I push the thought far back into my head. It's probably not the most brilliant idea.

He shifts so it slides in and the second he pulsates inside me I nearly lose it all right there.

"I didn't realize how experienced you were," I say as he thrusts into me.

"Oh. I uh, I'm not. I've never done anything like this before." He looks away from me, a blush creeping up his neck. Somehow his confession turns me on even more. I shimmy forward to get a better angle. I'm half off the desk with my legs wrapped around him. With him inside it's like one constant orgasm that won't stop.

"I hope this wasn't a cheap desk." I smirk.

His laughter is genuine. I want to hold on to it, save it for later. He leans down and kisses my neck.

"I'm pretty sure you know exactly what you're doing," I growl.

I've only had sex with two guys, and both times were not good. I'd sworn off men afterwards, because it never felt right, but with Luke... with Luke it feels fucking amazing.

He tenses under me, and I'm almost positive he's ready to let go. I want this to last, but I also want to let him know I'm ready to feel him release inside of me, so I pull him down so our naked wet bodies touch.

"I have a better idea. Go sit on your chair."

He freezes and leans back to catch my eye.

"It's my turn," I say.

Without another question, he pulls out, quickly making his way to the chair on the other side of the desk. He sits down, and I follow. I turn my back to him, and straddle over his legs allowing myself to sit on his lap. He wraps his arms around me as I use every ounce of energy and muscle in my legs to bounce up and down.

His heated hands on my slick skin, holding me in a protective way is all I need to get close. This is what I've been missing out on? If we had kissed during Seven Minutes in Heaven, would I have felt it then? I was so young and stupid. How could I deny this man of anything?

"Oh, Mill. I'm so close," he growls

"Me too. Oh, Luke. You feel so good," I whisper.

His body shakes as he releases and I stop moving all together, trembling from his release and mine. Wrapping his arms around me he pulls me into his body, kissing along my neck as he finishes.

"That was… that was…" He's lost for words.

"Whatever it was, I'm ready for round two."

I expect him to not smile, to be his serious self, but he does something unexpected. He smirks, like one of those good ones where his eyes sparkle. The sight of it takes me to a place I've never been. I pull him into me.

"Maybe not here though."

He laughs. "No, definitely not here. How about dinner at my place?"

"I'll bring the dessert." I smirk.

He grips on to me tighter like he doesn't want to let me go. I close my eyes allowing what just happened to sink in. I'm enjoying the comfort of him and love that he's a cuddler after sex. It makes me excited for tonight to see if he does it then too. It's funny after all these years, who would have known being with Luke felt this damn good.

"We should probably get up in case my dad drops by," he says, amusement clear in his voice.

"Oh, you're right. I hope he doesn't use this desk."

His exquisite full-throated laugh is the best thing I've ever heard. I wish he'd laugh more. I could listen to it all day long. He kisses my cheek and I crane my neck just enough so I can feel his lips on mine. We stay that way for a few moments before he gets up to discard the condom and clean up.

We take turns using the bathroom, and I'm the last one out. He's leaning on the desk with a mischievous grin on his handsome face.

"Hey, thank you," he says.

I step into his arms, needing the comfort of them again.

"Thank you?"

"For stepping in back there. Sorry I kind of lost my cool, I was afraid that guy would pummel me for thinking about taking half naked pictures of his wife."

"If it's not the direction you want for the studio, don't do it. No one is going to be upset. You take beautiful pictures and there's already a high demand for what you and your father do. So, not adding boudoir won't make or break you."

He lifts his hand and presses it to my cheek. I lean into his touch. "I know. I'm still thinking about it."

"Take all the time you need. It was just a suggestion, and I'm sorry if I pushed you."

His touch, his warmth, I never want to give it up.

"You didn't push me. I didn't mind taking them for you."

"Sure you didn't." I shove him playfully. He chuckles.

"You should probably get back to work," he says. "I hear the boss here is really strict."

"Oh, is that so? Well, he better get used to me slacking off, I'm not sure I can do much work after that."

Luke leans forward pressing his soft lips against mine. "I don't think I will either."

For a few more minutes we kiss, and I enjoy the simplicity of the moment. I hate when we finally pull away. What keeps me going is knowing tonight I'll be back in his arms, and whatever wild moment we had here will be replayed later. It makes the workday much easier to get through.

He looks down and scratches the back of his neck. "Millicent, there's something I need to…"

The phone up front rings and I know since we are still technically open, I need to answer it. "Sorry, I should get that…"

"Yeah. No. We can talk later."

I rush to the door, but before I leave, I give one glance over my shoulder. He's got a small smile on his face like something is on his mind, but when our eyes meet, he lights up again, and I love knowing I made it happen.

CHAPTER 27

The last time I was here I had planned on wearing sexy lingerie for a photo shoot. This time what's underneath is not for the camera, but for him. After I left the studio, I went straight home to shower and shave. At least this time I'll be prepared, but in all honesty, I have never felt so less prepared in my life. Not even for a biology quiz, and I sucked at bio.

I take a deep breath and grip the steering wheel tight in my hand. Liking Luke was never part of this plan. It was to get a job to tide me over, save money, move out of my parents' house, and eventually find a journalism job. The more I stay here, and the more time I spend with him, makes me want this life.

I shake the thoughts from my head. I'm on a mission, and this, this is just a side gig. I grab my brown messenger bag from the seat, and the rainbow cookie cake I picked up from Shop Rite on my way over. I promised dessert, although I think the most appetizing dessert will be devouring him again.

At the back door I lift my hand to knock when the inside door flies open. His dark black hair is slicked back, and although he's wearing his usual black T-shirt and jeans, he's gone above and beyond to neatly shave the scruff along his face. The scent of his flowery soap is stronger than usual; either that or I'm more attuned to his smell than before.

His cheeks flush. It's something I've grown to like about him.

"Hey," I say. My voice squeaks. Now I'm the one being shy.

"I hope you don't mind, I cooked us a pizza." He steps aside to let me in. The scent of his soap vanishes and a strong aroma of mixed herbs and tomatoes circles around me.

"Well now I feel like an asshole. You cooked and all I did was pay—" I pause and lift the plastic container with the cake. "Twelve fucking dollars for this mediocre cake."

His lips pull into a delicate smile. I'm taken back by the image and make sure I take a mental picture of it. Luke's smiles are rare, but when he does smile the whole room lights up with him. When did I even start to notice these things?

"This is my favorite actually, so it's perfect." He takes it from me, our hands somehow finding each other again. This time at least we don't drop anything. He shuts the door behind me and carries the cake over to the counter, placing it there. His oven timer goes off and he rushes to the stove to get out the pizza. When the oven door opens the scent becomes a hundred times stronger. I take it all in. There's more to nerdy Luke Parker than I thought.

"Now, it's not Ezra's pizza; but don't tell him, mine's better." He smiles, and tiny dimples pop on his cheeks. It's something you'd never notice unless you were really looking.

He sets the pizza on the stove top. All the ingredients are perfectly chopped and carefully placed. I come around the counter and take a chance by wrapping my arms around his stomach and placing my chin on his shoulder. His breath stutters as I rest my mouth against his jaw.

"It smells delicious," I whisper.

Standing like this with him feels almost natural. I expect him to stutter and ignore how close we are, but he doesn't.

Without looking he tosses the black oven mitt. It lands beside the cake on the counter. He spins and snakes his arms around me. His eyes meet mine and this magical feeling envelops around me.

"This isn't weird for you, is it?" he asks.

I blink through my lashes, observing the way his eyes scan my face. I shake my head. "Surprisingly, not at all. Is it weird for you?"

"No. It feels easier than anything I've ever done before." He pauses. "Wait, I didn't mean like you're easy, I meant like it feels natur—" I stop him with a kiss. There's no tongue or frantic motion, it's just a pleasant little peck on the lips.

He exhales. "Maybe we should eat first."

"Great. I'm starved!" I grin.

He steps back first and grabs utensils and plates from the cabinets.

"Do you mind if I grab us some drinks?"

"Oh, well I've got wine, or beer—or if you're totally not into drinking there's soda and water."

For some reason I don't want any alcohol in me. I'm a lightweight and even one glass of wine sends me into a weird state, and I want to be present for this whole night. Even with the nagging anxiety about our date, I don't need alcohol to control it, I only need good company, like his.

"Water is good."

"There's a pitcher in the fridge. I'll have some too."

We perch ourselves on top of the stools, facing the kitchen, and sit side by side. I'm in awe by the way all the ingredients mix to form the perfect pizza. We talk about random nonsense things, and I add two extra slices to my plate.

"Did you make the sauce yourself?"

He nods. "Yeah, I make a big batch on Sunday and freeze some, and mostly have leftovers for a few nights."

"It's amazing. Don't tell Ezra, but it's better than his. This entire pizza. I mean the crust," I say, lifting the last half of my third slice. "It's like the perfect combo of crisp and soft."

"Are you a food critic? What's my score?"

I chew on the piece in my mouth and smirk. "Ah... let's see, well this onion is a little burnt." I pick at a stringy onion lifting it off the pizza. He bumps into me with his shoulder. A nice buzz warms my body. "So, I'd probably give you a nine," I say, dropping the onion into my mouth.

His laughter fills the space around us. I lean into him, and he throws an arm behind me. His fingers find their way under my shirt and dance around my skin. Butterflies dance around in my stomach.

"You're different than I expected," I say, staring at my pizza.

His fingers slip from my back and I'm sure I've hit a nerve.

"I'm more than just my hobbies, Millicent." He takes an angry bite of pizza, and I fear I've lost him.

"Wait, no. I just meant, you act like women frighten you, and then you go and throw me against a desk with this determination I didn't know you had in you. Clearly, you're more experienced than you let on."

"I've never done any of that before." Shy Luke returns, and he can't look me in the eye.

"But—"

"I've only ever slept with one woman in my entire life."

I didn't peg him as a guy who slept around, but his confession still shocks me a little. He's definitely a one-woman kind of guy. He shifts in his seat, and he winces like the conversation is painful.

"Can I ask you something?"

"Shoot."

I feel like I've lost him. He's staring off. The one woman, it's probably Gretchen. There's so much uneasiness in his rigid posture. Maybe changing the subject will help. I wish he'd come clean about her, but I guess I can't expect it just yet. Our relationship—or whatever we have going on—is new. I won't bug him because for now, it's none of my business.

"It's D&D related."

He perks up a bit, sitting up straighter. His brows raise to encourage me to continue.

"The dice rolling kind of confused me." I chuckle lightly. "I feel like there are so many rules and so many dice, I had a hard time following along. The story line was amazing though. I love how you guys were on a mission to find out who was poisoning the kingdom. It was a cool touch. Patrick's character, the Rogue um, Neric, was that his name?"

He nods.

"He was very interesting. His ex-assassin background was neat."

He reaches out for my hand and takes it. Entranced by me, he's quiet and scanning over my features with his eyes. His thumb brushes my skin. I'm falling faster than I thought I ever could.

"Are you okay, Luke? I didn't mean to— I'm trying not to be her anymore." My voice breaks a little. "The girl you knew in high school. I don't want to be her. I hope you can see I've— I've changed." My voice wavers up and down.

He's still watching with almost admiration.

I try to blink away the moisture that has suddenly invaded my eyes.

He lifts my chin with his finger bringing us eye to eye. "I wanted you to kiss me," he says.

Tilting my head, I raise my brow wondering what he means. He clears his throat and swallows a whole bunch of times before he's able to speak. "That night. Seven Minutes in Heaven. I wanted you to kiss me so much. It was stupid of me, falling for the girl who made fun of me. How cliché, right?" He laughs despite himself, shaking his head.

His confession is not one I ever expected. I press a hand to my chest to steady my rhythmic heart. "Luke, I didn't..."

"I know." He looks down at our hands, pressing his thumb in harder. He smiles, a soft melancholy laughs breaks free from his lips. "There were times when I saw the you I see now. Times when we'd have real conversations and I loved having them with you. Sure, you pissed me off a lot, but I saw you."

My lashes become wet with the tears pushing their way out.

"I know you didn't like me," he says.

"I don't know what I felt back then. But that night has been on replay in my head for so long and maybe secretly I wanted you to kiss me, too. I'd thought about it, on more than one occasion. As the years went on I kind of got sucked into a world that I wanted and let go of home."

He closes the large gap between us by standing and putting himself between my legs. He gathers my cheeks in his hands and plants a slow passionate kiss on my lips. I'm more than wet. I've got hormones raging and a crazy feeling of love bubbling in my stomach and reaching my heart.

Resting his head against mine he sighs. "Mill, I've got to tell you—"

My phone dings with a text on the counter. I ignore it, even though I see Cheryl's name. I turn back to him. Another ding. I ignore it a second time.

"Mill..."

And now it's ringing. My shoulders fall and his eyes close out of frustration. It's Cheryl again. I press the button to turn my phone off completely. Cheryl can wait. I hate that we haven't spoken in a while, but with Luke in front of me all I want to do is get to know him.

"What were you going to say?"

He shakes his head. "Just that—" he doesn't finish his sentence, instead he kisses me.

I get lost in it, in the soft pecks he brushes along my skin, and then the aggressive way his tongue finds mine. He's hard, I feel him as he presses into me. I groan into his mouth. His erection making me forget everything. His fingers find their way under my shirt until they meet the peak of my nipples, and he rolls them between his fingertips.

"Luke," I say, tossing my head back. "Should we take this to your room?"

He lifts my shirt, rolling it up and then pushes up my bra while taking my breast in his mouth. I'm filled with fervor.

"We can take it wherever you want," he says roughly as he picks me up and carries me into his room.

The night is unlike anything I've ever experienced before. I wasn't expecting to stay, but like earlier in his office he holds me after. Peppers me with soft and sweet kisses. Runs his hands through my hair and whispers all these dirty yet wonderful things in my ear. Before I can blink, we're back at it, kissing, fucking, making love. All of it. And that's how Luke Parker stole my heart, and I don't think I'll ever ask for it back.

CHAPTER 28

I chug some juice to wash down the awful dry cherry pop tart I devoured. Running late was not in my plans this morning.

I've been working on my boudoir blog post, and just finished talking through email with someone I interviewed for it. He only had this time slot open, but he was very reliable in writing his feelings about what it was like when his wife surprised him with the pictures. He was grateful for the photos and said he even teared up a little. Said she is the most beautiful woman he's ever laid his eyes on. Stories like that warm my heart.

I'm uploading some of the images. Luke finally gave me a USB drive with the rest of them. I pull up the downloaded pic, the stiletto one, and I'm in awe. Like almost everyone I'm not very confident in my appearance. I don't think I'm ugly, but I feel like there's better looking women out there. I know, I've looked at them. But this picture, the way the lighting falls against my face, brightens my features, I look stunning.

Checking the time, I realize I have to finish up. We are doing an engagement shoot in the park at nine thirty and I can't be late.

Mom comes waltzing into the kitchen, a smug smirk on her

face, and a little blush on her pale cheeks. Her sky-blue nightgown is haphazardly thrown closed, and I won't even comment on the hair. Dad walks in behind her, adjusting his shirt as his eyes meet mine. The pop tart I just ate sits in my throat like it wants to come back up.

"Oh, hey, honey." Dad runs a hand through his own unruly light brown locks.

Mom clears her throat. "Oh, I'm glad you're still here," she says, tugging at the string of her robe to close it better.

They were not expecting to see me home.

"Yeah, but I'm about to head out." I start to close my computer when she struts over, eyes wide, glaring at my picture. Most people would be embarrassed to have their mom look at a boudoir shoot, but I'm used to it by now, especially after the vibrator incident.

"What— what are these?" she asks.

"I did a boudoir shoot for my blog."

"Boudoir sounds like something in a porno," Dad says.

Mom hushes Dad as he shuffles through the kitchen making his usual morning coffee, then turns to me. "Oh, like lingerie? And Luke was the photographer?"

"Yes, he was." My cheeks flush under her knowing gaze.

Dad chokes, and nearly loses his grip on his *Best Dad* mug, we got him one Christmas.

"Gerald, what on earth has gotten into you?" Mom says. Pulling a chair up she sits beside me. Her leg bounces up and down.

I click on the arrow to look at more.

Mom slaps a hand over her mouth, and her eyes shimmer. "My God," she whispers. "My daughter is the most beautiful woman I've ever laid my eyes on."

Dad puts the mug on the counter with a loud thud. "And those pictures are something you put on the net?" He eyes me down like I'm a kid.

"Parading around in undergarments is hardly something to worry about. I write about sex."

He's got more to say, but instead he goes to pour his coffee.

Mom sniffles, and tears roll down her cheeks. "It's no wonder he's head over heels, I mean look at you. My beautiful Millicent. I have seen such a difference in you since you've started working there. I love that you are home and love the glow on your face. I'm sorry." She wipes at her eyes. "I'm just— really happy you came back."

Mom's confession has me bubbling over the edge with so much emotion. "Mom." My voice catches in the back of my throat. "Now I'm going to cry," I say, sniffling. "And how did you — how do you know Luke and I..."

"From Jennifer. You forget it's Tony's office."

My heart lurches in my chest. There are no cameras there. Luke would know. My breakfast is still threatening to come up.

"He saw you two kiss the other day before you left the studio."

Dad coughs again, like he's sick and dying.

"My God, Gerald. Our daughter is a grown woman who writes about sex for a living, a little kiss isn't the end of the world."

Yeah, we did a lot more than kiss in that studio. I wish I could disappear at this very moment. She pauses, and I chuckle at Dad who is trying so hard to not get upset. I'm his little girl, I get it.

Mom shoos some more tears away. "Have I ever told you how proud I am of the young woman you've become? I don't care if some stuck-up magazine let you go; you're better than them and someday you'll take on the world all on your own."

My nose burns with the oncoming tears needing to be set free.

"I know things are rough right now, but I know you'll be okay."

When I first lost the job after I called Ezra, I talked to her. She knows how much that job and career meant to me. I remember a few times when we'd gone into the city. I was young, maybe ten or twelve. I would dress like I was going for an interview and walk around the city with a briefcase filled with articles I'd written for my school paper and ones I'd done for fun. I even made a fake resume after begging Mom to show me how. Manhattan, city life, journalism was— is everything to me and when I lost it, I broke. Somehow though, that brokenhearted feeling has felt repaired, but not totally. I'm not sure if it's being here with my family, Luke, or both, but things are changing and the crossroads I'm at has become my biggest enemy.

"Thanks, Mom."

"Love you, darling." Reaching around she hugs me. Her eyes flicker to the pictures once more before she sits. "Where were these taken?"

Closing my eyes, I bite my bottom lip. "His bedroom."

Now Dad is really choking, and Mom and I just sit there and watch shaking our heads.

"Mom," I groan.

And that's Dad's cue to leave. He walks out of the room without another word and Mom, and I snicker.

"Oh, so, I want you to invite Luke to dinner for Thanksgiving. I've told Jennifer and she thinks it's a great idea, but I think you should ask Luke yourself."

It's my turn to choke. "Th-Thanksgiving? You want me to invite him?"

It's not like he hasn't eaten dinner at our house before, but Thanksgiving feels much bigger. Are we serious enough for this? We just started feeling each other out, but he's also Ezra's friend and I'm sure he'd love to spend the holidays with him after being apart for so long.

"I'll ask him."

Mom claps her hands together. "I'm so glad. It will be nice to have everyone together." She smiles.

"So, you're dating your boss?" I jump as Dad reenters the

kitchen like he's been waiting to say something, and he's finally mustered the courage. "Here I thought he was just being kind, changing your car battery." His soft hazel eyes narrow at me.

"Uh, I— It's— We're something, I guess."

"Be careful, honey. It can get very sticky if things don't work out."

"I'm not sure how serious we are, and plus this isn't a permanent job. I want to write, not be someone's assistant."

Dad sighs and reaches for the sugar beside the coffee pot. "I'm just looking out for you. I know how fragile your heart is."

"Dad, I'm an adult, and you don't have to worry about my heart. It will be okay."

"I know, baby. I'm just being a dad." He gives me a brief yet worried smile.

"I love you guys more than anything. I promise I'll be careful. Okay?"

Dad's not completely convinced, but we can work on it. Mom on the other hand... she's glowing like a Christmas tree.

When Astra stopped calling, and showing up during school holidays, my parents began to question what happened. I'm close to my parents enough that I told them everything, and ever since then Dad has been determined to keep my heart safe. So, I do understand where he's coming from, but I don't think I've fallen deep enough yet for it to hurt like it did with my heartbreak over Astra.

"I really have to go," I say, shutting my laptop and tucking it under my arms. "I don't want to be late."

I give them both a kiss on the cheek before heading out.

MY PHONE RINGS as I get into the car. Pulling it out of my purse I see it's Cheryl. I forgot to call her after dinner with Luke.

"Hey, Cher. What's up?"

"Oh, thank God. I thought the aliens snatched you when you didn't answer my texts or calls."

"I am so sorry. I've been so busy with work and such..."

"You're working?"

I start my car and wait for it to warm up a bit. It's a cold brisk November morning. The trees are almost void of leaves and it's sad, but knowing the holidays are around the corner make the transition easier.

"Not in journalism. I got a job at a local photography studio as an assistant. I'm learning a lot. I think I might take some photography classes, get a little better. I've got a great article for my blog too."

She's quiet for a few seconds. "That's great, sweetie. Are you thinking of coming back to Manhattan?" she asks.

I freeze up. Am I? Of course I am. City life feels like another life. I do miss the constantly blaring horns, the chaos, the smell of city trash on the city streets, even.

"Mill?"

"Sorry, I uh—" I put my car into reverse and back down the driveway, keeping her on speaker. "That's the plan to come back. What's with all the calls?" Maybe if I change the subject, she'll drop the one I've been avoiding thinking about.

"Your girl got the cover article for the December issues."

I feel as if I'm a balloon that's been popped. The sting of a needle pricking through my skin and initial explosion of the pop has me gasping for air. My dream. She got my dream. I know I'll have other opportunities, but this was... Fuck.

"Can you hear me? Did I lose you? Hello? Millicent?"

"I-I'm here," I say, softly.

I stop at a red light and my vision blurs. I'm nearly at the studio and there's no hiding the waterfall about to pour from my eyes. Hands shaking on the wheel, I try to hold myself together, but it's all coming crashing down.

"That's really amazing, Cheryl. I am so, so happy."

"But wait... there's more. Word on the street is *Violet Press* is looking for writers. You should totally apply."

"I did," I say sullenly. "It was one of the first places I applied to."

"You'll get it, I know you will. Look, I've gotta go. Meeting in ten. Miss you."

"Miss you too."

I swipe at my eyes with one hand, keeping my other on the wheel. When I pull up to the studio, Luke is already filling his car up with everything we need. I check the time on my dashboard. It's 8:50. We are headed to the same park as last time, so I hope I got here with plenty of time to spare.

"Hey," I say, meeting him on the sidewalk.

He must notice the waver in my voice as I speak, because he immediately stops what he's doing. His brows knit together, and he shuts the trunk and moves quickly to the sidewalk where I'm standing. He takes me in his arms, kissing my salty lips. Pulling back, he holds on to keep me steady. "Millicent, what's wrong?"

My lips twitch up in a quivering half-smile cry thing. "My friend Cheryl, she's going to get the cover story. The day I got fired, I was going to pitch an idea to my boss, and I had all the confidence in the world striding in there and— and I never even got that far."

Chest heaving with sobs, I shake my head and try to step out of Luke's grasp, but he only holds on tighter.

"Am I crazy to think this blog will attract attention? Or that I'll find my place back in Manhattan again? I love it here and working with you, Luke. I love it so much. I just— It's my dream," I say, pointing west. "Manhattan is my dream."

He holds on tighter. "If that's what you want, then go for it. I'm living my dream right here," he says, eyeing the studio behind him. "You don't have to feel bad about wanting to live yours. I'm here. I'm not going anywhere. If you want to go back to your life before I'm not going to stop you. We can still do this; be us. It will just be at a distance."

His emerald eyes pull me in. He's serious. Luke's not holding me back. He doesn't want to. It's way too soon, but this man has me falling for him further and further with each passing second.

"I like you more than a lot, Millicent. If you haven't realized it already."

I snort-laugh, some snot surfacing from crying. My cheeks burn. He doesn't look disgusted. Not in the slightest.

"We may have just started this, but I want you to be happy. I've made so many mistakes in my last relationship and I need to try and be a better man."

"Who would tell you that you aren't? Luke, you have been there for me, even when you hated me."

"I could never hate you," he whispers, planting a soft kiss on my lips.

His words mean the world to me. The kiss is short, but amazing at the same time. He pulls away.

"Come to Thanksgiving with my family. Your parents are already invited by my nosey Mom." I laugh.

He grins.

"So, will you uh— will you come?" I shut my eyes, squeezing my lids tight. My stomach vibrates with tingles as his soft fingertips dance along my jawline.

"Of course," he says, planting tiny kisses along the same places he touched moments ago. "I'd love to."

My eyes flutter open. "Really?"

"You're cute when you're flustered," he says, pressing his lips to my forehead.

"Hush! I was nervous. I didn't know where we were in our relationship, what step we had entered, and figured a family dinner was a really big one."

"Do you want to take the step?" he questions.

Without hesitation, I stare up into his brilliant green hopeful eyes, and nod. "Yeah. I mean we don't have to label it, but moving forward would be okay with me."

We stand there quietly, enjoying each other for a few long lingering moments. "We're going to be late," I whisper.

He pulls his phone from the back of his jean pocket, and smirks. "We have plenty of time."

CHAPTER 29

"*W*ow! You look, wow!"
I'm startled by Luke's edgy voice as he enters my room. He's trying not to stare too much, keeping his eyes trained to the floor. I laugh.

"You don't look half bad yourself." I wink.

I'll never get tired of seeing him in a tux. I'm all hot and bothered and kind of wishing I could just let him have me here and he can leave the suit on. I can feel the warming sensation in my lower abdomen. Feeling this way is so new to me. Sure, I've had plenty of sexual urges, but he does things to me I can't explain.

He steps inside my room, closing the door behind him. Standing at the foot of my bed I attempt to put a black choker necklace on. Tonight, we have a wedding to shoot. It was a last-minute addition Tony booked. Luke said the mom of one of the brides called desperately seeking a photographer since theirs bailed; and luckily, he happened to be free that day.

It's a fall wedding at a vineyard out east. A dream set-up in my eyes. It's a bit of a drive, so he was happy when I offered to go.

"Can you help me with this?" I ask.

He's quiet as he steps behind me and grabs hold of the clasp. I lift my hair up to make it easier. As he fumbles with it his fingertips gently dance along my neck, and before I can get a word out his lips are there. He pushes at the black jacket of the suit I'm wearing and nibbles a little harder.

I smirk. "Someone is feeling feisty tonight."

He spins me around and takes in the rest of the pants suit. The pants are a little long, so I've compensated with one of my chunky heel shoes that provide comfort, unlike stilettos. I've almost matched his height. My eyes finally reach his nose instead of his chest.

With a single finger he lifts my chin a little higher. "I'll admit, I'm a dress and skirt man, I don't normally find a woman in a suit sexy, but you... you'd look sexy wrapped in toilet paper." He chuckles.

"Toilet paper?" I ask, grinning.

"It was on-the-fly thinking." Luke is radiating the same confidence that shows when he's behind the camera. "I could look at you forever like this."

His confession gets me a little misty eyed. I rest my hand on his trimmed scruff and press a kiss to his soft lips. It's brief, but there's so much emotion behind it from both ends.

"I love how open you are becoming with me. It's like there's this whole side to you that was buried in there."

He runs a hand through my hair and his eyes scan my face, like he's taking a mental picture of me and storing it in his head for later. I've never had any man or woman look at me the way he does. How did this go from; *oh my God I can't believe I'm working with nerdy Luke Parker* to *oh my God Luke Parker is sexy and I want to keep him forever?*

"As much as I would love to show you what you in that suit does to me, we should probably hit the road." I grab at his silk black tie and pull at it. The back of my knees hit the bed, and I carefully tug him down with me. He crawls over me and kisses my neck in soft gentle pecks. I roll my eyes and head back onto the bed and moan.

"Come back to my place tonight," he whispers.

"Oh. A sleepover. How exciting. I should pack a few things, but yeah. I'd like that."

His lips meet mine and for a few brief electric moments I'm caught up in him. There's a hunger so intense in his kisses. I want to tell him screw the wedding, let's just go to his place, but it's for work, and we don't have a choice. When he pulls away, I'm breathless. It's weird falling for someone you never imagined yourself with. The idea swirls around in my head, and I can't help wanting to store it there to write about. He inspires me more than anyone has before.

He gets off me and holds out a hand. I groan with displeasure. He pulls me up and into him, then leans in, whispering in my ear. "To be continued."

THE VINEYARD IS BEAUTIFUL. It's a little chilly, being almost mid-November, but since it's late afternoon and the sun is still strong enough to grace us with its warmth, the ceremony will be outside. I don't have to do much, but I'm excited to go around with the Polaroid camera and get some shots of guests having fun.

We enter the main building. It's more of a large house. Luke knows where he's going. The old floorboards creak below our feet as we make our way through. There aren't many people here yet. We step inside a room with gorgeous floral decor hanging from the ceiling. Light pours in from the large windows along the back of the room. I love the wooden tables and flooring, it's so rustic and perfect.

When we reach the outdoor area behind the house a woman

waves us over. She's chatting with another woman who looks our way. Her short dark curls fall in front of the beautiful, freckled face. There's something familiar about her.

"Millicent, darling. I didn't know you were coming."

CHAPTER 30

*T*his isn't any wedding, it's Astra and Katherine's. My body, minus the pounding pulse in my ear, slows down. Everything is distorted and there's an itch in my nose, making my eyes tear up.

The voice is Astra's mother, who's strolling over with a wide smile on her face. Luke is in professional mode and doesn't notice what is probably a shocked look on my face.

Her mother, Ann, is wearing the most stunning long teal dress with a slit up the side. Her mom was supermodel beautiful back in the day and looks the same as she had when we graduated high school.

Luke's eyes fall on me, and I try my hardest to plant the kindest smile on my face. I truly do miss Astra's mom. She was like a second mom to me. She steps forward ignoring Luke for a moment and wraps her arms around me. "I've missed you. What are you doing here?"

She pulls away. I clear my throat and stare down at the trimmed grass at my feet.

"I'm working with Luke, the photographer." I shift the

backpack on my shoulder. *Don't show any emotion, you can handle this*, I say to myself.

"Oh. Luke." She finally turns to him.

"Luke, this is Astra's mom," I say.

"Hi. I'm sorry I didn't recognize the name. I went to high school with Astra and Millicent."

"Luke, it's lovely to meet you. Thank you for doing this on such short notice. I'm surprised you were open, you're the hottest photographer in town." She flashes her pearly whites at him.

Luke blushes and grins. I stare at him trying to make myself feel better about this situation. I love watching Luke's eyes light up when someone compliments his work. He deserves all the compliments in the world. He really is an amazing photographer.

"I used Astra's first name, Marie. Her middle is Astra and I for the life of me can't understand why she still insists we call her it." Ann rolls her eyes. "She is still a little mad at me for interjecting and getting a photographer she didn't research first. I told her I got her nothing but the best. Seems I was right." While Ann was a sweet motherly figure in my life, she was stubborn and refused to give in until it was her way or no way.

"I'm so glad you are both here to celebrate with us today." "And Luke, you are a lifesaver. Marie and Katherine came to us in tears when their photographer bailed on them."

"It's not a problem at all; we are both happy to be here."

He glances back at me, and his brows knit together, concern flashes behind his green eyes. I shake my head at him and try to keep my composure. It's obvious he wants to comfort me, but knows he has to remain professional.

"Well, come with me. I'll take you to Marie. She'll be so happy when she sees you."

Astra's mom is in the dark about how much I loved her daughter. I'm assuming she only believes we had a falling out because of college.

Luke and I follow Ann. My sights are set on the ground before me and the sway of her teal dress. My heart is fluttering and pumping so hard it almost hurts. Soft fingers graze mine and I gasp.

"Hey," his voice is a whisper. "If you can't do this, you let me know. Okay?"

"I-I'm fine."

He wants to say more, but holds back, and gives me one last touch before moving on.

Ann disappears behind a bush. There's chatter on the other side.

"Marie," Ann sings. "You are going to be so happy with the photographer."

Even through the large bush I can hear a heavy sigh from Astra. "Mom," she grumbles. "I still can't believe you went behind my back—"

"Stop being so stubborn, Marie."

"And stop calling me that. I want to get through this day without—" She stops short when they round the bush.

There's never been a moment where she hasn't looked stunning. This girl looks good even when she's sick. Today she's gone above and beyond, and I can't help my wandering eyes. Her beautiful lace sweetheart dress hugs her body in all the right places. Her hair is pulled back a little, there are small silver clips in her hair. They shine in the fading sun, and her beautiful dark curls cascade down her neck. My heart is in my stomach. When her eyes meet mine, they widen.

"Can you believe we booked Luke from school. Who would have known your best friend is his assistant." Ann's smile is wide.

"Hey, guys."

Astra balls her hands at her side, but still politely smiles. She shakes her head at me, and I bite down on my trembling lip. This is so stupid. How can my heart be torn between two people?

"Hey, Astra. It's nice to see you. Are you ready to take some photos? Millicent is just going to help me out."

"Oh. That's wonderful. Were you the one to take her photos?"

He nods. "I did. They came out great. The makeup was fantastic." Luke rambles on happily, like they are old friends catching up.

Astra's cheeks turn rosy. "May I see them? Do you have any, maybe on your phone? I'm sure they are beautiful."

He looks over his shoulder to me, I give a slight nod of approval. I'm trying to hold it together and be polite.

He pulls it up to show her. Astra's eyes are glued to the screen. "They're beautiful, just like she is," she says.

God that hurt so bad. I shouldn't be so affected, I'm with Luke and I'm falling fast and hard. There should be no pain when a woman I used to love calls me beautiful.

"I think so too. So beautiful," he says, eyeing me.

Hearing her say I'm beautiful stung, but hearing Luke say it, makes everything okay again.

He pockets the phone. "So, let's get started since I have to take pictures of your soon-to-be wife too. I would have come to the house to take pictures of you getting ready—"

"Oh, no it's okay. We just wanted the ceremony and reception to be remembered." She lifts a finger and I swear she's wiping a tear from her eyes, but when she pulls her hand away, I see no trace of one at all. I can't believe this is happening right now, if I would have known I probably would have made Luke do this alone. He has no idea what kind of impact Astra had on my life. I'm not afraid to let him know, but I don't want him to get weirded out by it. I'm terrified.

"Millicent, my backpack."

I shake my head and blink a few times. Luke's worried eyes narrow on me. As I shimmy the bag off my shoulders, he closes the gap between us and whispers in my ear, "Hey, I'm worried about you. Are you sure you're okay?"

I nod quietly, the lump in my throat returning with a vengeance. He's not buying it, but also doesn't push me. We spend twenty minutes taking photos of Astra. I stand back and let Luke do his job. He's so amazing as usual. He's soft spoken and courteous towards Astra as he positions her for photos. He's gentle with the train of her dress and makes everything look easy. There are a few moments where he calls me over, asking me what I think, and then distracts me by teaching me some photography tips. His fingers brush against mine, and I am forever grateful for the love this man is showing me tonight. I'll have to thank him later.

WITH ALL OF the photographs being taken, there's not much time for Luke and me to talk. I'm relieved mostly because my brain is trying to reason with my heart as to why witnessing this moment is wrecking me. I'm happy for her, but for some reason my heart is still breaking.

Luke gives me the side-eye every time he passes. He continues to brush his fingertips against my hand. The gesture calms me. With the arrival of the guests and the ceremony starting we finally make our way out back to where it will take place.

A beautiful wicker arch with a fall-like garland woven into it sits in front of the aisle; a long white carpet leads up to it. Guests are seated on both sides taking up all the chairs. Luke stands off to the side, while I take the very back. The sky grows overcast and a fall chill soars through the air. Guests are bundled up, trying to stay warm until we get inside.

The first few beats of Ed Sheeran's "Perfect" play. I swallow hard as my eyes land on the bridal party beginning to walk down the aisle in delicate orange dresses. Their flower girl and ring bearer are so young they have to be escorted down the aisle in a shiny red wagon. The image of the two adorable kids makes me smile.

Everyone stands as Astra steps forward. Katherine is waiting at the front. Her dress is similar to Astra's, and I wonder if they had planned it that way. There are some minor differences in the laced pattern, and Katherine's did not have lace sleeves like Astra's, but both have sweetheart necklines. She's as beautiful as Astra with her long wavy dark hair positioned over her shoulders.

Some guests whimper and wipe their tears. There's a large knot stuck in my throat, but I haven't felt the urge to cry.

Both her mom and dad walk her down. Everyone sits except Luke who is capturing all the shots of their ceremony. I'm surprised at how fast everything goes. It's short and sweet. They wrote their own vows and by the time they get to it, I'll admit I'm a little weepy.

"I've never loved anyone, the way I love you. You're my perfect match, my best friend," Astra says, droning on.

Ouch. Fucking ouch.

"The only person who ever got me."

Triple ouch. Astra's words sting more than I want them to. The part that hurts the most is growing up we went to each other for everything, and I got her, at least I thought I did. Maybe it's why this is hard for me, because my best friend pushed me away when I needed her the most. When I was just discovering who I was and she just— She left me high and dry.

The thunderous applause catches my attention, and by the time my eyes wander back up front, the two are happily walking down the aisle. Luke is close now, snapping shots as they step forward.

When they finally retreat from the area, Luke strolls over holding out his hand for his backpack. He rests the camera strap over his neck and takes the pack from me. Kneeling he gets what he needs, then gets to his feet.

He leans in and brushes a simple kiss to my cheek. "Hey," he says, softly.

Out of the corner of my eye I catch sight of Astra and Katherine kissing and turn away. "I'm going to slip away to use the bathroom. Is that okay?"

"I'm not going to stop you from peeing." He chuckles. "The girls are going for a small break anyway, and I have to change the card in my camera."

"Okay."

I start to walk away, but I'm stopped by his hand gently closing around my wrist. I gasp at the spark of electricity shooting through my veins. Luke shimmies us behind the trunk of a tree. We aren't fully hidden, but the guests are all facing the other way. He twirls me back into him and wraps his arms around me. Bending down, he whispers into my ear, "I'm looking forward to tonight."

My lips twitch a little, and I suck in a shuddering breath. I hug him back, needing to feel close. He goes in for a simple, sweet kiss. Then he checks our surroundings to make sure no one is watching and gives me one more for good measure.

"Me too. Now let me go or I might pee all over you."

He chuckles. "Okay."

THE SCENT of lavender drifts around me as I place my hands on the counter in a resting area. There's a couch and a huge mirror. It's amazing for a bathroom at a vineyard. It feels like I should be at some fancy wedding hall.

I observe myself in the mirror. When I had come out to Astra, she was happy for me, but there was still something about her reaction that will always plague me. Like, when I said I was bi, I felt like I was not enough. Me liking both made it hard for her to accept me as a potential partner.

The door opens and as it does my eyes do too. Staring back at me are familiar brown eyes. I gasp and spin. "I didn't know it was your wedding," I whisper, backing myself up against the counter.

"I didn't realize Mom booked Luke either. I told her I wanted to do it, but she insisted, and I couldn't back out once she booked it."

Silence passes between us. I can't stop staring at her in that dress. My hands shake as I try to steady them on the counter behind me. "The ceremony was beautiful. Congratulations."

The air around us is becoming too thick and I find myself taking large deep breaths to compensate. She takes a few steps closer, so we aren't talking across the bathroom. "Are you and Luke—"

"Yeah. We are. It's new and we aren't sure where it will go, but I'm truly happy."

I mean every word of it. When I lived in the city, I thought I had all the happiness I could have ever wanted. The truth is… something was missing. I've found it with him. The broken piece of my heart is healed. So then why, while I'm standing here in front of Astra, do I want to cry?

"It's obvious the boy is in love with you. It always was."

Love. Luke. I keep trying to fight it. It's too soon to fall, but my heart is already there, and I think it has been since the lanterns. My lips twitch as I try to control the tremble of my jaw.

There's so much I miss about our friendship, well before the kiss. We spent almost every hour of every day together. If we weren't together, we'd be on the phone or chatting online. When she left me hanging, I fell apart and I used the city as a band aid to cover my pain.

"You don't have to pretend to be okay. It's been years, but I know you better than you think."

"Was our friendship not enough to overcome my moment of poor judgment?"

Astra's eyes close for a split second, then she reaches for me.

Now she wants to comfort me? After she abandoned years of friendship? My hand pulls back and slams against the counter behind me.

"Fuck!" I swear under my breath, shaking out my hand.

Her hands rest back at her side, and she sighs. "You wanted more from me. What was I supposed to do? We would have never worked out."

"You don't know that." My voice shakes and I hate the effect she has on me. I clear my throat, pulling myself back up. "That's not the point though. The point is we could have moved past it. College was hard enough going into it without knowing anyone. Then you drop off the face of the earth. My best friend in the whole world, the one person I could count on, just vanished. I think it stung more than the rejection of your love."

"I did it for your own good."

"I thought our friendship meant more to you."

"It did, but even you have to admit that things got weird. I pulled away because it was for the best. I called less while we were apart, and eventually just not at all."

I blink, trying to keep the incoming tears at bay. "But those things you said—"

"I said them because they are what you wanted to hear. You were still figuring yourself out, you were more into—"

"More into what, Astra. Guys? If you're going to insult me just do it. You know what, forget it." My body heats up like it's on fire. The tears fall before I can stop them. I shake my head, my vision blurring like a windshield on a rainy day. I put my heart out there on the line for her, and she crushed it more than once. "I have to get back to work." I wipe my face attempting to keep my composure.

"Millicent, I never meant to hurt—"

I hold my hand up. "Don't. Okay? I have to get through this night for Luke."

She tries to grab me as I brush past, but I tug hard and her dark eyes flash with hurt. I hate that the image will be burned into my head. I'm done chasing, and as much as I hate how this went down, I needed closure. I deserve better, and I have better.

I exit the room and attempt to get myself together before heading into the ballroom where it's now cocktail hour. Taking several deep breaths, I give myself some time. Once I'm ready I march forward. It's time to move on.

CHAPTER 31

$\mathcal{T}$he reception is winding down. I made it through the night. After the incident in the bathroom, I knew I needed to move forward with my life. As the night went on, I realized although we had an amazing friendship, she was never going to believe I belonged and seeing me with Luke tonight solidified that. I'm not going to lie, it hurts.

"Hey, I'll pack up my things and we can get out of here. Okay?"

Luke's warm breath dances along my ear. I straighten as he puts his hands on my hips. I just packed away the Polaroid camera. The guests absolutely loved it. They were happy with their pictures, and I actually had somewhat of a good time despite the urge to cry, which is returning.

"I should probably say goodbye."

It would feel wrong if I didn't. A warm wet tear escapes the corner of my eye, but he catches it before it falls.

"We'll do it together then. Will that make you feel better?"

"Maybe," I say.

He drops his hand and connects it with mine. Our fingers lock together and suddenly every upsetting thought in my head vanishes. We head to the table set aside for us, and he packs away his camera and equipment. I expect him to have me hold it, but he throws it over his shoulder with a reassuring smile.

As we walk over to say goodbye our hands stay linked. Astra spots us coming over. Luke says, "I hope you both had a great evening. Millicent and I are going to hit the road. I'll have some previews later in the week. Would you like me to email them?"

Astra grins, but there's a little hesitation behind her smile. "Yes. Thank you. We really appreciate you stepping in."

"Yes, so grateful." Katherine's beautiful face lights up.

"Congratulations," I choke out. I clear my throat, and Luke holds on tighter.

Luke pulls me from the goodbye, and we go and find her mom. She gives me a giant hug and tells me to keep in touch. I probably won't, but I tell her I will.

When we get to the car, Luke opens the door for me. He goes to put his things in the back, then walks around to his side of the car. The second his door closes a loud sob breaks through. Guilt rides heavily on my shoulders. I thought I had enough in the restroom earlier, but I guess there were still more feelings bubbling.

Being the kind, gentle soul he is, he wraps his arms around me and holds on tight. It's uncomfortable here in the car, but his hugs are powerful, and with every tightening grasp I sink into him, never wanting to leave.

"I'm sorry, Luke."

"What's there to be sorry about?"

"I-I'll understand if this is all too much for you. I don't know if you've ever dated a bisexual woman and if you're uncomfortable w-with…"

"Mill," he says, in the calmest voice I've ever heard him speak. "Millicent. No. Why— How could you— Did she make you feel this way?"

He forces me to look at him, by taking me by the shoulders. I can't turn away. His eyes are wide with concern. "That's who you are. It's a part of you. A part I've embraced, a part I love. I like you exactly as you are." He pauses to take a breath. "Hey." A soft smile tips up the corner of his lips. "We have something in common, right?" He gives a light playful push at my shoulder and it kind of helps ease the tension.

A small feeble laugh comes out of me. "You just want me to admit the waitress with the sliver of a tattoo showing at the hem of her sleeve was hot."

Luke's laughter fills the car and connects all the missing pieces of my heart. I grin. Luke is making me feel so at ease. I love him for that.

"I just— I always feel so invalid. Tonight, I realized Astra would never accept me..."

"I could never not want to be with you because of your sexuality. Unless you decide you only like women because well then... you wouldn't be dating me, but even then, I'd still like you. And you are more than valid. Don't let anyone make you believe otherwise."

"I'm sorry I still have those lingering feelings for her too. I think some small part of me always will."

"She was your best friend. I get it. I'm not mad. I swear. I know what's in your heart, Millicent. I trust you."

I smile and throw my arms around him, shedding more tears. I am beyond grateful for this man and whatever forces brought us back together.

When I finally get myself together, I pull away. He holds me at arm's length, making sure I'm okay before letting go.

"Do you want me to take you home?" he asks.

I shake my head and wipe some extra tears with the back of my hand. "I don't want to be alone with my thoughts. You keep them from destroying me."

He reaches over, squeezing my leg. "Okay. Let's go home then."

I like the way the word home rolls off his tongue. It makes this... us feel official.

The car ride is quiet, but it's exactly what I need. The only noise is his humming to the radio. He drives with one hand and holds on to me as if he never wants to let go, and I don't want him to.

When we get back to his house and step inside, he awkwardly stands there for a moment, then places his backpack by the door. His hands are balled up at his sides, his cheeks flush a soft crimson color, like he's holding back. After blankly staring out into the dark night as we drove home, my head is somewhat clear, and the only person on my mind is him, and how much I've grown to like him over the past few weeks.

"Millicent, there's something I need to—"

I take the initiative and push him up against the front door, pressing a kiss to his tender lips. "Save it for later," I say, parting only slightly, before crashing back into him. We both gasp in sync with each other and gently open our mouths. His tongue glides along my lower lip. He wraps his arms around the lower part of my body and lifts me in the air. I wrap my legs around him, and he walks with me to his room.

Our kisses are soft and loving, nothing rough. It's what I need. Lust is great, but sometimes I need calm passion that takes my breath away. His compassionate touch sets my heart on fire. Lowering me onto the bed, he straddles my body. He sucks on my neck, sending shivers of chaotic pleasure rippling through me.

"I'd love for you to leave this on." He tugs at my suit. "But there's too much fabric in the way," he murmurs, as his teeth find the outer edge of my ear.

The nibbling causes tension in my lower half, but it's the good kind. All the sadness I was harboring is left behind and tucked away, hopefully forever. Here in the moment the only thing I care about is the man I love. His sparkling emerald eyes meet mine. I'm hypnotized by their fierceness. Love.

He helps me shimmy off the jacket and I wiggle out of it. While undoing each button of the white dress shirt his mouth presses against the exposed skin of my chest. Luke says he's not an expert, but then why am I so wet for him?

The dark scruff on his cheek tickles on the way down. When he gets to my waist, he pulls down my pants, the underwear coming along with it. My shoes fall off the edge of the bed. His eyes wander down my whole body, he's taking a picture in his mind again. I want to tell him he doesn't have to take one, because I want this for as long as he'll have me.

I'm desperate to feel his skin against mine. We both work on his clothing, discarding it to the floor. Shimmying up the bed, he leans over and pulls out a condom from his drawer. He can't get it on soon enough. The moment it's wrapped, he slips it inside and I scream out in pleasure. The one thrust was enough to trigger a mini orgasm. Who needs a sex toy when I have him?

I love how all his focus is on me as we slowly rock back and forth in a steady rhythm together. This time for some reason it feels different. He's laying every emotion right there on the bed, like he's baring his soul to me. I could stare at this man for the rest of my life.

He lowers his body so he can rest his lips against my neck. His slick skin meshing with mine is such a turn-on. I arch up and into him and he hisses. "Millicent," he whispers. His trembling hands find my cheek. I focus on him and only him. The world around us fades away as we continue to rock into each other.

"Millicent—"

I blink away the fog, trying to read what he's going to say. He closes his eyes and bites down hard on his lower lip. He pauses briefly. I don't mind. I love the way he fills me. Now it's my turn to reach up and touch him. His scruff tickles my hand as I lay it against his perfect flushed skin.

"I-I love you," he says. His confession charges the air around us with passion.

He moves slightly and my whole body feels the orgasm. I shake.

"I love you, Luke. I've fallen so—"

He doesn't let me continue. His lips are against mine and his body starts rocking again. With each movement I'm drowning in him, loving every second. Sex has never felt like this with anyone before. His entire body trembles as he lets go inside of me, and I quake for a few extra minutes, the fading orgasm lingering.

He crashes down next to me, throws the condom into the small wastebasket beside his bed, then wraps me in his arms. I suck in a breath.

"I love you," I say again, like the words will never be enough.

"You don't know how relieved I am to hear you say it back."

"Why, did you think I wouldn't?" I ask.

He looks away. His cheeks flushing in embarrassment. "Because of our past, and other things that aren't out there yet. Because I fail..."

I look up, trying to understand the last comment, and adjust to lie on my side. Taking his face in my hands I hold on as best I can. I press a soft meaningful kiss to his beautiful swollen lips.

"I feel like I still have some residual fears from my relationship with Gretchen and I don't want to make the same mistake twice."

Still holding on to his face, I give him another kiss. "You and I can make each other forget. I feel like in some ways you already have for me. You know when I first moved back in with my parents? I felt like I'd failed. More than anything I wanted to be back in the city, writing for a big magazine again. Being here with you, though, it feels so much better than how I felt out there in Manhattan. I couldn't believe I'd been missing this in my life. You made my heart whole again. I'm sorry for tonight, I hope I didn't hurt you."

He sighs and kisses my forehead. "You didn't; it was my own insecurities."

"I'm yours and this thing between us is something I never want to lose."

He smiles, a true genuine Luke smile. It reaches his eyes and there's a glistening shimmer there.

"I should clean myself up, but I really just want to lie here with you."

His smile never fades. "Then let's shower, get into something comfortable, and go to bed."

The grin on my face hurts. "I'd like that. A lot."

For a moment I stay on the bed as he rolls off and gets to his feet. I watch him spin and face me. Whatever happened tonight was magical. I love this man with all my heart, and I'll do whatever it takes to make him happy. Even if there's a voice inside my head with the idea of writing about this precious moment, and leaving to pursue my career again, but as usual I try to push it back, because hurting him is the last thing I want to do. If it means losing my writing career then so be it, this is what I want. Forever. At least I think it is.

CHAPTER 32

*M*y Phone pings with a message.

> Hey, it's Nora. Jake gave me your number. I spoke with him, and he says to plan on a one-shot during Christmas break. Teacher life. Lol. But I wanted to reach out, because I thought that maybe we could get together, and I can help you with your character. I'm not free for another few weeks, but let's make plans. I'm thinking Warlock for you.

Smiling I type back a response.

> Hey, it's good to hear from you. The guys tell me nothing, not even my own boyfriend. Haha. Anyway, that sounds great I've been doing some Warlock research, actually.

Not even seconds later she responds.

BTW, I read your blog post. Damn girl, you look amazing! Seriously. And Luke, he's a kickass photographer. Yay! We're on the same page. I'll touch base soon, and in the meantime, I'll send you all the good websites for research. Talk soon?

I can't help smiling. While I have Cheryl, she's got her own life right now in the city and I'm here on Long Island. Sure, we aren't far, but it feels a lot farther, especially since we've kind of drifted since I left. It's nice to have another female friend in the area.

Nora reading the article is also the cause of my smile. Yesterday I hit the publish button on the boudoir post. I read it over and over to make sure it was perfect. It's only been up for twenty-four hours, and I've already gotten a massive number of comments and reshares on platforms like Twitter and Instagram. It feels like I did something right and after Cheryl reached out, I haven't been alright, but this is kind of helping. Also, Luke's photography on my post is getting A LOT of buzz, I mean a ton. People are commenting on his style and how they wish he'd taken their photos. We had an influx in phone calls. People interested in not so much boudoir but everything we do there.

It's only been a few days since Astra's wedding, but I'm feeling okay. Luke. I don't even know what to say about him. He loves with all his heart, and I am so grateful we got this second chance at being together. Even Ezra is on board and texted me a ton of winky emojis with flames.

Luke's coming in a little while to pick me up for work. It makes sense to just take one car, especially with gas prices the way they are.

I've been contemplating my next article. My fingers are itching to write about us. Falling in love unexpectedly is a rush, like the kind you get on the first drop of a rollercoaster. I want to write about every emotion I'm feeling.

I've decided to distract myself from writing it by rummaging through the vibrators. They are sprawled out on my bed, in a heaping pile. Dildos, vibrators, even panties that buzz with the help of a remote. When I asked what kind of posts my readers want to see, this is the top one I received. Sure, I've tried to write this article before, but with the number of comments recently, I figured why not dive right in.

A lot of women question which is the best, for single player use, or for in the bedroom with their significant other. Men have even reached out asking which is the best one for their partner too.

Flipping on the switch to a small palm sized vibrator, I let it buzz in my hand. The thing shakes my hand with a force more rapid than I've ever felt in one before. I'll have to test them later, Luke should be here shortly, for now I shut the switch and toss it into the try pile.

My phone buzzes beside me, I jump from the vibration thinking one of these has a mind of its own. An unknown number flickers across the screen. I don't normally pick up random calls, but I decide to answer anyway.

"Hello?"

"Hi, is this Millicent Gibson?"

"This is she," I say, picking up a vibrator resembling a microphone.

"Hi. I'm Maggie Thompson, from *Violet Press*. We are a women's magazine located in Manhattan. I apologize for not reaching out sooner, I've been out of the office. Your resume was given to me by my assistant, and I did a little digging and found your latest blog about boudoir. It blew me away, not only that, but you're a beautiful woman."

"Oh, uh—" My heart grows heavy in my chest as it punches me from the inside. A few months ago, I would have felt less anxious about a phone call for a job. I haven't applied for anything since the first week I was working for Luke, the idea of working somewhere other than the photography studio isn't as appealing as it once was.

"Thank you. It was a lot of fun to write. My partner took the photos."

"They're wonderful too, if we were searching for a photographer I'd hire them on the spot; those pictures were phenomenal. I'm calling for you, though. I know your articles from *Forever Twenty* and they always blew me away. When your résumé landed on my desk, I knew I had to have you."

"Oh, wow." I can't help smiling, because hearing that after being let go, and having to start over, is exactly what I needed to boost my confidence.

"When are you available?" she asks.

Luke gave me Thursday off; he said he had some errands to run. It's the only day I can sneak out without him knowing. I know it's wrong to not tell him, but I don't even know if she'll hire me. My heart twists in agony as my brain contemplates the job.

"Thursday."

"That's perfect, my meetings are in the afternoon. Can you be in Manhattan by nine?"

Manhattan. The sounds of the city come rushing back into my head, even though I'm trapped here in suburbia, the atmosphere of the city is always with me.

"I can."

"Perfect. Let me email you all the details. Is your email still the same as it was on this résumé?"

"It is."

Maggie speaks with me for a few more minutes, giving a brief overview of the job and the magazine itself. It's one of the top competitors of *Forever Twenty*. I hang up the phone and someone knocks at my bedroom door.

I grab my chest. "Come in."

The door groans open and we lock eyes.

"Hey, can we talk before we…" He nods his chin towards the display of sex toys on my bed. "So, you weren't going to call and ask for help with those?" His face lights up and my body swells with hundreds of emotions all at once.

I shrug my shoulders and tilt my head slightly. It's like I got caught doing something I shouldn't. I'm hot all over, as the thought of him using one of those on me riles me up.

"They were test products to try when I worked at *Forever Twenty*. It wasn't just relationships I wrote about."

"I know." He grins.

"Y-you know?"

"Yeah, baby. I looked you up."

I wince, and chuckle softly. I love how since the wedding he's been so much more open with me and seeing the real Luke has been eye opening. With narrowed eyes he shuts and locks my bedroom door, then comes trudging towards me.

"My mom is down—"

"No, she's not." He smirks.

He crawls onto the bed and over to me, his legs steady on either side of my body. Having him here with all the want and need lingering in his eyes almost makes me forget about the interview. Telling him would be the right thing to do, but I'm so lost in the moment, and the fact that he's just picked up the remote to one of the many samples beside him. With a wide grin, he flicks on the switch, and the thing roars to life. It's a small bullet type, but has many different settings, and he's ramped it all the way up.

With a gentle ease he reaches under my skirt and brings the toy to the outside of my underwear. At full blast I gasp. His lips meet mine and immediately I open my mouth for him. Slipping the toy beneath my underwear the sensation vibrates through me. On top of his kisses, it's the easiest orgasm, and most intense. Several twitches later, my tense shoulders finally fall against the soft sheets behind me.

"My boss will be mad if I'm late." I grin under his soft kisses.

"You can tell him you were occupied."

"Occupied with this..." I grab hold of him, and he groans under my touch.

Luke discards his pants like they're on fire.

"Condom in the drawer," I say.

I reach over, attempting to grab the handle, but can't quite... and there goes another orgasm. I shiver under him, and I can't help staring at the pleasure on his face as I twitch endlessly. For a brief second, he gets off me and grabs a condom from the box, then rips it open like he's eager to get started.

I take over the vibrator with my own hands, while he preps the condom. He watches me as I lay there, eyes flickering from open to closed.

He pumps himself a few times while sliding the condom on. "Watching you playing with yourself is such a turn-on. I love your job." He grins.

For a second, I lay there frozen. My job, the interview.

"Hey," his hand grazes my cheek, "you okay?"

"What?" I ask.

"I lost you there for a minute."

"Oh, no I'm okay," I say.

I attempt a reassuring smile, but I'm not sure he buys it. Even if he doesn't, he slides himself in, while I allow the vibrator to chill on the outside.

We both don't last long, but when we are finished, we lie beside each other panting in sync.

"Do you get to keep those?" he asks.

"I'm thinking about writing about which one is best."

"I think you found your answer..."

I grin.

"How late do you want to be?" he asks.

"Someone's a bit excited today."

"I can't help it." He props himself up on one arm and allows his fingertips to dance over my bare stomach. "Knowing we can finally be together like this makes me happy."

"When did you kind of like me? You know, back then?"

So many emotions flicker in his eyes. I see them all pass by like a quick summer storm. He quietly contemplates what to tell me, like maybe the memory hurts?

"I think I was a freshman. You were a junior. Jason's crew tripped me in the cafeteria, and without any hesitation you helped me pick everything up and made sure I was okay. We had lunch together that day, and I was so grateful that you were there."

My fingers find their way through his soft locks of hair. I kiss his scruffy jawline, and he rolls his head back releasing a subtle moan.

"Jason Geiger was an asshole. His whole group was. I'm sorry I was mean."

He lifts his neck so I can kiss the spot where his pulse is wildly beating under my lips. "It was a lifetime ago," he whispers, as I crawl on top of him now, letting my lips trail down his chest.

"But I never imagined being able to do this to you. There were times in high school I had to hold back, and when you'd come down to the basement during *D&D*, in my head I pictured myself crossing the room and sweeping you off your feet."

I huff out a laugh, grinning enough to make my cheeks ache. "If you had kissed me back then, the way you do now, who knows, it might have worked."

The second I say those words I want to invent a time machine to go back and erase all the things I said. He didn't deserve any of it, even if I didn't mean it to hurt him, I only meant to be playful. Adult me hates teen me. While I could make every excuse under the sun, like how those were the years I was most at war with myself because of who I was becoming and the fear of being accepted. Yet, there I was bringing him down over a love for a game. We both craved approval from others. For me it was having people see me as valid. For him, it was to not be judged over his hobbies, and for who he was.

"Millicent, I forgive you. Stop doing that."

"Doing what?"

I'm afraid to look but when I do, I'm seeing a different Luke. A confident and sexy version. I would have seen it if I wasn't so—

He kisses me. Trying to erase every lasting bad memory.

"Retreat into your head like that, rehash the past. Don't live in it. Live in the now. Be here. With me. Okay? I'm all in."

"Me too," I hum softly.

"So, should we go for another round?" He grins and slowly strokes my face while pushing stray hairs aside, making me love him even more.

"You're really trying to get me in trouble with my boss..."

"Oh, you're in big trouble," he teases.

I cringe playfully. "Well then I guess I need to be punished."

Laughter fills the space between us as he grabs me and flips us so he's on top. For the next half an hour I get lost in him again. While I'm holding myself together on the outside, my insides are screaming to tell him about the phone call, but I never do, not because there's no time, but because I chicken out.

CHAPTER 33

*E*verything about Manhattan excites me, from the disgusting scent of urine to the pollution-induced headache. It's not home, yet it calls to me. A siren blares a few blocks away, and that combined with the impatient taxi drivers would drive most people nuts; but for me it's like a song to my ears.

Luke hasn't texted, but I know he had a lot going on today, so I'm not worried. Although, he has been acting a little strange. I can't let anything get in the way of this, so I put on my brave face and trudge forward. Guilt is killing me. I'll tell him after the interview. If I don't get the job then it won't matter anyway.

I step inside the large glass building a few blocks from Times Square. Women's heels click on the green marble tiled floors. People rush by, and I've gotten nudged in the shoulder a few times. I'm acting like a tourist visiting for the first time but stepping back in feels like it's new all over again.

There's a heaviness this time, and it makes my body tight, causing the tension in my lower back to pinch. I rub at the spot while I wait to step up to the large desk in the back of the main lobby. Elevators ding in the background, and voices collide, echoing around the large open space.

"Hi. I'm here to see Maggie Thompson. I have a 9am interview."

I step up to the desk, a big burly balding man stares down at me like I'm trouble. His eyes scan the screen.

"Name?"

"Millicent Gibson."

He leans over and writes something on a large sticker. It's weird coming here and needing a guest pass, but I shake it off. He hands it to me and gives me directions.

The elevator fills with the scent of various perfumes and colognes as it races to the top. Men and women get off at different floors, and when I finally step out on floor nineteen, the *Violet Press* door catches my attention right away.

The nerves have settled in, with shaking hands I open the door and enter a small waiting area. Chairs are lined up on both sides. The dim lighting makes it feel dark and unwelcoming, but I chalk it up to being unsure about the whole thing.

The woman at the small gray desk glances up from her large coffee. She doesn't smile when she greets me. I introduce myself and she barely acknowledges I exist, just hands me a clipboard, and asks me to take a seat. Jenna, the receptionist at *Forever Twenty* always greeted us with a smile, even guests who weren't a part of our team. Sometimes I miss her bubbly personality, and I'm reminded I should reach out and see how she is. I've slipped off their radar, including the other friends I made while I was there.

"Millicent, darling!" a boisterous voice calls out.

I lift my gaze to find the door across the room partially open. A tall, thin woman with bright fire-red hair stands there watching me with a wide grin. Over the years I've learned how to tell a fake smile from a real one. Her jaw is clenched, like she's trying too hard.

Following her through the office, it's quiet. Everyone in the room beyond the door sits in their cubicle in the center of the room. As Maggie walks through, they all keep their heads down. Not a smile on a single one of them.

My stomach is in knots. It feels surreal to be here back in the city. I don't know what to expect, but I also know this is my dream and if I can have another chance at achieving it, I'll jump through hoops to get it.

We enter a large conference room with a long white table. There's not much space between the walls and the table. I find a spot across from the windows, and finally feel somewhat at home again.

"I'm glad you could come in today. I'm looking for a writer who's not afraid to be bold and daring. Your articles have this spark about them. The one you wrote when you were with *Forever Twenty* about sex positions, flawless."

If only I could tell her it was written from zero experience. I had to interview some co-workers to get the story, because of the dry spell I was going through, and because I hadn't experimented with multiple positions prior to dating Luke.

"Thank you."

On the outside, I'm showing the professional Manhattan girl version of me, on the inside, everything about this feels wrong. Luke's face flitters across my mind, and all I want to do is stand, say thank you for this opportunity, and jet out of there to him, but the Manhattan girl stays put.

"I want more pieces like the boudoir one. I love how you got the perspective of the significant other."

"Thank you. It was one of my favorite to write."

"I'd love for you to model for some of our articles too, you've got this look about you. This wholesome small-town girl who took Manhattan by storm vibe. I love it!" She practically growls.

I nod, with a smile, trying to stay as professional as possible. She opens a booklet on the table, and scatters some papers, one being my résumé. After talking about how much she loves me, she dives right into the nitty-gritty. It's been a long time since I've had an interview, but some of the questions get a little personal. The vibe radiating through this office doesn't feel right.

"I have a few more candidates, but you are who we really want. I will call you when I'm finished to let you know the decision we have made. We are doing interviews right up to the holiday. Just know, we'd love to have you on board."

This gives me time to come clean to Luke and to be honest with him about the interview. We can figure out everything and hopefully it will all just fall into place. I could commute too, but it depends on the demand, and it will get pricey after a while.

"Sounds perfect. It will give me a chance to figure out transportation and possibly a move."

She smiles, clapping her hands together. "This could be the start of a beautiful thing." She presses her hand to her mouth. "I almost forgot. I have a meeting. You can find your way out, can't you?"

"Yes, of course." I manage my most polite voice.

We shake hands, and part ways. Once back out on the city streets I gasp for air, sucking in the harsh air of Manhattan. A knot forms at the back of my throat and I try to swallow it, but the cold brisk temperature doesn't help and forces my eyes to water. My phone vibrates in my purse, it's Luke.

Finding a spot against a neighboring building, I lean back against the cool brick, and finally answer the call.

"Hey," I say.

"Hey, where are you? It's loud," he asks.

"I went to Manhattan. Visiting someone. You gave me the day off and she called, and I hadn't heard from you, so I just went."

"You— oh." The melancholy tone in his voice makes me think there's something wrong.

"Are you okay?" I ask.

"I will be. I was going to see if you wanted to get a bite to eat, but you're busy, so I'll just—"

Something is wrong. The panic in my chest is so tight it hurts. Maybe it has to do with Gretchen. She hasn't been around and I'm not sure if it's a good thing or a bad one.

"Luke..."

"No, don't worry about me." He sniffles. Is he crying?

"I can be home before one. I'll hail a cab and meet you somewhere."

"It's okay, Mil. I—" He pauses. "I'll see you tomorrow."

"Luke?"

He's silent and I check the screen to make sure I haven't lost him. My phone is always finicky here.

"Yeah." His voice is a silent whisper.

"I'm worried about you. I can come home. I don't have to stay here. If you need me, I'm here."

I push off the wall and rush towards the street to get a cab. Something tells me he needs me.

"No, Millicent. Don't cut your time short. Stay. Okay?" Again, he sniffles. "I'll be fine. Promise. I need some time alone anyway. Don't worry. I love you."

"I love you too."

I want to believe his words, but they're robotic, and not at all the way he's sounded before. I bite my lip to control my own emotions. Between the interview and the return of Luke's cold behavior I'm feeling like I could break any moment. My mouth opens to say something, but there's a click on the other end, followed by the dreaded dial tone.

"Fuck!" I say out loud, kicking the wall.

People stare, but I ignore it. It's the city after all. I'm not the only one cursing to myself. Instead of heading back to Penn, I take a day for myself to be a tourist for once in my life. Maybe being surrounded by the sights and sounds I'm used to will help guide me with the big decision I'll have to make come next week.

CHAPTER 34

*L*oving the city during the day is one thing, but night is when the entire place comes to life. The lights twinkle from buildings, and even in the cold brisk nearly winter wind, the night is beautiful and clear. I stumble from the old familiar bar with Cheryl. I wasn't planning on telling her I was in the city, but I needed to unwind.

Technically I'm not lying to Luke now. I'm hanging out with an old friend. It started with some lunch, sight-seeing, and is now a full-blown drunken city night. Cheryl's soft hazel eyes find mine in the bright lights.

"This was a great idea. I'm so glad you're contemplating a job here again. We could take on this city."

Laughter laced with liquor fills my lungs. "We'll be like the *Sex and the City* gals."

"You know I always thought it was Sex in the City," she says, her voice sounding like she's in a far-off daze.

"Right? Me too." The giggles return.

We walk down the street, arms hooked together, observing the beautiful night.

"So, you've been okay back on Long Island?"

We come to a slow steady pace, matching each other's stride.

"Yeah. Really good actually. I'm dating."

"Oh. Who is she—"

"He."

"Look at you. What's his name?"

We stop on the street corner waiting for the light to change so it's safe to cross. Normally I'd take a chance with the other daring New Yorkers, but tonight I'm not in a rush.

"Luke. He's a friend of my brother. He's kind of my boss right now." I chuckle.

"The boudoir pictures?"

"Yeah. He took them. That's when we had our first kiss."

She squeals. The little man on the sign changes to white. We step forward into the street, a taxi nearly clipping us, forgetting to stop. She pulls me back. My heart races and her arms tremble in mine.

"You okay?" she asks.

An image of Luke's smiling face flashes before me. I bite hard on my lower lip, trying to bite back the tears. We reach the other side and continue walking.

"Yeah. Are you?"

"Gotta love New York, right?"

"Is it love?" she asks.

"It's everything," I say with a sigh. I'm not only saying it, because I'm wasted off my ass, I mean it. Every word. I feel something with Luke. It's much deeper than any relationship I've had before.

In the corner of my eye, I catch her watching me.

"Aww, you're glowing." She grins.

"That's the lights from the billboards."

"No, it's not." Cheryl bumps into my hips, her body moving closer. I rest my head on her shoulder, and we continue to walk.

"So, he's the one."

"The one. Maybe. I dunno. He just got out of a complicated relationship," I whisper.

"Damn."

"Shit. Am I the rebound?" I want to blame the alcohol for that conclusion, but now I can't get it out of my head. Luke's only been with *her*—Gretchen. What if this is his way of experimenting with what else is out there. No. That's not him. Not him at all. I have to stop thinking that before it consumes me.

A car honks at us, and Cheryl pulls me back. "Should I ride the train back home with you, make sure you get home safely?" We step in front of Penn Station.

Signs of the upcoming holiday are everywhere. Next week people will be lined up across the street from here, while they wait for the parade to pass through. I went one year with another co-worker; it was so cold, and we had to sneak away early to use the bathroom and lost our spot.

I glance back over at her. "I'll be okay. I'm glad you were available today. It's been a lot of fun."

"Yeah. Please don't let another two months go by before I hear from you again, okay?" She wraps me in her arms, making me almost miss city life. Pulling back, I catch a whiff of her cinnamon scent. Each season she changes her perfume; it's getting close to Christmas, so cinnamon is her go-to. In the fall it's this lovely scent of pine, and her spring-time perfume is a strong sweet floral.

"Of course. Maybe I'll be back in Manhattan soon."

"That would be wonderful. Goodnight." She leans in and kisses my cheek.

On my way down the steps into Penn Station my phone rings. I pull it out and nearly face plant as my ankle twists on the step. I grab hold of the rail, and wince.

"Hello?" I press my lips together, trying to suppress the pain. I didn't even see who it was.

"Where are you?"

It's Ezra.

"I'm in Manhattan."

"Luke said you were supposed to be home hours ago. I went to Mom's to get something, and she said she couldn't reach you."

Once at the bottom step, I let go of the rail and hiss in pain. My ankle rolling only slightly.

"You okay?"

"Yeah. I'm a little tipsy. I'm fine. I met up with a friend."

"Luke's in a mood. We ended our game early. You're in the same kind of mood. Are you two fighting?"

"It's none of your business. I'm about to get on a tra-*ain*." *Damn it hurts.*

There's some chatter on the other end, but I'm more distracted by my ankle. It's not too bad but will definitely feel a little sore in the morning. "Look, I'm on my way, but I might need a ride. I'm so wasted."

He sighs. "Hold on."

He's mumbling to someone. There's a buzzing in my ear and the muffled voices on the other line are hard to make out. I listen harder over the sound of a musician ripping it on guitar. The tune echoes in the underground space.

Ezra asks what time I'm coming in and I relay the train and track information, and he promises to be there. After I hang up, I have a feeling it won't be him there to greet me.

"EXCUSE ME, MISS." Someone pokes my shoulder.

Blinking rapidly my eyes slowly open, then scan the area. I'm on the train. *Shit. I hope I'm not in the train yard.*

"Miss. This is the last stop. I was checking the train. Have you missed your stop?" he asks.

I blink away the sleep and get a better look at the man before me in his well-polished blue conductor's suit. The electronic screen above the inside doors says: RONKONKOMA. Shit, I did miss my stop.

"Oh. Thank you."

"Are you feeling okay?"

I stand forgetting my ankle hurts a bit and that I'm still drunk as hell. Groggily I nod.

"Yeah. Thank you."

"Would you like some help?"

"No thank you."

He's an older gentleman, probably around my parents' age. His white hair and matching mustache make him seem a little older. "Do you have someone to come and get you? It's nearly one in the morning, not the best time to be on your own."

"I'll call them, they should be two train stations in the opposite direction."

He wishes me a good night and I step off the train and out onto the platform. My ankle hurts, but I don't think I did any damage as I can walk perfectly fine. The train beeps as the doors close and the sound whooshes by me. I wait until it's gone before I pull out my phone and call Ezra.

"Where the hell are you? The train you said you were on passed by ten minutes ago?"

"I fell asleep. I'm in Ronkonkoma."

He sighs. "Which side?"

"Airport."

Again, another sigh, this one is long drawn out and clearly annoyed. My hangover is in full force; my temples throb. He says nothing, then hangs up.

I shiver, which increases the tension in my head. Sharp zinging pain starts at the front, zipping backwards, squeezing my skull like it's in a vice. I lean back and close my eyes, gripping my purse tight in my arms. This isn't like me, getting myself into a horrible situation. Even living in the city and partying with my work crew, it was never this bad. Guilt is a powerful thing. I convince myself it's okay to close my eyes, even though it's not safe.

I'm jostled and lifted into the air. Instincts tell me to fight back, but warm familiar arms tell me otherwise. Luke. My hands automatically wrap around his neck.

"Where's Ezra?"

"He and Jake took care of getting your car back to the house. They used your spare key."

"Why didn't they just come and get me?"

"Because you're coming home with me." His tone is dreadfully dull, like he was roped into it.

"You don't have to take care of me, I can handle myself."

"Clearly you can't."

I roll my ankle out of frustration. It's stiff, and when I move it, the pain shoots up, making my head throb again. A moan escapes my lips, and he holds on tighter. I swallow hard to push down the impending sob rising little by little.

"Are you okay?" I ask, my drunk brain somehow remembering how upset he was on the phone.

"I don't care to talk about it." He's on edge; his tone is sharp. Having him mad at me is disheartening. Maybe being forced back into my parents' house made my maturity level drop. This is why I've stepped away from relationships. I was never good at the fighting or the disappointing moments, and maybe it's what makes me immature.

He lowers me to the ground and opens the door for me. Once inside he cranks the heat and pulls out of the lot. There are no words exchanged as we head for the expressway, there's only the quiet hum of the engine. I keep my eyes closed, even in the dark the anger is radiating off him, and if I look it will be more real.

Back at his apartment he gives me some of his clothes to sleep in. I change in the bathroom, while he gets me some Tylenol and some ice for my ankle, which feels okay, but Luke insists so it doesn't swell.

Crawling into his bed beside me in the dark, I'm aware of the harsh way the bed dips beside me, and his heavy annoyed sighs. I can't sleep on my back, so I lie awake. He's not sleeping either, his breaths are too uneven.

There's pressure building in my chest. It's so tight I honest to God feel pain. It's stupid to cry, but the building sob releases causing tears to roll with it. I wipe it away, but Luke beats me to it. The softness of his skin rubs against mine. His hand falls to where mine now lays between us, and he holds on with a strong grip.

Soft moist lips caress my cheek in a tender touch, then linger over my ear.

"I love you, Millicent."

Twisting my head, I can make out his outline in the hovering darkness. I lean forward and press my lips to his, causing more tears to fall.

"I love you," I manage to say in a high-pitched squeak.

He sighs and kisses my trembling lips. "It's okay," he says, holding my chin with his pointer and thumb. Again, he caresses my face with his fingers. "It's been a long day for both of us. Get some rest. I'm right here, and I'm not going anywhere. We have time to talk about what is plaguing us both. It doesn't have to be tomorrow or the next day."

"Okay," I say into his chest while I breathe in his soapy scent.

He presses a long, lingering kiss to my head and holds me tighter than he ever has before. The tension in my body finally deflates, allowing my shoulders to fall, and the heaviness in my eyes take over. Out of all the arms I've been in, I've never felt more love than when I'm in his.

CHAPTER 35

*I*t's been a very strange week. Luke is still not himself, but it hasn't stopped us from spending time together and enjoying each other in bed. Work has kept us insanely busy, giving me hardly any time to think about the job, but I think in a way it's a blessing in disguise.

His dad has been helping a lot. He's giving Luke pointers on how to combat the holidays. He's worked for his dad for a few years so he knows it can be crazy, and next year will be the first year Luke is at it on his own.

Dread shatters me. Leaving Luke alone without someone to help him is going to be hard. If I take this job, he'll have to search for someone else. He'll have to train them and get them used to all the equipment and routines.

In between edits Luke and Tony have taught me how to adjust the F-stop or F-number, which controls the size of the lens aperture. They even let me take a few pictures of them to practice. I feel like there's so much more to learn, and Luke even promised to show me how to take product shots for my blog and I'm really excited to learn.

Thanksgiving is in two days. Mom is going nuts trying to

make sure she has every single item she needs. Plus, we have a few more mouths to feed this year, so she's really pulling out all the fancy recipes for this one.

I rub the sleep from my eyes. It's just after seven. Luke should be here soon to pick me up.

There's a soft knock at my door.

"Come in," I say, groggily.

Ezra peeks his head in.

"Hey, what are you doing here?" I ask.

"I dropped off some extra stuffing for Mom. The store near me had it, so I grabbed it for her. I also came up to check on you."

"Hold on, Mom actually trusted you to get something?"

Ezra chuckles as he crosses the room. "Well, she literally walked me through the whole thing over the phone, down to what aisle it was in, how far down the aisle it was on, and what shelf, and what space it was in. I swear she has a map of every store on Long Island. So, yeah. I guess that's the only way she trusted me."

Even with all the stressful thoughts in my head I find it in me to laugh. I can picture Mom giving him directions as if she's sending him on some magical treasure hunt.

"Luke called out of D&D tonight. He claimed it was for work. I know he's busy this time of year, but something felt off, so I came to check up on you. Did you guys break up?" he asks.

"No, but he's been off lately." Admitting it to Ezra is easy. I sit up and straighten myself as he takes up the spot beside me.

"Want to talk about it?"

"I don't even know where to begin. We photographed Astra's wedding."

"You what?" His lips part, and eyes focus in on me, curiosity dancing in them.

"Yeah, surprise."

Ezra scoots as close as he can to me.

"I'm okay now." I'm being honest with him. I spent all this

time missing someone who clearly did not accept me for who I was. After Luke and I spoke, I felt better about myself and who I am sexually. While there will always be this place in my heart for Astra, I don't love her the way I thought I did. Maybe I've just moved on and it took seeing her to do that, but I know in my heart Luke is it.

"And as for Luke, he's been acting funny since last Thursday. Do you know anything about his ex?"

"Ex?" Ezra looks baffled.

"Oh. I guess you guys don't talk about things like that, do you?"

"Not really. We engage in other conversation, but not about past relationships."

"I feel like it's something to do with her. She came in a few times and talked shit to him, and then on the phone. Tony doesn't like her either. But uh, maybe he found out about me…"

"What about you?"

I hold my breath for a moment before letting out an exhale. "I wasn't in the city last week just visiting Cheryl. I had a job interview at a magazine. I kind of want it. Luke said we would make it work if I ever got a job in the city again, but I'm just… afraid to come clean."

"When do you have to make your decision?"

"They should be calling this week." I wince.

"Millicent! Talk to him! He deserves to know. I'm your brother and I love you, but don't leave him hanging."

"You think I don't know that?" I run a frustrated hand through my hair, tugging hard on the ends. "Am I the bad guy here? It almost feels like it, but then he's also very protective of whatever is happening inside of his head. If we are going to make this work, he has to talk to me too. It works both ways."

"You're not the bad guy. Neither is he. Do you love him?"

"So freaking much. He's the first guy who has shown me any kind of real love. Being with him is like… being home. He's home for me, Ez. I just wish he'd talk to me more, tell me what's up, but he shuts down and I can't penetrate that wall."

"I know he loves you, but you both have to do a better job communicating. That's what works with Jake and me. We are honest with each other. He's never kept a secret from me. Secrets can destroy love; don't let it destroy you."

I allow a few tears to escape. "It's like, I envision us here, on Long Island together. Maybe not in his small apartment, but it feels right, ya know? Thinking about moving back to the city and going back to that life is far from what I want. I love working at the studio."

"So, then tell them no. Stay here with us. Mom and Dad would love having you here. When you moved to the city, they were beside themselves."

I cover my eyes and lean forward, allowing the tears to fall and the short sobs to reach the surface. Ezra wraps me in his arms; the warmth of his body is comforting. I love my brother and my family, and more than anything I want to be here with them too. It's not just Luke holding me here; it's them, this place is pure happiness.

"Maybe you're right. I still want to think about it. I'll just talk to Luke about it later; what can go wrong, right?"

"It's an excellent plan. I'm sure it will be fine. I have to head out, okay? If you need me, don't hesitate to reach out. I'm always here."

"I know." I wipe the remaining tears and give Ezra one last hug.

When he closes the door, the tears dry up. I don't know what I'd do without Ezra in my life. He's the best brother and always helps me see things in a better light.

I'm going to tell Luke everything after work today. Then I'll call Maggie and tell her being with my family is more important than some job. I want to start a life here. I don't have to live in Manhattan to be a writer. I can do that here with everyone I love.

CHAPTER 36

$\mathcal{T}$he back room door slams against the wall. I jump.

"You did it again!"

The tone in his voice is icy cold like a mid-winter's day. I spin in the chair and face him. He grinds his teeth and stomps over. I move aside as he pulls up the schedule on the computer. His shoulders fall.

"The client you put through to me called to confirm everything for November twenty-eighth for their engagement shoot. I checked the calendar and you squeezed in a school picture shoot the same day, within an hour of each other."

Shit. I made the mistake the day after my interview. I remember setting it all up. I sink back into my chair. My brain was so distraught over everything.

"Luke, I didn't—"

He holds up his hand. "I'll take care of it," he growls.

I know it's not my first mistake. He hasn't been this mad since I first started. There's something different about it, almost like everything is about to end. If he was a cartoon character, there would be flames surrounding him. This morning when he picked me up the anger building over the past week felt astronomically larger, but I brushed it off, because I figured it was all in my head. Something is bothering him, and I wish he'd talk to me rather than keep it all pent up inside.

He tried to talk to me the other day, but clients came in, and then we had multiple shoots, so any serious conversations had been pushed aside. Including what I'm hiding from him.

"I'm sorry."

He glares at me, then retreats to the back room. The door bangs shut, and I jump again from the echo in the open space. My breath catches in my throat, a knot forms, making it hard to swallow or breathe. I slide my chair back in and stare off at the screen where I'd made the error. I have been so cautious since the first time it happened. Maybe being in a relationship and working together is not a good idea.

My head is aching with more intense pressure. I felt the sting of an oncoming migraine this morning but pushed it off as just a headache. The auras are bad, and I almost want to tell him to take me home so I can rest.

A tear falls as the front door opens.

"Alright, home-wrecker, where is he?" Her high-pitched nasal voice reminds me of Janice from *Friends*. Her mouth moves furiously as she chews on some gum.

"What do you want, Gretchen?" I hear his voice before I see him. I didn't even know he had come up front. He stalks forward, clenching his fists at his side.

"We need to talk." She touches his chest and pushes him back into the room. I hate the twist of jealousy in my stomach as he glances down at her long fingers. Realization smacks me in the face. What if she is what's been plaguing him all week. Are they back together? No. Luke would never— The door shuts behind them.

I fight the urge to check up on him. There's no way I can concentrate on anything but what's happening back there. Voices carry out through the place, but they are muffled from behind the wall.

My feet are heavy on the solid concrete floor as I carefully navigate my way through.

Waiting outside the door I attempt to ignore the consistent throb at my temples. Everything goes quiet, and my gut tells me to check in. My hand extends towards the handle, but I hesitate as if it might bite me. I shouldn't interfere, but at the same time our relationship is on the rocks, and if there's something going on, I want to know. I need to know because it will solidify my decision to stay.

"I said, no. As of last week, we are officially divorced. There's nothing else I want from you but for you to go away."

I grip my chest hard. I shouldn't be listening to this. *Walk away now, Millicent.* This is not— It's not my battle but it suddenly feels as if it is. He's quiet for a few lingering moments. His errands were not just going to the grocery store or bank. All this time he was still— Holy shit! Up until a week ago he was *married?* Luke? How did I not...

"He's not mine, so no. I took the fucking paternity test you asked me to. We both know who the father is." He's banging on what I believe is the desk with tiny staccato beats. "I understand it's hard to be a single mom and I'm sorry he's not stepping up, but we're over. You really need to stop coming here. I'm not afraid to put a restraining order on you."

Single mom? There's a kid involved. What did I just get myself into? I lean against the wall. I'm seeing stars.

"Luke, I love you—"

"No, I told you, I'm not interested in trying again." A pause.

"Why?" It's the softest I've ever heard her voice.

"Why? Because I don't want my fucking heart broken again. Is that what you want to hear?"

Not because he's in love with someone else, but because he

doesn't want her to break his heart. I knew getting myself involved with someone would do this to me.

What pisses me off the most is I've been working with him for almost exactly two months and this entire time he never mentioned Gretchen was his wife. He said ex. Never wife. And here I've been feeling an insane amount of guilt over taking this interview and leaving him.

It feels like I've been slapped in the damn face. The hurt starts in my chest, making it tighten, then it radiates out, amplifying an oncoming migraine, and spreading into all of me. Here I thought my secret was big.

"Oh, I get it, you're sleeping with your receptionist. She's nothing. Just a rebound looking for some."

There's the icing on the cake. Rebound. Just as I'd said when I was drunk. The sad part is Luke doesn't say a word. It's quiet. Too quiet. I don't care if he fired me for this, but I can't stand here listening to this.

Without thinking I barge into the room. Luke's back is to me, but from here I catch Gretchen's flustered face and how close she is to him. He has his hand stretched out, like he's trying to keep her away. He dips his head as a blush forms on his neck and travels up to his ears. What did I just walk in on?

She catches me over his shoulder. Luke's head lifts, and he turns. His lips part. It's like I'm here but floating outside of my body looking down on the situation.

"I asked you to leave," he growls, curling his hands into fists at his side. "I'm tired of being taken advantage of." When he says it, he looks from me to her. Why would I be a part of that statement?

I'm not sure how much more of his insecurities I can take. I was willing to look past it because he had been hurt. This is why I've avoided relationships for so long. They can be complicated, even when they don't mean to be. I see the love in his eyes, but

Ezra is right. Without the proper communication even the strongest love can die.

Gretchen rolls her eyes, flicks her hair, and walks out. "Fine. If that's how you want this to go."

"I've been trying to tell you for months. We. Are. Over. For. Good. Stay away." He's trying so hard not to let his voice tremble, but I hear it loud and clear.

"Good luck with him." She shoves her thumb over her shoulder and walks out.

He glares at the doorway after her. His shoulders rise and fall in large swift movements. His eyes glaze over, some of the anger dissipates as he realizes what I saw. From what I gather he didn't want to kiss her. She forced herself on him, so it's not entirely his fault, but there are other things at stake that need to be brought to light. Looks like I'm not the only one who was lying.

He doesn't say anything to me, his focus is still on the path she took to leave.

"So, y-you were married? And you never thought to tell me? You were still married while we were dating."

He crosses his arms at his chest. His eyes shimmer against the fluorescents above.

"Two fucking months, Luke." I'm unsteady on my feet. His hand twitches for me, but he pulls back. Everything is spinning and the aura is getting worse. Bright colors hum around me.

"I have been working here for two months and at any time you could have told me. Hell, it doesn't matter about the before you and me— What matters is you didn't after. I spilled my guts to you about Astra. Told you everything I was feeling. I didn't want you to feel as if…" I scratch at my chest under my green sweater, probably making red marks along my skin.

"I told you about my feelings because I didn't want there to be secrets between us. I wanted to be straight with you. My feelings for Astra were what deterred me from every relationship and it's why I haven't been with anyone in years. You were the first and I trusted you to be honest with me, like I was for you."

"Are you going to let me speak, Millicent?"

"I dunno, should I let you?"

"I tried to tell you." He steps closer, hands balled up at his side. I lean against the door to support my weight. The world tilts again and I wish it would stop. "Yeah, when?" I stumble a bit but catch myself.

He jumps forward ready to catch me. "Mill, what's wrong?"

"Just don't, okay. I'm..." I shake my head, "fine. Answer my question. When?"

"When we had dinner together for the first time. You had several texts and a phone call, and it just didn't feel like the right time. Then again after the wedding, and a few other times... today even, every day this week, in between. The 'I need to tell you something' I've been trying to get out the past week—"

"Excuses, that's all I'm fucking hearing." I rub at my face, massaging my temples to ease the terrifying lightning bolt pain surging through my aching head.

"I thought I could trust you. And who were you referring to a few minutes ago, huh? It seems your eyes said it all when you said you were being taken advantage of."

"When were you going to tell me about the job?"

"I dunno, Luke. Today, maybe. I didn't even know if I was going to take it or not or if they were going to offer. And when were you going to tell me about fucking being married? I think your secret is a little bigger."

Crossing his arms at his chest he looks me square in the eye.

I shake my head. "How did you know?"

"I overheard you this morning. When I came to pick you up, I headed upstairs, and Ezra was over. I went back down, and your mom stopped me to chat."

He what? There's no way. I run a trembling hand through my hair and tug hard at the ends, enough for it to sting. This is not how this conversation was supposed to go. I had a plan. This is not it. "Well, I was going to tell you."

"Save it, Millicent. I was just a temporary fix until you got back out into the real world."

"You have trust issues," I spat back.

His dark laughter is something I've never heard out of him before. "And now you see why. The women in my life like to lie."

I cringe. How dare he compare me to her. I want to bring up what I caught them doing, but we'll get to that later.

"You really think I didn't want to tell you?"

I'm so angry, but I have to get this off my chest.

"Maybe I was scared. I hadn't told you yet because I couldn't decide what to do. I was ninety-nine percent certain I was going to tell them no. Being here with you feels like home. I love writing, and I always dreamed of being a well-known journalist. I had it all, and when it was ripped out from under me, it broke my heart. But then I fell in love and there was nowhere else in the world I'd rather be. And I had my family back too. The city, while it was fun, was lonely. I was ready to take the dive and put the magazine writing behind me, because I love you."

My voice breaks at the last part. His expression softens from my confession. But my anger is only beginning. I've said what I had to, now it's his turn to talk to me, but I have more questions.

"What happened before I came in here?"

His lips part like he wants to speak, but nothing comes out. His eyes dart all over the room, making it obvious something did happen. Even if he didn't expect it to, I'm a little disappointed in how this all went down.

He could have come to me this morning and asked about the job instead of blowing up on me. I can't help thinking maybe Luke isn't ready for love and taking the job would be better. The thought of leaving this behind makes it hard to breathe.

I scoff. "That's what I thought."

After a few beats, I speak. "Maybe we need a break. It will give me some time to think over what I want. And will give you time to process what happened here today."

"So, you're breaking up with me?" His lips tremble, and it takes everything in me not to step forward and hold on to him. Before I can do that, he needs to work on his trust issues.

"I didn't say forever. I said I needed a break. If you can't tell me what happened in this room, then maybe you have some issues with lying too."

"She kissed me."

"Okay. Well, you could have just said that. If I never would have come in here, would you have told me? Even if it wasn't your fault, even if she was the one to initiate and you pushed her away. Would you have told me?"

His eyes narrow down to the floor again, and I have my answer.

"I gave you plenty of time to be open with me. I understand it's hard to talk about and she fucked you over, but this is a big secret to keep."

I've got more to say, but the knot in my throat is preventing me from speaking. Coughing clears it a little, so I decide to continue. "I say we need a break, because if neither of us can tell the other these important things, then maybe we both have a little growing up to do. Relationships are about trust and telling each other things that scare us, but we both failed."

"Fine. If you want a break, then we'll take one."

His distant eyes give no indication if he'll forgive me for this break.

"I'll still come into work. I won't screw you—"

"Don't bother. We did fine before you, and I'll be fine without you," he says, eyes cold and unwavering. He crosses his arms at his chest and presses his lips together. His harsh tone and demeanor take my breath away.

I gasp in response. A twinge of pain stabs me in the chest, it's not a physical pain, but it sure as hell feels like one. "Goodbye, Luke."

"How are you getting home? I drove you here, remember," he asks, his tone lighter, sadder.

"I'll..." I realize it's still mid-day and everyone is at work. "I don't want you to have to worry about me anymore. I'll be fine. I've been on my own before and I can sure as hell do it again."

I try to swallow but a vomit sensation hits my throat. It burns at the base, and I press my hand to the spot to try and control it. I feel my eyes roll back from the intense pressure in my head. *Don't puke now, please.* I hiccup. Oh no.

"Mill, you're not okay. Please, are you—"

Blinking away some unshed tears, bile shoots up into my mouth. I cover it and run past him. He's calling my name, but I can't stop, I need the bathroom. I make it just in time to slide into the toilet and empty the contents of my stomach into it.

Crying and puking at the same time is not fun. Emotionless puking is so much easier. This burns and stings and it's not just my throat. It's my damn heart. Home is slipping away. I can feel it. Maybe I wasn't meant to be here in the first place. I counted down the days until I left Long Island and made it into the city. Life was a bit easier there. No emotional connections to drown me. Just Cheryl and I taking on the city and our jobs. The only damage was working on articles until four in the morning and then waking up an hour later for work.

Losing Astra hurt, but the thought of losing Luke after making things right... it hits a little differently. I never wanted to find love again. Didn't care if I ever did. I was married to my career. Maybe it was better that way.

I jump at Luke's warm hands on my back. Hot, plump tears stream down my face. He pulls my hair back while I hack up another helping of my lunch. It takes a few extra minutes of heaving before I slump back into him. His hands are on my forehead as he runs his soft fingers through the strands of fallen hair. The back of my head lays against his hard chest. Warmth envelopes me but I can't let it drag me under.

"I'm taking you home. Don't argue with me."

My headache is worse. I have no fight left. He somehow gets me to my feet. With an arm tossed over my shoulder he leads me into the studio.

"M-my stuff," I say, groggily reaching for it, then wincing when pain shoots through my head.

"I'll come back and get it."

With no energy left, I allow him to help me into his car and wait while he goes inside to grab my things. I don't know what he's doing, but even with my eyes closed it feels like forever before the car shakes with his presence.

The ride to my house is silent. When we pull into the driveway Mom is impatiently awaiting our arrival.

"You called my mom?" I ask.

"Yeah. When I went inside to lock up. I told her you weren't feeling well. She said you get migraines, and you left your meds at home."

I grab my bag but linger for a moment.

"You should still come to Thanksgiving because my mom is expecting you. I promise to stay out of your way, but don't disappoint her, please."

He doesn't look at me. "I'll be there. I try not to break my promises." His voice cracks.

It's hard to pull away. What's even worse is the tear that falls down the side of his face. He doesn't even try to wipe it away.

I don't say goodbye, neither does he. Maybe it's because goodbye feels too final. There's a sliver of hope in my heart this could work, if we both grew up a little, but I won't hold on to too much hope.

My phone buzzes as I step out. The number is from the city. My heart lurches in my chest and without thinking I answer.

"Hello?"

"Hi, is this Millicent Gibson? This is Maggie's assistant, Carolyn. I'm calling because she is offering you the job if you want it."

A sliver of hope radiates through me, but the dread of what I just lost devastates me. I turn back, but Luke has already sped off. I knew he had, I heard him leave but ignored it.

I swallow hard. "Tell her I'll take the job."

"She is going to be thrilled. Thank you, Millicent. I hope you have a wonderful holiday. I'll reach out on Monday with the details. You'll probably start around the first?"

"Great. I-I'm looking forward to it," I say, biting the side of my cheek to keep from crying. I've done way too much of that this past week. I'm done.

When I get to the door, I collapse in Mom's arms. My head is worse than before. The aura around my vision is so bad I think I might puke again. She gets me to my room and into bed with some medicine. After I swallow the pills and in between tears I drift off to sleep.

What a mess this has turned into.

CHAPTER 37

I don't want to ruin Thanksgiving, so I don't allow anyone to see my dismay over my break with Luke. I didn't tell Mom what happened. She thinks I only had a migraine, but she's suspicious. I know her looks all too well, but if she does sense something, she doesn't say anything. She's probably too busy worrying about making everything perfect. And I want it to be for her. She lives for holidays and having people over.

I've been keeping myself busy. This morning I got up at the crack of dawn and started the turkey a half an hour before Mom woke. By the time she did, it was almost ready to go in. I even shoved her out of the kitchen at one point and told her to go take a nice long shower and enjoy herself before the craziness of the holiday.

When she returned, I was already making her homemade cranberry sauce, and boxed stuffing. Now, we are both finishing up on the little things like setting the table. Dad comes wandering in, his sights set on the gravy that permeates the small kitchen.

Mom smacks him away, and when she does, she gives him this loving look. They stop for a moment to stare into each other's eyes. He bends down and takes her into his arms. They must forget I'm here. My shoulders are weighed down by this tremendous cloud of gray sitting over me.

"I'm going to set the table," I say, my voice an octave higher than usual. I flee from the room before they can speak, so Mom can't see the tears.

In the living room Dad set up the large table we pull out for occasions such as this. Against the wall is a large hutch filled with Mom's most expensive holiday dinnerware. The doorbell rings. As I open the cabinet, I hear Mom's voice beaming through the house. "Hi, Jenn, Tony. I'm so glad you could make it," she says.

Tony and Jenn's voices echo through the house. Their laughter and happiness. It should be a nice sound. It guts me to think of how perfect this day would have been.

I pull the dish in my hand back so fast and hard it shatters in my hands and the pieces fall to the floor around my feet.

Mom comes rushing in. Her feet heavy on the wooden floors. "What was that..."

Dad stops behind her, eyes wide at the scene. I'm not sure how crazy I look, but they immediately focus on my eyes. Next my lips tremble and holding it together seems nearly impossible.

"I'm so sorry," I say.

They were my grandmother's plates. Mom inherited them after she passed, they are older than me.

"Oh, sweetie, those are old plates. Don't cry, it's okay."

I wipe my eyes. Mom doesn't even realize the real reason behind my mini meltdown, but I don't correct her. I need her to believe at least until Luke leaves, that everything is okay.

The doorbell rings again. "I'll get it," Dad says, but his eyes remain glued to me.

I turn and clean up the pieces. More muffled voices enter the house, it sounds like more than two.

"We pulled up at the same time," Ezra says.

"I brought this wine for dessert." *Luke! Fuck!* A sharp shard knicks my finger leaving a small trail of blood.

I try to hide it as Mom brings over a garbage bag. "I'll get this, you should go greet our guests. Go say hi to Luke," she says, bending.

"N-no it's okay. You go, I'm going to finish cleaning."

She gives me a once-over, before deciding to listen to me. A few moments later voices mix into one chaotic mess of noise, but Luke's is more pronounced than the rest. And my heart breaks all over again.

"You're bleeding."

I suck in a breath as Luke stands behind me.

"I'm fine, it's nothing." I suck at the bloodied finger, pull it away, and hold it up. "See, it's good as new," I say, as a trickle of blood cascades down my thumb.

"I'll take over," Ezra says, shooing me away. "Go get something on that cut."

On wobbling legs, I stand. Luke holds out his hands ready to steady me. With his arms around me he leads me out of the room. Once out of ear shot of everyone I snap. "You can stop the act; we're alone."

When I get a good look at him, I see my own reflection in his face. The sad swollen eyes, the purple bags. He looks as if he lost his world. I can't give in, though, and we can't talk about it. Not today, not here.

"I can take care of myself," I say, for what feels like the millionth time in two days.

Luke doesn't listen and follows me to the bathroom. He holds his hand up catching the door to stop me from shutting him out, then steps in, and grabs for the first aid stuff inside the cabinet. I turn on the sink below it and rinse my finger, he bumps into me with his body, and we gasp in sync. We pause for only a heartbeat before we move again.

In silence we find ourselves falling in line with each other's movements. I sit on the closed toilet, and he kneels in front of me. My attention is on him as he investigates the cut. He doesn't say anything as he works to dab it with medication, then wraps a bandage around the finger.

"Nothing too deep. You're good."

The knot in my throat prevents me from getting any words out. I stand, grabbing the items and placing them back inside the medicine cabinet above the sink. I leave the bathroom before he does, and when I get back into the living room, the plate is cleaned up and Ezra has set everything out.

"Thanks," I say, finally finding my voice.

"No problem." Ezra steps in my view, blocking the way. Brows knit as he waits for me to say something.

"What?" I ask, my voice as quiet as a mouse.

Ezra shakes his head, his attention flicking to someone over his shoulder, then lands back on me. I can't find it in me to look at him.

"I'm going to help Mom."

It's obvious the person behind me is Luke. It's like my body is hyper-aware of him, even if I'm looking in the complete opposite direction.

I feel somewhat relieved as I reach the kitchen and can keep myself busy with preparations. Jenn helps us too, I'm glad she and Mom are talking about something unrelated to relationships and are instead fangirling like teens over one of the men from the *Supernatural* show.

Once everything is ready, we all head to the table. I should have prepared myself more, sitting beside Luke at the dinner table and not being able to reach out and touch him is awful. I can't give in because what I said was true. We both have a lot of growing up to do, and I don't want to be in a relationship if we can't tell each other the truth.

Ezra and Jake are across from us, Jenn too, and Tony sits on the other side of Luke. Mom and Dad sit at opposite ends of the large oval table. Everyone is passing around food and getting lost in conversation.

"Potatoes?" Luke asks, holding the large bowl out to me.

"Yeah." I go and reach for it, but he takes it upon himself to plop the potatoes down on my plate.

He does this with all the food being passed around.

"I'm so glad we were all able to spend Thanksgiving together. The start of, hopefully, a beautiful tradition," Mom says, gushing.

Luke's shoulders stiffen beside me, and I'm sure I mimic his exact position. We both stay quiet eating what's on our plate.

"So, boys, how's work going?" Mom looks over at Ezra and Jake.

"I'm just glad to have this break," Jake says, wiping his forehead. "Middle schoolers are a tough crowd."

Mom chuckles, then turns to Jenn. "Jake is in his second year teaching social studies at the middle school."

I get lost in the muffled conversation. Adding some things here and there. Luke does the same. We're here but not.

"And Luke."

I perk up at his name.

"How's the studio? I'm sure you will be busy next month squeezing in holiday photos."

I take a deep breath, and swirl around the gravy, mixing it with the potatoes to make a swirl of brown and white. I spot him out of the corner of my eye, swirling around his own potatoes.

"Yeah. There's lots of good ones coming up. I have Santa coming to the studio the first and second weekend of December. I had a limited number of spots and they filled up fast."

"Oh, isn't that lovely. I can't wait until there's children running around here waiting for Santa."

Luke nearly chokes on the scoop of cranberry he shoveled into his mouth, and my fork slips from my grip with a loud ring as it hits the plate. I catch Ezra watching me. He tilts his head, worry lines creasing his forehead. I bite my lip, shaking my head

247

at him, and it's like we have some sort of sibling telepathy, because his eyes soften as if he knows.

"So, Jake and I are thinking of getting a dog," Ezra says, attempting to change the subject.

"Oh, what kind?" Jenn asks.

The conversation turns into one about pets, and the moment Mom's attention is elsewhere Ezra checks back in with me. I'm not okay. The hairs on my arm stand on end and I find Luke watching too.

Dinner goes on and every time Mom attempts to bring up something relationship-wise, Ezra deflects it for us. I'm forever grateful. I'm not sure how much more of it I could take.

After dinner Jenn and I help Mom clean up and do the dishes while Dad recruits the guys to watch football. I try to busy myself and let Mom and Jenn talk. Anytime Mom gets close to asking about Luke I deflect by talking about all the delicious food we have eaten.

When everything is done, we bring in the pies and other desserts that Mom and I either baked or bought. Everyone comes back to sit at the table. I keep checking the time, wishing this torture would end. Everything is too raw.

"Millicent, how do you like working at the studio?" Tony asks.

"You've really been a huge help," Jenn says.

I look over at Tony, and he nods in agreement. Everyone's eyes are on me, including Luke. I muster the best smile I can.

"I love working there. Tony and Luke have both welcomed me with open arms. I'm learning so much. In fact, the other day Tony showed me the trick to product photography, and we took some shots of this mini-Christmas tree and I learned how to set up softbox lights."

Tony finishes chewing. "Your pictures came out phenomenal. I may have you use a few shots for the social media pages. I'm still learning my way around Instagram, but Millicent is a pro." He turns to Mom and Dad. They both gleam with pride. "She has been a blessing with those pages, she's brought so many people in through our accounts. Oh, and remind me after the holiday, you can borrow the D3500 for your blog."

I choke on nothing. I can hardly eat the cake in front of me. I've been poking it with my fork for the past few minutes. "Yeah, that sounds—" I peek over at Luke. He's quietly eating. I close my eyes briefly. "It sounds good, Tony. Thank you." I hate how weak my voice sounds.

"Well, I'm so happy to hear your doing so well, sweetie," Dad says.

I give Dad the best half-smile I can muster, which isn't much. No one but Ezra seems to notice.

"Millicent, what's the matter? I thought you loved that cake," Mom says.

It's hard to pretend everything is okay while I can't keep myself busy with something. When I had dishes to do, or things to bake and cook, it was easy to hide my emotions behind it, but now sitting here without anything but pie, it's much more difficult.

"I'm tired. No big deal."

"Mom, this pie is delicious," Ezra says.

"Yes, Mrs. G. Perfection," Jacob echoes.

Mom blushes. "Aw. You guys. Have you had the crumb cake? That was all Millicent."

Beside me Luke takes a bite of the piece on his plate. "It's the best crumb cake I've ever had," he comments.

I inhale sharply at the smile he gives me. It doesn't reach his eyes. Doesn't even light up his face. There's not a single emotion behind it. I grab at the fabric of my shirt and keep my eyes on my uneaten food, missing how he used to smile for me.

The conversation continues, mostly about cooking and baking, and everyone's favorite Thanksgiving meal. I'm grateful the night is almost over. The darkness peeks in through the partially opened cream drapes. I help by gathering the empty plates on the table.

"Well, it's been a lovely evening, I truly hope this becomes a family tradition. Luke, Jenn, Tony, you are all welcome to our home next year as well. Christmas too, I don't know what you do on Christmas Eve, but I make a ton of pasta, and I love having extra mouths to feed."

"Oh, that would be wonderful. What do you say, Tony, Luke? We don't do anything on Christmas. I'm sure Luke and Millicent will be spending the holidays together anyway," Jenn says. She flashes Luke and I a smile.

I'm standing between Dad's chair and Jake's. My eyes land on Luke across the table. He nods his head to appease his mom.

"You are all like family, and maybe one day we will be…"

I drop the dishes onto the table, this time none of them break or crack, but the noise is loud enough to stop Mom from talking. Luke is staring at me wide-eyed. His lips part like he wants to say something. He's holding back again. Why can't the man just speak to me and tell me how he's fucking feeling.

Everyone's eyes land on me, and the building sob is so intense I might lose it right here in front of everyone.

"Millicent, what is with you today? Are you still not well?" Mom asks.

I back away from the table, my words get caught in my throat. "I'm going to wash these," I say, picking up the dropped dish and adding one or two more to the pile. I swiftly exit the room.

When I get into the kitchen, I place the dishes in the sink and grasp the edge of the counter. A soft tap on my shoulder jars me. My chest trembles as I check and see Ezra.

"Not now, Ez. Please." My words are barely above a whisper.

He nods in understanding. "I'm here, Mill. Okay? When you're ready."

"K."

"Millicent, everyone is leaving, come say goodbye to your boyfriend and his family," Mom shouts.

I wince and stop drying my hands on the towel. Ezra sighs beside me but doesn't say anything. Taking deep, uneven breaths I turn, and as I'm about to take a step Luke appears in the doorway.

"Goodnight, Millicent."

"Night, Luke."

Without another word he spins on his heels and heads back in the direction he came. There's no way I'm going to be able to stand there saying goodbye to his parents when my chest is about to explode with a sob. I sneak past everyone and race up the stairs to my room.

Once I'm alone, I unleash everything I've been holding in. There's a knock, but it sounds distant. Moments later familiar arms wrap around me. It's Ezra. He doesn't ask what happened, just holds me and allows me to get whatever is left inside out in the open. I know I'll have to explain what happened tonight to my family later, but for now, I'm too tired to think. I close my eyes and listen to the sound of Ezra's heart. It's comforting, and with how tired, exhausted, and heartbroken I am the sound has me slowly drifting into darkness.

CHAPTER 38

$\mathcal{A}$fter a long holiday weekend of tears and explaining everything to Mom, I step up to the door of Parker Photography ready to call it quits. Luke told me I didn't need to come back, but I knew Tony would be in today and I wanted to thank him for everything he'd done.

I start work on Thursday and I'm already planning a possible move. Cheryl's roommate moved out and there's an extra room. For now, I'm going to commute to make sure the transition is smooth. I'm terrified, and I can't decide if this is really what I want. I'm second guessing everything.

Ezra and I had a long talk. After I discussed it with Mom, I drove to Ezra and Jake's. I laid it all out for them. I told them not to be mad at Luke, I couldn't bear to see their friendship die because of me. Ezra says he's going to talk to Luke, he feels like he has to or something. I want them to work things out.

I take a few uneven breaths as I embrace the small town around me. It's quiet and it's to be expected after a long holiday weekend. Everyone is either hung over or exhausted. Most are back to work now. The town has decorated the black lamp posts with green garland and white lights. It looks phenomenal at night. A large sign hangs over the roadway from one side to the other promoting the Christmas tree lighting next weekend. I want to be excited for the holidays, but I don't have it in me.

The door jingles and Luke's eyes meet mine. He's sitting behind the desk where I usually am. He looks worse than he did the other day. His hair is all disheveled, his shirt is wrinkled, and he's wearing his glasses. Like the ones he did in high school. The ones with the black frames. I'm transported back in time, wishing more than anything I could go back again.

"I thought I said you didn't have to come."

"I know. I-I'm here to see your dad." I swallow. "I need to thank him for allowing me this opportunity."

He stands but pauses for a second to hold on to the desk. His lips are pulled straight. I inhale and my chest wobbles with the threat of sobs, but I won't let it control me. Part of me wishes we could sit down and discuss this like adults, but I don't think either of us are ready to hear what the other has to say. That's okay, I guess. I'll give it time.

"I'll— I'll go get him."

He turns his back to me. When he moves his body holds no definition. He's just making the motions like he has to exist in this new reality.

"Lu-Luke." I sound so weak.

He stops and hangs his head. I bite my lip to keep from crying. When he turns I see the tears in his eyes too. He doesn't speak, just stands there watching, waiting for me to say something.

"I-I should thank you too." My voice breaks and the dam in my eyes does too. "You took a chance on me, and I am so grateful. You gave me a job, a home, a place for m-my-my h-heart." I look down and away from him.

"Th-thank you." A small sob is released.

He's still standing there watching me. His heart breaking as well as mine. Silent tears roll down his cheeks. He wipes them away, then turns to get his dad. I close my eyes allowing myself to feel everything some more. I grip my stomach as a sob escapes.

The back door opens, and I try to pull myself together. Tony comes out, but there's no sign of Luke.

"Hey, Millicent. Luke said you need to— Are you alright?" He rushes to me, placing a hand on my shoulder.

I bat him away and sniffle. "I w-wanted to thank you. For giving me a chance here. I got a job back in the city and I feel terrible leaving you guys hanging... But..."

"That's great news, Millicent. I'm sure we'll be okay here."

I try to tell myself everything will work out, but I'm having a hard time. I wipe at the annoying build of another sob in my chest.

"I'm sorry, Tony. I— This is... I know you'll be okay. Make sure Luke is. Please."

He scrunches his brows. Understanding finally dawns on his face. I guess Luke doesn't talk to his parents about things either, because he looks confused by what's happening.

"Thank you," I say one last time before I retreat from the studio.

The cold fresh air hits my face. I know I'm doing the right thing. I want this. I love the city and the life I had while living in it. This is the right choice. I know it.

Without another glance at the studio, I get in my car and drive away and just hope I'm doing the right thing.

I'M restless and can't focus. My blog is long forgotten and I pace my room with what feels like purpose, but it's not. I'm a shell of myself as I try and prepare for my first day of work. Mom's concerning glance at dinner was enough to make me spiral. I hate that I'm angry with Luke but miss him at the same time. It feels weird not seeing him every day and Tony too.

It's not late, only a few minutes after eight. I go downstairs with the intention of finding something to snack on. My stomach is gurgling at the lack of food I had tonight, but I'm nauseous. I'm also hoping work will be able to throw me into a daily routine to make me forget. Move on.

There are hushed voices coming from the kitchen. One is Mom. The other... It's Jenn. Her head is hung low, and Mom's hand is on her back. She looks as disheveled as I feel. Her hair is tossed up into a messy bun, the side of her cheeks hold a hint of black, most likely from her makeup.

They lift their gazes as if they can sense me.

"Hi, sweetheart," Mom says.

"Mom. Jenn. Everything... is everything okay?"

Mom's smile is meek, and it worries me. She pats the table. "Come sit."

"Hi, Millicent," Jenn says, cautiously, like she's treading lightly over my broken heart.

I sit beside her and wait for one of them to explain why she's in my kitchen crying. The itch to reach out and comfort Luke's Mom is strong.

"I'm sorry, I know I'm the last person you want to see..." I open my mouth to speak but she holds up her hand. A tear slides down her already wet-stained cheeks. Resting my hand over the one she pressed against the table I give her an encouraging smile.

"When Tony called me to tell me he suspected you and Luke had a falling out, I had to reach out to your mom because I feel guilty for holding on to this secret. While the gossip mill in this town is strong, you all have somehow not been in the loop and I should have come sooner, but it wasn't my story to tell."

Mom puts a hand on Jenn's shoulder and squeezes it. Mom's eyes hold nothing but forgiveness for her friend's troubles.

"I didn't know Gretchen had come back into Luke's life. There were some gossip queens who had targeted Luke. *How dare he leave a pregnant wife.* They didn't know the whole story.

Everything happened in California but upon his return it wasn't easy. Months passed and it seemed as if they'd forgotten. Things had settled when I ran into your mom, and it felt nice to have someone to talk to again and not have that lingering over my shoulder."

She inhales then exhales. "I should have been up front with your mom, but I wasn't. I needed a friend and should have shared my worry over the situation. I thought it was taken care of. I also thought Luke had told you. So, for that I am so sorry. He's a good man, Millicent. He didn't deserve what she put him through."

"No. He didn't. I met her and she's brutal."

"I know you don't want to hear this right now, but when you came back into his life, I saw a spark in him again. He truly loves you and I do hope maybe one day you can work things out with him. But what I do hope is that you will forgive me too—" She chokes on a sob. "I'm grateful your mom has. It was so hard to talk about. I kept feeling judged and I knew she wouldn't, but it was still so hard."

I don't hesitate to take Jenn in my arms where she cries softly, wetting my T-shirt. This woman loves her son with everything she has. I know she had no ill intent and Mom seems to have forgiven her too, as I peek over Jenn's head and see a soft smile on Mom's lips.

I still love Luke with all my heart, but I'm not ready to forgive him yet. I need the time to process what has happened. To figure out if the lie was too big of one to trust him again. It really wasn't Jenn's story to tell. She is not at fault. I let her know that and she, Mom, and I spend another half an hour talking.

When Jenn leaves, Mom stops me before I go upstairs. She gives me a look I've seen so many times in the past. Her eyes asking over words.

"I'll be okay, Mom," I say, giving her a kiss before retreating to my room and preparing for what tomorrow will bring.

CHAPTER 39

*F*or the longest time I thought writing was what made me happy, and it did—I mean, it does—but writing for someone else isn't fun anymore.

It's been almost three weeks since I took the job. I expected to be able to write some of my own ideas, but instead I got stuck writing about the best shaving cream for your legs for my first article.

Since I started Maggie said I could come to her with ideas, but all she does is shoot me down, and today, she did it again, in front of the entire team. I thought maybe, *Communication as a Love Language*, or once again the *Falling for Someone Unexpected* popped into my head. I thought it was a good idea for a future issue. I'd be able to write it from my own experience and speak from the heart. She said it would never work.

After a long hot shower, I find myself rummaging in the kitchen for something to eat. My bags are packed; they have been for a few days. I've been sitting on moving in with Cheryl. The job has had me questioning so much about my life, so I haven't made the transition yet.

The screen on my phone lights up with an incoming message.

Aside from work I have been meeting with Nora at local coffee shops recently. Although things with Luke and I aren't resolved I have been using this time to delve deeper into the world of *D.&D* and learning how much I love it.

With Jake's guidance about the world he's creating for our game and Nora's teaching skills, I've learned so much. The thought of playing the game and Luke being involved scares me, but I can't allow what happened to affect Ezra and his relationship, and if it means sitting down and playing a game with Luke in the room then so be it. I don't know if he plans on joining us or not the week of Christmas, but I do know that I'm excited to play.

> Sent you some more videos. Check them out when you get a chance.

I type back quickly.

> Thanks. Will do.

My stomach rumbles, but I have no desire to eat. I rest my elbows on the counter and lower my head into my hands. I hate feeling this low. Deep breaths don't keep the tears at bay, they threaten to fall, tingling my nose, causing me to sniffle.

When I lost my job a few months ago, I imagined getting back on my feet and staying in Manhattan. I swear I went forward a step, and now I've had to take two back. There are moments when being with him is a distant memory, but then my heart defies me. It wraps me in a need so tight it strangles me, making it hard to breathe. Like now. We never got to talk things out and I hate that.

"Mill?"

I jump at the sound of Ezra's soft voice behind me. His eyes narrow as I spin, and even though he's already seen the tears, I try to avoid his gaze.

"Hey, what's wrong?"

Ezra takes a few big strides across the kitchen, and when he reaches me, he scoops me up into his arms. I bury my face into his maroon sweater, trying to steal its warmth, and trying to find some comfort in my brother.

"Don't worry about me, just having my hundredth meltdown in a month. Stupid shit."

"It's obviously not shit to you if you're crying."

"Working for this new magazine has been..." I pause, trying to collect my thoughts. "It hasn't been what I expected. It's like the moment you go from high school to college, and everyone seems like they are way out of your league. That's how it is there, like they all look at me as if working for *Forever Twenty* makes me less of a journalist."

"So quit!" He steps back but keeps me at arm's length.

I can't keep hold of his stare again. I'm embarrassed. I went from a woman with a direction and goal to this. I haven't felt any kind of joy working at this new company, as I felt when I was with *Forever Twenty*, or even writing my blogs, those gave me joy too. Mostly, I was at my happiest when I worked for Luke.

"I can't just quit. I'd be back to square one."

"You could ask Luke for your job back. He's looking for help, but don't tell him I told you. He hasn't called back a single person who he interviewed. He says they are all missing something. Clearly what that boy is missing is you."

I snort and shake my head, vision blurring as more tears prick at my eyes.

"I'm serious, Millicent. *D&D* has been rough, he's there but he's not."

"Nora might have mentioned that too. I doubt it's because of me, and he'll find someone."

Ezra sighs.

"I'm not sure I'm ready to talk to him."

"Well, that might be a problem..."

"What do you mean?" I ask, feeling my brows squeeze together.

"I mean, I'm proposing to Jake this weekend."

I jump back and my jaw goes slack. The frown I wore seconds ago transforms into a smile and it's lighting up my cheeks so much I feel the burn.

"You're what? You mean on Christmas?" I stare at him slack-jawed. "But really? And how am I just finding out about this now?" I shove him playfully in the chest.

He chuckles. "I had been thinking about it for a while, but this was kind of spontaneous. Luke is putting the whole thing together. Um, and I need you there. I have this cosplay for you—" He pauses. "What's that look for?"

My lips curl up into a teasing smile. Of course he'd make it something nerdy. I love it. "Nothing. What am I dressing up as? A Dragon-born? Gnome? Oh, what about something really cool like a Tiefling?"

Ezra chuckles. "Have you been doing your research, Millicent?"

I shrug. "Maybe."

"Is just an Elf okay?" he asks.

"Oh— I like that. Can I be a Warlock Elf?"

I don't miss the huge smile on my brother's face. I initially started combing for *D&D* information because of Luke, but when everything came crashing down, I started researching for myself. Which is where Nora comes in. She looked over my character sheet and shook her head at my poor attempt, but now it's all coming together.

"You can be, but I already got your costume." He takes out his phone to show me a picture of the costume. It's better than I expected, the olive fabric of both the shirt and the tight pants is a color that goes well with my complexion. There's also a sweet little brown corset leather vest, and pointy ears.

"I can bring it over tomorrow for you to try on."

"This isn't too bad, but what does it have to do with Luke?"

"He's setting up the whole thing, he's got props, and I know it's nearly December and freezing, but I plan on doing it at the park by the lake where we used to LARP. Jake thinks we are going to do just that."

The pain of the past month vanishes as if it never happened. For a brief moment I'm excited, because my brother is getting his happy beginning. I don't say ending, because it's truly not an end, it's like a new chapter, his story isn't over, it's just getting better. I've always considered Jake family, even before they dated.

"How can I help?"

"I need hands to help set up, and—" He bites down on his lip. "Please, Mill. I want this to be perfect. Jake is— he's my everything and I love him with every fiber of my being."

Happy tears prick my eyes. My baby brother is growing up. He's got his life together and I would do anything to be a part of his day. Even if it means having to face Luke. I miss him more than I care to talk about. Are there third chances? I don't know.

"First, let me process this. My little brother is getting married, and we are all going to run around in costumes?"

He chuckles. "Pretty much."

"Okay. I'll do it."

"Really, Mill?"

"Of course, Ezra. You're my brother and you've been there for me more times than I can count. I love you and I'd do anything to make your day special."

"The whole thing was Luke's idea. I told him I wanted to propose, and he just laid it all out there. All I did was ask to have photos taken. I know it might be hard to see him, but I really need you. Plus, there's no return on the costume."

"Really? You just thought you'd get away with me cosplaying because it's not refundable?"

"Well yeah."

I throw myself at him and wrap my arms around his neck. His

pine-scented cologne wafts in my nose. He's right, one hundred percent. It's not about me and Luke; this is about him and Jake. There's nothing I wouldn't do for my brother.

"I can put aside my silly drama for this once in a lifetime moment to watch my brother ask the man he loves to marry him."

"You don't know how happy that makes me."

"Are Mom and Dad coming?"

"They sure are. They're going to be part of your Elf family too."

I'm trying to imagine my dad in costume, and the image makes me smile. "And they are both cool with this?"

"Secretly you all wanted to role play, admit it."

It feels good to smile.

"Are you sure it's okay Luke's involved? I don't want to upset you..."

"It's fine. He's your friend. I said if something happened between us, I wouldn't ever let it ruin your friendship with him."

Neither of us say anything for a few seconds. He hurt me with his lies, but at the same time I know it's not Luke. There's something more he's not saying. I wish I could ask, could find the courage, but I'm not sure I can.

"I miss him." I glance up, my lip trembling. "So damn much." Leaning forward I dip my head and cover my face with my hands.

Ezra throws his arm over me. "It hurts worse than when Astra told me she only loved me as a friend. And much worse than when I saw her walking down the aisle to the girl she loved. I think Luke was it for me. I fought it so hard..." I blink away the tears, but it's not working.

"He misses you too. I promised him I wouldn't say anything, but he broke down last week at D&D. I said something about you, and he stood and walked away. I found him outside on my front step in the freezing cold. We had a long chat. I think you two should talk. Even if it's just to get closure. You both need it."

I remove my hands from my face and meet my brother's eyes. I know he's right. Emotions swirl with images and thoughts about Luke. I want this to all be about Ezra not me, but I also want the dust to settle before the wedding. They found each other again after all these years. Their friendship is important, and I won't destroy that or take it away from them. No matter how hurt I am.

ell, Ezra is right, the costume is perfect. I'm surprised by how excited I am to wear it in a few days. I send a picture to Nora and her reaction is a ton of heart eye emojis. I definitely needed the boost.

I come downstairs and Mom, Dad, and Ezra all turn to me. Ezra's jaw drops when he sees me.

After Ezra left yesterday, I looked up some cosplay pictures to get a better idea of makeup and appearance. The shirt comes down at an angle dangling at my knees. The corset is my favorite part. It presses my chest up just enough to make it look like I actually have one. I found black knee-high boots in my closet. My French braid flows down my back, setting off the elf ears.

Dad turns up in his costume. I never in my life expected to see him dressed like an elf with pointy ears. I grin. Him and Mom look amazing. Mom's costume is a little less revealing than mine, just a vest goes over the front.

"Wow, these are actually cool. If I would have known dressing up for role play was this fun, I would have joined you a long time ago."

Dad chuckles as the doorbell rings.

"Oh, I'll get that." Ezra disappears and Mom eyes me. "Sweetheart, you look lovely."

I stare at Mom and her wavy hair, her elf ears sticking out through her hair. "I should say the same to you."

"Of course, man, it's no prob..." Luke's voice catches me off guard. I'm facing Mom but can feel him behind me. My skin pricks with goosebumps. I close my eyes briefly, only to be brought to by my mom's delicate touch. She gives a small smile, and I take a chance and turn.

He looks— he looks like Luke. Although his eyes tell a different story. They are heavy and not at all like the bright-eyed stares he gave me while I was under— *no, Millicent. Don't go there.*

"Hey, Mill," he says. His lips twitch a bit, as he takes me in.

"Luke." I wish my chest would stop trembling.

"Mr. and Mrs. G." He pauses then looks back at me, his eyes roaming the whole length of my body. They stop on my chest, but seconds later continue their observation.

"You guys look amazing." A hint of his usual smile appears, but it disappears quickly.

"Um, I'm going to go and change. I love the costumes, Ez." Truth is, I need a moment to grasp the fact that Luke's here in my house and that what I feel for him has not changed, no matter what we went through. I brush past him and Ezra and take two steps at a time up. My door slams a bit harder than I expect it to, making my heart race.

I need to breathe for a second. I sit on the edge of the bed with my hands on my knees just taking deep inhales, counting to five, and exhaling. I'm about to suck in another breath when there's a knock on my door.

"Millicent?"

Luke.

"Yeah?" I close my eyes tight. There are no tears, but there's pain.

"May I come in? Are you decent?" he asks.

I chuckle at that. "Yeah. You can come in."

He opens the door slowly. At first, he doesn't come fully in. He peeks his head around the door frame to check. I didn't notice earlier because that's not where my attention was, but he's wearing a black hat with a red D20 dice on it. It makes me smile. I love that about him. His passions.

"There are no vibrators hanging around this time are there?"

I snort and maybe sob a little, but I control it enough where it doesn't get me. "No, Luke. No vibrators."

He steps inside and shuts the door carefully before crossing the room. Without hesitation he sits beside me on my bed. I almost smile. I can feel him, he's so close. He's freshly showered, his Dove soap scent lingers, and I find myself breathing it in.

"Are you okay with this?"

"Of course. It's for Ezra. We've worked together when things weren't so good between us before. We can do it again."

I close my eyes. "What if Jake's mission is to find the lost human Paladin of the great nation of Ashor?"

Luke bumps his shoulder into me. I bask in it, needing more.

"It will be like a treasure hunt."

He's watching me now with the same curious eyes he had when I stayed for their game that one night.

"What if he has to collect items to make a ring? I mean not the actual ring—but this magic ring is going to save the Paladin."

"Okay, so how about the first part, a golden band is guarded by a bronze dragon. Played by... Sean," he says.

I touch his arm. "Yes!" He doesn't move my grasp, and I swear he closes his eyes for a second.

"To slay the dragon and retrieve that item you have to hit him where he's weak. His heart. All of us will get a chance to slay the dragon, Jake will be the last and Sean will fall to his death and a large band will drop," I say.

Luke's face lights up as we talk. This moment feels so easy

between us somehow. I should be chewing him out, but I don't want to.

"The second is diamonds, the Orc, aka Patrick, will be guarding it, and for him you must put him to sleep with a special magic powder that you have to purchase from the old haggard lady, erm, Nora can be her. Be careful, she might sell you the wrong one."

"Oh, that's really good," I say. "And the powder that puts him to sleep is orange, she may try to sell you the red."

"Should we be writing this down?" He chuckles.

"Oh—maybe." I stand from my bed and cross the room to my desk. I've got several notebooks out already for notes for my articles. I find a blank page and bend the book, then swipe a pencil and find my place next to him again. Where I belong. I shake the thought.

I try to quickly jot down everything we said. Luke makes a few comments to help remind me.

"Once the Orc is fast asleep you will be able to steal its diamonds. And then, you know that huge rock in the center of the park? Ezra should be waiting behind it. Then we'll have Jake trade the items for Ezra's—the Paladin's—life. Could it be an evil Elf that takes him captive? Like maybe he was wronged by Ezra or one of Ezra's parents killed his—"

Luke chuckles.

"What?"

"Nothing, it's just— Your face, it uh, it kinda... never mind." He shakes his head, grinning at me.

I feel like there's some sort of truce passing between us.

"Maybe you should be a DM," he jokes.

"Hush, you! Let me finish before I lose my thoughts."

"Go ahead," he says between his laughter.

I open my mouth to speak when the alarm on his phone goes off. He leans to get it, bumping into me and I wish he'd just stay there, but he sits back normally and sighs.

"I have to go to a photoshoot. Can we— Are you free tomorrow? We... can solidify everything. You can meet me at the studio if that feels more comfortable to you."

"Yeah. I'll be home by five. I have some things to do."

He stands and I do too. We're so close but standing feels a little more intimidating. Luke clears his throat and scratches at the back of his neck. His eyes are on the space between us, downcast and unsure.

"Cosplay looks good on you, Mill." With his smile directed at me I feel my heart wanting him.

"See you tomorrow," I whisper.

"Yeah. Tomorrow."

He takes long slow strides across the room but stops just before he gets to the door. I gasp as he turns his head to find me. Our eyes meet and his lips part like there are words, but he can't quite say them. I get it. I have them too. He gives a soft smile before retreating, closing the door softly behind him.

For a few seconds, I hug the notebook to my chest. I don't cry, only stand there. My heart is talking to me, saying everything I should have. I walk towards my desk, plop the notebook beside the keyboard of my computer, and sit. Like I'm on autopilot I turn the computer on and pull up a blank Word document. I might not know how to say these things out loud, but my fingers do, and I let them.

CHAPTER 41

$\mathcal{T}$aking a large breath, I make my way into the *Violet Press* offices.

When I finished writing last night, I went back to look at my blog page. I haven't checked it much since the boudoir post. I was so oblivious with everything going on I didn't realize how big it had blown up. I came back to over a thousand comments.

You look amazing.

Beautiful photos!!

My girlfriend sobbed when I gave her my photos. She said I'm the most beautiful woman she ever laid eyes on.

I love your articles. They are so informative.

You make me want to do boudoir.

Seeing all of it filled me with a joy I wasn't expecting, and now that I think about it, maybe I don't want to be a staff writer. When I write what I want I do so much better, and maybe if I take some time and do freelance for a bit life will make sense again.

I have the support of my family. I don't have to move out. I've come to realize being in the city doesn't mean you've made it. You've only made it when you're truly happy or content with what you do. And I'm happy writing what I want to write. If it takes me nowhere it does, but I don't need to work for a big press to feel accomplished. I felt more accomplished working for Luke and being with my family. Home is where my heart is. It's not here in Manhattan; it's back on Long Island with the people I love the most.

All around me people are buzzing about the weekend. I'm feeling the holiday high as well, because in two days my brother is going to ask the love of his life to marry him, and I couldn't be more thrilled to be a part of it.

I'm about to get up from my desk when Nora sends me a text.

> Good luck today with the job. Also, send me all
> the details on your reunion with Luke. Hehe. And
> let me know what I can do if anything for the
> engagement.

It's so nice to have a friend again who I can talk to daily. I told Cheryl I wasn't moving back, and she still hasn't said anything. It sucks that our friendship flickered out like this, but maybe it's for the best.

Maggie's office door is closed as I approach. I never set up a time to speak with her, I wasn't even sure I was truly going to move forward with this, but working here has been anything but what I imagined for myself. I miss my blog, but most of all I miss working at the studio.

I mentally prepare myself for what I'm about to do. I'm heading back to square one, but this time I'm ready. Knocking on the door I don't feel the least bit sad about my departure from *Violet Press*. It's almost like a weight has been lifted.

"Come in," Maggie calls from behind the door. "Oh, Millicent, just the journalist I was looking for. I have this story that..."

"Actually, Maggie, we need to talk."

"Oh. Shut the door then," she says, tipping her chin in the direction behind me.

I square my shoulders and do what I'm asked.

"What's going on? Everything okay?"

"Not really." I blow a breath out of my nose. I've never been so sure of something, but at the same time, I'm terrified. "I no longer wish to work for *Violet Press*. I have decided I want to freelance for a while. I want to see where it takes me."

"Oh. Was it something that happened here that helped you come to this conclusion?" She leans forward in her chair, rests her elbows on the desk, and watches me carefully.

"I'm just not happy. I want to write things and I keep getting shot down. I had this amazing job back home and if he'll have me, I'd like to go work for him again."

She rubs her chin. "Millicent, dear." Her tone is almost condescending.

The power I was feeling when I first walked in is slowly fading. My leg shakes fervently. *Come on, Millicent, buck up.*

"I had big plans and high hopes for you. These articles are just the beginning to show us what you're made of."

"I understand it's—"

She holds up her hand. "Look, all I'm saying is stick with it, write some more shaving cream articles and sex toys..."

"Sex toys?" A hallow laugh escapes me. "I've done sex toys. Over and over. For *Forever Twenty* and my blog. It's a tired subject."

She narrows her eyes at me and crosses her arms at her chest. Her chair tilts back. I'm not backing down. I know what I want, and *Violet Press* is not it.

"I'm sorry, Maggie. I appreciate the opportunity you gave me here. I had high hopes because you had sought me out after seeing my work for *Forever Twenty* and my blog. I figured you'd see my potential."

She leans forward in one swift movement. "But I have seen it, Millicent." My name comes out sharp on her lips. "And all I'm asking from you is to spend a few more months writing these types of articles. We all must start at the bottom."

"Been there and done that. It's time for me to grow and not be held back. I know my potential and my talent is enough to write more. If you can't see that, then I'm sorry, but I can't work here."

Right then it clicks, there's no guilt riding over me. "Thank you for taking a chance on me. I appreciate the opportunity."

"You're making a huge mistake."

I stand and stare down at her "The only mistake I've made was taking this job."

"Well, if that's the way you feel, please clean out your cubicle. There's no reason for you to stay."

Without another word I retreat from her office, but as I slip from the threshold of the doorway, I swear I hear her say, *you'll be sorry.*

There's not much in my cubicle, so it's a quick clean up. Most of it gets tossed. I wave goodbye to a few people who were nice to me, but I didn't make any friends here, so I have no attachment.

Out on the city street I reach into my pocket for my phone to find a message from Luke.

> Can we talk when you get here? I feel like I have a lot to say, and I'm sorry I took so long to say it.

My heart flutters and I don't hesitate to text back:

> I'm ready to listen.

CHAPTER 42

*M*y stomach is twisting and turning and not in a bad way, but the nerves have settled in and I'm not sure how to handle this. I park right outside the studio doors. I don't see him, but I know he's there. His car is beside mine.

It's dark out, the sun has set, winter is fully here. I shut the heat, and a shiver rakes through me. Turning off the ignition I stare at the building. The lights are on inside. It's now or never. I thought I wanted to be a city girl, but nothing compares to this, and the pull Luke and this small little shop have over me. This place brought us together and while it could be the place that ends us, I'm hopeful it won't.

After fighting with myself I step out just as the door to the studio opens. I stop short at the sight of Astra and Katherine. She sees me and smiles.

"Millicent."

I wait to feel something. Anything. The pain over her is non-existent. So, I give her a real, true smile. "Hey, Astra. Katherine," I say, as Katherine falls in line beside her.

We stand under the light of the streetlamp. All of us bundled up. I tighten my scarf to keep the tiny specks of snow from touching my neck.

"I sprung a last-minute call to Luke. We were supposed to get our pictures a few days ago, but Katherine wasn't feeling well."

"Oh, how'd they come out?"

"Luke is phenomenal. His work is genius. He captured these moments between Katherine and I that are just—" She looks over at Katherine, eyes focused only on her.

I truly am happy for them. "He is pretty amazing, isn't he?"

"He sure is. And he's a lucky man for capturing your heart," Astra says.

I shake my head. "I was the lucky one."

As I speak, familiar green eyes meet mine through the glass door of the studio.

My heart reacts to him. I hope whatever we talk about today can either give us the closure we need or maybe give me the fuel to forgive.

The cold is stinging at my eyes, making them water, but my heart knows the true reason.

"We should go," Astra says, breaking my thoughts. "Millicent, it was really nice seeing you again."

I nod and smile. I miss her. I miss our talks, our friendship, but that was all in the past. The memories of all of it will always be something I'll hold on to. It's time to move on. We say our goodbyes and when they walk away, I find Luke again.

He holds open the door, just like he did on the first day. His lips are parted as I approach. He's taking deep steady breaths and then scratches the back of his neck.

"It's you," he whispers.

"It's me. Hey, boss." A trembling laugh escapes my lips.

He moves away allowing me in, then locks the door. I take it upon myself to sit in my spot at the desk. Luke comes around and leans against it to my left.

He looks down and releases a soft exhale. "Do you remember how it felt when you were fired?"

When his eyes find mine, I catch the haze glazing them over. "Of course. It hurt like hell."

"Didn't you say you felt like a failure?"

"Yeah. That was the second worst day of my life," I whisper.

"What's your first?"

"When we thought keeping secrets from each other was a good idea." My voice breaks, but I don't cry.

"Mine too."

He's quiet as he lets his tongue wet his lips.

Swallowing hard, he finally finds the words. "When things went down with Gretchen, I felt like I failed. I failed her, failed myself. I wasn't good enough to be a husband. I couldn't meet my wife's needs. How could I make you happy if I'd failed before?"

"Luke…"

"Let me finish, please." He blinks back the moisture in his eyes. "Apparently, she found someone who could fill her with that need. It had been going on for years. Years. Under my nose she was seeing some guy while we were married."

I want to reach out and hold his hand, give him some kind of comfort, but I hold back.

"I met Gretchen my first year at college. We were engaged by twenty, married at twenty-two when we graduated college. California was our home. I had planned on staying for the long haul. We were serious. We talked about starting a family and everything."

Another break.

"We stayed together up until last spring. She told me she was pregnant." He scratches his neck a little harder.

"I'll admit I was scared, but I was there for her. Three months into it she tells me he wasn't mine. She had cheated on me. In my head I knew it couldn't be mine since we hadn't had sex in quite some time, but I went along with it, because I—"

"Because you loved her."

He nods. "I got the paternity test, and her son is not mine. She kept wanting me to be a part of his life, but I don't see what the point is. So, I filed for divorce and moved back home. We married too young. It felt rushed but I was blinded by what I thought truly was love. She stayed there and I was here. For a while things moved forward with the divorce. She was fine with it or so I thought."

Inside of Luke is a broken man. I kind of see why he kept it from me.

"The first day you were working here was the day she returned. It's why—"

"Why you were moody and had to close up early."

"Yeah," he whispers.

There will still always be some sort of resentment over what he did, but I get him having a hard time and I see why he's so hesitant to lend out his heart.

"She said I wasn't bold enough, and was too boring. She wanted to spice things up, but apparently, he wasn't any better, because every time there's a rift in their relationship, she's right back to pleading with me to take her back. But she hasn't come back, not since that day."

He swallows hard, eyes flickering in every direction until they land on me. "I'm sorry I didn't tell you. I didn't want you to think I was anymore of a failure then you already—"

I don't want to waste another minute. I push the chair out from behind me and stand in front of him, inches away. He's so close for me to touch but still, I don't.

"Luke, I don't think you're a failure. Even back then. You were just my younger brother's friend that I loved to nag. I liked getting under your skin. I'm sorry you took the brunt of my jokes. I hate myself for it. I truly do." My voice cracks under the pressure.

He quietly watches me.

"God, if anything you're the best damn thing that's ever happened to me. You're far from boring, and sex with you—" I roll my eyes back like I can feel the pleasure that rips through me every time, even without him touching me. It's been a while, but I never forgot his touch. "Luke, it's the best sex I've ever had. But it's not what I love most. My favorite part is your passion for the things you love. Like with D&D and I see it in your eyes when you're behind a camera, hell, I even saw it when you were with me. You didn't fail."

I want to shake some sense into him so he can see everything good about himself.

"You're about to take over this place and people love you."

Sure, it's his dad's studio, but the reviews on Yelp and other websites all mention Luke. I've looked. He's just as well-known around here as his father.

"In fact, on the phone, they would request you over your dad. I might be selfish, but I'm glad Gretchen wasn't your one. You want to know why? Because if she had been I wouldn't have had the pleasure of being your girlfriend. I never would have known what love was. So, I don't think you've failed. I think it was a bump in the road. Just like mine was."

"Millicent, I am so fucking sorry." His chest heaves with each word. Tears he's been holding in release, and right there I think I've forgiven him. "So sorry."

He folds in on himself, covering his face with his hands. I hate the way his shoulders shake with sobs. "I don't want to fail you anymore."

With one step I take him into my arms. He shed only a few tears when we said goodbye, but he didn't cry like this in front of me. His whole body trembles as I hold on, keeping him from going over the edge. I run a hand through his familiar soft hair and close my eyes, reveling in it.

I want to tell him that I failed him all those years ago, but I know he's forgiven me for that, so I stay quiet on the subject.

"You didn't, Luke. I love you. I never stopped."

"I didn't mean to hurt you." His voice is muffled in my shirt, tears wetting my neck. "I love you. I love you so damn much. I want to do better for you. I want this to work, and I want to be a better man…"

"You're already the best man you could be for me. I'm sorry I didn't give you a chance to explain. I'm still a little upset that you kept it from me. I think part of me always will be. But I get it now. I don't want to go another minute without you in my life."

He lifts his head, eyes meeting mine again. "Are you forgiving me?"

I take his tearful face in my hands and hold on. "You gave me a second chance. Now it's my turn to give you yours. You didn't have to love the girl who stepped on your toes, but you did. You loved her so fiercely and she fell hard, and there's no turning back. I want you in my life. I want this life. Here. With you. With my family."

"I love you," he whispers.

"I love you."

I press another light kiss to his mouth and hold him until he's ready. If there's anything I want to do from here on out, it's to show him he's not a failure and he's loved and capable of so much.

"So, I uh, quit my job. Are you still hiring?"

His smile makes me giddy. I did that. Again.

"I dunno, what are your qualifications?"

I release his face and he wipes his tears, sniffling.

"Well, I worked for this photographer once, he was kind of a nerd, but he uh, taught me to plan my depth of field… to make sure everything is in focus and clear. And I think everything is finally coming into focus. Oh, and I'm pretty good at taking phone calls."

I love the smile on his face, and the way he leans in, and how his lips touch my ear as he whispers, "I'm seeing pretty clearly right now."

"Me too," I whisper.

"You forgot one thing…"

"Oh yeah, what's that?"

"My hot chocolate."

I tap his arm and his melodic laughter grabs me and holds on. Our lips collide and I'm not sure who went in for the kiss first. It starts off with hungry scrapes of our tongues, moves to soft and sensual, then back to hungry. He lifts me up off the ground and walks towards the back.

"Did you clear your desk off for us at least?" I ask.

He chuckles into my mouth. "Nah. Too much work."

I bury my face into his neck, kissing along his sensitive skin. I take in his soapy scent and suck a little harder with each bite. His moans drive me crazy. He pushes through the door, then sets me on the edge of the desk. Standing between my legs he presses his erection into me.

He grips the back of my neck, pulling me in for another kiss. I fidget with his belt, tugging it off him. I push his jeans down to his ankles and he kicks them off along with his shoes. He's so hard when my hand finds his length. His breath hitches as I take it and stroke gently.

"Millicent," he moans.

Pulling back, he unbuttons my gray peacoat tossing it behind me. He unravels my scarf from around my neck and places it in the pile with my jacket. He slowly moves his fingers over the buttons of my navy-blue suit.

"What did I tell you about wearing this around me," he growls.

"Why do you think I did?"

He grins as it all comes undone, then removes my shirt. I reach for his pulling it up and over his head, then drop it in the same spot his pants have landed.

"You don't know how long I've waited to feel you again," he

whispers, trailing his fingers down my arm and then tugs at my pants. I lift my bottom as he pulls down, taking my stilettos off with them. He grins at the memory. They are the same shoes. I've gotten kind of used to them.

"I'm all yours, Luke. Touch me, kiss me, fuck me, make love to me, do it all. I've held off for too long," I whisper.

"First, I'm going to make love to you, because you deserve all the love in the world."

He plants a kiss on my lips.

"Then I'm going to take you to dinner and kiss you some more."

My neck.

"And then take you back to my place where I'll fuck you all night long."

My breasts.

There's a confident growl in his tone, turning me on more than I have ever been in my life.

"And it won't stop there."

Lower, he goes much lower, and I gasp. Tugging my underwear slightly he kisses above it.

"I'm in. I'm all in. For as long as you'll have me."

He stands back up but allows his fingers to dance along my lower half.

"How does forever sound?"

My lips twitch as I shiver from his words. "It sounds amazing."

Without another word he kneels on the floor, discards my panties in one of the many piles of clothes and presses his lips to my center. I grip the sides of the desk and my head flings backwards. I nearly lose myself when he pushes two fingers inside of me while his mouth lingers. He's never done this before and it's ecstasy.

I grab a fistful of his hair as I let go into his mouth. He comes up grinning, his lips sparkling with me. He lays me down on top of the papers, grabs a condom from his wallet. It feels like forever before he finally climbs on top of the desk with me.

"I hope this desk is strong," I chuckle.

He grins. "We're good."

He pushes up and into me. I've missed him so much. He said he was going to make love to me here. And that's exactly what he does. His eyes flutter closed every few minutes, pleasure raking through both of us. I writhe under him as he drags kisses up and down my body, making sure no spot goes left untouched.

I'm engulfed with flames and fire and passion. I know in order for this to work he and I need to learn to communicate better. He's already trying, already telling me things, not only with his words but with his body, how much I mean to him. I couldn't ask for anything better. I'm home as he screams my name and I scream his. We finish together, panting and satisfied. There's no rush as he lifts me up, stands and then tugs me into his chest. It's quiet with the exception of our beating hearts. I'm not sure how long we hold on for, but when we finally pull away and get ready to go to dinner, I know in my heart I've made the right decision.

CHAPTER 43

*T*oday is the day, and of course it's snowing. Whack! A snowball flies at my head, pelting me. It's way too early for this shit and I'm freezing. Aside from it being a holiday, it snowed last night. Setting up was a bit of a task, but somehow Luke and I managed.

This is the place where they used to go as teens to play. They have done a few live action role-playing sessions since then, but not so much anymore. It's a beautiful park with a small lake, and in the summer the tree line behind it is beautifully landscaped. Now all the trees are bare and filled with the last frosting of snow.

Mom, Dad, and Ezra should be arriving soon. Since Luke and I had to be here bright and early I slept at his place, and we came together. Later, Jenn and Tony are joining us for Christmas dinner, and we're going to celebrate all the good things happening.

I pack a ball for myself but before I can get it round another one pelts me. Laughing I manage to finish and toss one in his direction, but he jumps out of the way.

"You suck, Luke!"

He grins. "Yeah, you weren't complaining earlier."

Even with it being the coldest day of the year, I find myself heated up by his comment. I trudge through the snow towards him and when I'm close enough I scoop up what I can and throw it at him. It's all over his heavy black winter jacket and all over his black beanie.

The sun is peeking through and when they do arrive, we plan on taking our jackets off and freezing our asses off to get pictures and go through the tasks, which shouldn't take too long.

Luke wraps his arms around me, holding tight. Looking up into his eyes I get a little lost. This is all so surreal. Just a week ago I thought I'd be on my way back to the city to live with Cheryl, but now I'm here and I feel like I've lost nothing but gained everything.

"I want you to read something," I say, wrapping my arms around his neck.

He leans down and takes my bottom lip between his teeth. I yelp, but grin. Luke's changed over the last few weeks since we were apart. While I do see a lot of hesitation and fear in those beautiful green eyes of his, there's also the relief of knowing he'll always be enough for me.

He pulls away slightly. "Maybe in the car? Where it's warm."

"Are you going to be the one to heat me up?" I tease.

"Didn't we just do that a few hours ago."

I look up towards the sky and try to create a sly smile across my lips. "So, we always have a little time to spare."

He laughs. "Come on. Let's go. I'll keep you warm alright."

We slide into the backseat of his car. He leans his back against the passenger side window, leaves one leg up on the seat the other down, while I squeeze in between his legs. I hand him my phone, the web browser open to my blog.

"What if you wrote blogs for the studio? I mean you're already our social media whiz..."

"Are you going to give me a raise?" I snicker.

"Oh, I'll give you something."

He takes his hand (which had no gloves while we were outside) and sticks it down the top opening of my jacket, unzipping it a little. It's hard with the corset but he manages to rub the top part of my breast. His hands are ice cold and I yelp. His laughter in my ear is the best thing I've heard in a while.

"I think it's a fantastic idea."

I groan when he releases his grip on my breasts.

"Later?" he asks.

"Mmm... yes. Now read. Please. I know we're okay now, but when I wrote it, I didn't know if we would be, so sorry."

He presses a kiss to my cheek, then lifts the phone to read while I lie in his arms.

For Him:

Finding love when you least expect it. It bites you in the ass when you're not looking. This fall I found what I've been searching for all this time. I was walking around thinking that happiness was making it in Manhattan, having the highest paying job, living miles away from my family, and just getting by. And then, I lost all of that, and I thought I'd never recover, but I did. Being home made me see what I was missing. Like my family, having weekly dinners with my brother and his partner, having a shoulder to cry on when I needed it, knowing it would always be there, and finding someone that I could picture spending my whole life with, even if it meant ditching the painful heels, and the lifestyle I once craved.

Losing that job was not failing, it was a wake-up call. Then unexpectedly I found a job. It wasn't a writing gig, and at first, I thought I'd only do it for a week or two before I'd find a real job again, but there was nothing fake about it. And there certainly wasn't anything fake about how I felt towards the man who let me into that world. It was more real than seeing my articles published monthly for the world to see.

My life started to become less about the money or the fame, and more about the man who knew all my faults, yet he still loved me.

As a teen I regret a lot of what I did and who I was. I hurt someone who I liked. I'm not making excuses for my behavior, but I was discovering who I was back then, and feeling more invalid than anything. I pushed all that anger and fear onto him. I think it was my insecurities talking. Back then, I didn't understand the feelings I had for him, but I'm sure they were always there. He thought I was the stuck-up troublemaker, and to me, he was the boy in tights eating Funyons in my mom's basement, while he played *D&D* with my brother and their friends. I used it as ammo to poke fun, something now I wish I could take back.

I'm not that girl anymore and haven't been for a long time. There was one night that changed it all for me, and I've lived with the guilt since then. It is possible for people to change because I know I did. But then after we gave each other a chance at love, we both screwed up. We failed at communicating with each other, and once again the past felt like it was back to haunt me.

I had been carrying heartbreak from a previous relationship with me, and for many years I pushed away anyone who got too close, but him, I just wanted to pull him closer. I lied, because I was afraid to hurt him, but in the end it backfired. Hurting him was far from what I ever wanted to do. I'm ready to start this life, the one where we work together, and never hold on to a secret. I want to tell him everything, because up until that point I had. I spilled every fear and every emotion out for him, apologized profusely, and he still loved me.

If you're reading this now, and realizing that there's someone in your life who you never expected to love, but you somehow do, tell them. Don't hide it; let them know, because sometimes those people are the ones that need us too.

Luke, I love you. I understand why things happened the way they did, and I'd love more than anything to put it in our past, move on, and start brand new. We have something that doesn't come around every day, and for the first time, I want to dive in headfirst. I want to love, and I want to be loved. I forgive you, and I hope that maybe you forgive me too.

Luke rubs his fingers against my face and gives me the phone. I place it between my legs on the seat and turn, putting my feet on the floor.

"Everything worked out just the way it was supposed to."

"It sure did," I say.

He kisses me. Not just a regular kiss; he puts his whole heart into it. My lips part and his does too. Our tongues gently get tangled in each other. I grip a handful of his jacket to pull him closer. As I roll the zipper down an obnoxious horn honks several times.

"Ezra," I mumble.

Luke chuckles. "Come on, you. It's time." He gives me one last peck before we retreat from the car.

Ezra gets out of Dad's Corolla all decked out in shiny silver armor, like he just stepped out of a fantasy book.

Dad and Mom look stunning in their Elf costumes too. Dad holds on to her, keeping her warm. I watch them closely. Their love has always been strong. I wasn't sure about love for a long time, but even when I wasn't, I knew it existed: I lived with the most loving parents. They used to dance in the kitchen late at night when they thought no one was watching, but I saw them. Loud and clear.

"Don't wanna know what you two were doing in there. The windows are fogged." Ezra crosses his arms over his chest.

He's right. "Making up for lost time." I stick my tongue out at him.

Luke is shaking his head, an amused smile on his face.

Ezra searches the lot. Jake spends Christmas morning with his dad. He suffers from Alzheimer's and lives in a nursing home. Christmas is his favorite holiday and was always their special time together. So Jake's coming straight from there to here. He thinks the guys are getting together to LARP in the snow but has no idea what's in store.

Sean and Patrick pull in in Patrick's car, followed by Nora in hers. She's going to play our old lady. After Luke and I made up we called everyone with our plan.

"Luke, this could be a perfect post for the Parker Photography Blog. If that's okay with Ezra of course."

I turn to him.

"Blog?"

"Yeah. We are starting one for the studio. I get to be in charge of it. Because I'm a kickass blogger. Says this guy." I point over my shoulder at Luke with a grin.

"That's because he's blinded by love."

I shove Ezra and laugh. Luke joins in.

"Oh, baby, I packed the 85mm; that's what you needed, right?"

"I love when you talk lenses to me," Luke jokes.

"And on that note..." Ezra grins, making us all laugh.

Nora comes over and putting her arm around my shoulder she leans in. "So, looks like you two have made up nicely."

I bump her hip with mine, and she chuckles, withdrawing her arm. When she pulls away, I get a good look at her. She's no half-elf Bard today, but somehow makes an old lady look good. She's even using a fake long nose. I'm a little jealous because her costume looks much warmer than mine. Especially the brown sweater and tattered wool blanket sitting over her shoulders.

With everyone here, dressed and ready, it's time for us to buckle down and get started. Jake should be here soon.

"Okay, guys, Luke and I came early and set everything up. Sean."

Sean places on his really cool cosplay dragon mask. It's so realistic with scales and everything.

"You need to go by the oak near the playground. And Pat..."

Patrick's green makeup and Orc-like features are even more awesome. We look like legit cosplayers and honestly, I'd do this again. "You are near the small lake. And Nora..." I point to the path to the lake, which Luke and I tried to uncover from the snow as best we could. "You'll be there, on the path."

Jake's car pulls around the corner, and my heart leaps into my stomach. "Shit, Ez, go now, he's coming."

The others scatter quickly, but it's Ezra who I have to nudge. He hesitates, turning to me for reassurance.

"You got this." There's no stopping the smile spreading across my face. "I love you, and you'll do great."

His eyes meet mine, and I give an encouraging jerk of my chin. I watch my brother run off towards the huge rock to the left. I'm getting a little teary-eyed knowing in just a few minutes we'll be celebrating with some of the most important people in my life. The past few weeks have been rough but being able to stand here and share the moment not only with my family, but with Luke makes it all worth it.

CHAPTER 44

I walk to Luke and touch his shoulder. He's still fiddling with the camera, taking random shots, and checking the focus. White steam pours from his mouth as he exhales. I'm lost in him. Luke shivers. His eyes solely on me. A single breath catches in my throat.

"Hey, guys!" Jake says, interrupting the moment. "What are you all doing here?" he asks. Jake is so handsome in his dark brown leather armor, and black dress shirt tucked underneath.

"It's a family game today," I say, with a knowing smile.

"Oh. That sounds fun, I'm glad you could join us. You two," he says, turning to my parents, "look amazing by the way." Then he looks at me. "And you. You are a stunning Elf."

I curtsey and grin. "Thank you. I kind of like it." I twirl a little for him. The hairs on my neck stand on end, and my eyes flutter back to Luke.

"It's suits you well." He bows to me, earning a giggle, and it feels good to laugh.

Luke clears his throat and hands Jake a large scroll. "You have been given a task..."

His role-playing voice makes me think I might melt the snow with how hot I feel.

We all walk together and come upon a black wrought-iron gate, which makes the scene so much more real. We strung white twinkling lights along with a garland of ivy intertwined through the gate.

Jake investigates the scene, stopping for a moment to take it all in. He touches a finger to his lips. He's becoming more suspicious by the minute.

Sean is the first stop. He roars in the best dragon voice he can muster. He could be an actor with how well he pulls off his part. Once we finish with the dragon, Sean quickly removes his head and swaps it out for some ears. Mom and Dad wanted to observe rather than be an actual character, so Sean offered to play the part of the evil Elf who has captured Ezra as well as the dragon role.

I'm sort of paying attention, but the other half of me can't help focusing on Luke. He's taking advantage of each moment by snapping photos. He's in his element, and I love it. Jake turns to him as we walk away from Sean. "Why the pics, Luke?"

"For the studio. Trying something new," he says. Technically he's not wrong, the pictures are going to be worked on, but little does he know the pictures are for him and Ezra.

Everyone is nearly frost-bitten by the time we get to the Orc.

"You cannot pass!" he says in a low rumbling voice.

"Have you any information on the lost Paladin of Ashor?" I love the accent he's chosen to use. It reminds me of a mix of Shakespearean and fantasy all tied into one.

When Patrick's character becomes difficult, Dad shouts, "Use the powder!"

Jake mistakenly throws the magical dust, aka kinetic sand, into Patrick's eye. He makes light of the situation and falls to the ground in a heap and loudly snores.

Our last quest is to speak to the Elf guarding the large rock.

Around the rock is the beautiful display of roses and lanterns. Luke and I went to several dollar stores searching for just the right stuff for this.

Sean makes it to the rock just before we do. He had some trouble with his ears, and Nora had to jump in and save him.

"Have you brought the items required to enter?" he asks in a smooth velvety tone. He drove the girls mad in high school. I can see why.

"I have, sir." Jake bows in front of him; Mom, Dad, and I follow. Jake hands him the items.

"Ah. Thank you, good sir. You may enter."

Sean moves aside revealing the lit pathway. It lights up in the darkness from the overhead sullen sky. Luke is taking photos as he follows Jake behind the rock. We all remain close so we can capture the whole thing. Mom is already sobbing and when Jake stops short, I know he's found my brother.

I step to the side so I can get a better view, Ezra is on his knees with tears streaming down his face. Jake's hand is covering his mouth, his shoulders shake with sobs of happiness.

"Jake, there's no perfect way to say this, but I want to roll a D20 with you for the rest of our lives."

A swirl of laughter between everyone captivates me. This moment is so special to them. I've never rooted for a couple to be endgame so hard in all my life.

"When I met you in first grade and you threw sand at me, because I didn't share my Oreo with you, I knew I loved you even then. I may have been young, but sometimes you just know these things. When I came out first you supported me, and then you did, and I did the same for you. I knew I needed to kiss you then. We spent years back and forth, convinced we couldn't date, but here we are, and you're the best thing that's ever happened to me." Ezra's voice breaks as he holds up the box with the ring inside.

"Jacob Michael Collins, will you do me the extraordinary honor of being my husband?"

Right there, the moment Ezra's tears become a full-blown waterfall is when I lose it too. My younger brother is pouring his heart out to the love of his life, and we are all here to witness this beautiful moment. Even Patrick and Sean have tears in their eyes, and Luke, he's hiding behind the camera, but I catch a sliding tear cascading down his bright red cheek.

Jake nods his head, still unable to speak or uncover his mouth. My brother gets to his feet, and carefully removes the hand, placing a gentle kiss on Jake's lips before sliding the band onto his ring finger. Jake wraps my brother in his arms, and everyone claps for them.

We all take turns hugging the happy newly engaged couple. Ezra wraps me in the biggest hug. "Will you do me the honor and be my best woman?"

I chuckle. "Is that even a thing?"

Pulling back, his eyes meet mine. "It is now, and I don't care if it's ridiculous, but I want you standing beside me when I say my vows. You stood by my side when we told Mom and Dad I was gay, then I stood with you when you told them you were bi. I don't think I would have been able to do it on my own. We have been through everything together, and it will mean the world to me if you'd take the role."

A happy kind of sob escapes my trembling lips. "Of course I'll be your best woman." I wrap my arms around him. "I love you."

"Love you too, sis."

To say this was the best Christmas ever would be an understatement. It was more than great, more than the best, it was fucking wonderful. I take another peek at Luke who's got the camera pointed at Ezra and me. I shiver from the cold, but the second he lowers the camera my entire body heats up. He gives me that nerdy-Luke smile, the one I can't resist and deep down I know I've made the right choice.

EPILOGUE

EIGHT MONTHS LATER

"*A*re you almost ready?"

Luke steps into the back room. I've got my hand up over the back of my head, looking like some crazy monkey trying to scratch my back. My eyes meet his and he grins. He takes in the forest-green off-the-shoulder dress, then floats down to my bare legs, and the black low-heeled pumps on my feet.

"A little help here?" I ask, still stuck in a weird, contorted position.

Shaking his head, he crosses the room. Instead of doing what I ask, his lips find the nape of my neck. I shiver at his touch. He zips it, spins me around, and presses his mouth to mine. His fingers slide up the soft fabric of my dress. It's late August and the heat is unbearable, so I've decided to forgo the pantyhose.

His fingers slip under my underwear as he presses his fingertips against me in soft circular motions. My head falls back in response as a gasp leaves my lips.

"We're going to be late," I hiss.

"No, we're not. We've got time." Luke grins. I can't resist him.

I take a step back and take a moment to relish in his attire.

The brown vests over white button downs and khaki or brown pants are somehow more attractive than a regular old suit.

He leans me against the desk, lifting the skirt of my dress. Reaching out I unbutton his pants, and they fall to his ankles. I grab at him, greedily, and hold his length in my hands and stroke him gently. It's his turn to feel pleasure, and I'm enjoying every minute of it.

I lay back and reach into the drawer of the desk, grabbing a condom, and throw it at him. It's now his studio, so he keeps a stash locked away.

He chuckles as it bounces around in his hands for a few seconds before he holds it steady. Once it's on we don't waste any time.

"This desk is getting much more use than you intended it to." I giggle.

Luke laughs into my mouth as he pushes into me. I tighten around him, the feeling of him inside of me will never get old. I lay my hands flat on the desk as he thrusts forward and let out a moan so loud it echoes through the room.

I get onto the desk, he follows, and looms over me. He dives in and kisses along my jawline. With time not on our side, we both finish together. For a few lingering moments we lie there, panting in each other's arms, until time runs out.

THE PARK LOOKS MAGICAL. The treetops are at their fullest, awaiting the return of fall. A large wooden arch sits in front of the lake. White flowers and green vines wrap around it. It's not frozen over as it was last winter when we were here for the proposal. The water is flowing and filled with wildlife. We've transported to another time and place for sure.

Ezra is talking to Sean when he spots us. My brother's eyes

light up as he races over. He's all decked out in an outfit similar to Luke's, only his vest is black and so are his pants.

"What took you two so…" Ezra stops.

No doubt there's a soft blush on my face.

"On my wedding day?" He crosses his arms, jovially.

I grin. "Sorry."

"It's the dress, man," Luke says.

"And that's my sister, man," Ezra teases back.

After the two go back and forth for a few minutes, they finally realize it's time to do the big reveal. Mom and Dad make their way over. Tony is waiting for us, camera in hand. He's kind of officially retired now but offered to do the wedding so Luke could enjoy himself, but of course Luke offered to jump in if his dad needed the extra hand.

Nora bounds over, excited for the big reveal. She says her hellos to Luke then comes over to me.

Luke pulls a blindfold from his pocket and wraps it around Ezra's eyes. Beside the rock where Ezra got down on one knee is Jake. He's not looking in our direction. Pat has drawn his attention instead. Luke walks beside me as I guide Ezra over to where his handsome husband-to-be is waiting.

Ezra halts for a second.

"Everything okay?" I ask.

"It's uh, it's perfect." He takes a deep breath. If he wasn't blindfolded, he would be staring right at Jake. It's almost as if he knows exactly where he is.

"You're about to marry your best friend; of course it's perfect."

"What if I suck at it?" he asks.

"Suck at what?"

I reach for Ezra's hand, it trembles in mine and is a little sweaty. He squeezes, like he's holding on for dear life.

"Marriage."

"Are you kidding me? You two have been together even before you were together. You conquered one of the hardest obstacles, you overcame all your insecurities together, and now here you are about to marry the love of your life. You've been living together, and in my book it's like you're already married."

"So, then you and Luke are already married."

I growl at him. I moved into Luke's place back in March and it's been perfect, just how I imagined. I'd never want to go back to the life I had before, the lonely, going-home-to-no-one life. We have talked about our future and what we want, and it's on the cards for us one day.

"What I'm saying is you've already been living a married life, just without the piece of paper to make it official. This is just one more step in your journey together. It's your happy beginning," I say.

"And this is why you're my woman of honor." He chuckles.

I catch a stray tear sliding down his cheek and wipe it away for him. "Now come on, let's go get your man."

After situating the two to be back-to-back, Luke and I step back, standing side by side. Tony lingers waiting for the moment. I count backwards from ten, and when they turn to face each other both of their faces light up. It's not a huge reveal since they both knew what the other was wearing, but it's not the clothes that make the difference, it's knowing they are about to embark on a bond that for them will last forever.

MOM AND DAD happily clap their hands as we all watch Ezra recite his vows under the beautiful wicker arch. To be funny, Ezra and Jake rolled a D20 dice and whoever rolled the highest got to go first.

Luke was appointed as Jake's best man. He stands beside him, giving him the ring.

Jake pauses before and wipes his eyes. Searching the crowd, I don't think there is a dry eye in the park. In the distance a woman wearing scrubs pushes a man towards us. Ezra reaches for Jake's hands.

"Before you tell me how much you love me..." he says, a wide grin on his face.

Jake rolls his eyes and playfully bats my brother away.

"We have a guest of honor here today." Ezra jerks his chin towards the man and nurse.

Jake's eyes follow. A gasp escapes out of his mouth. There are more tears as he turns to my brother. "How did you...?"

"It wasn't easy, but we were able to bail him out to at least see the ceremony."

Everyone watches as Jake takes off down the aisle towards his father. He looks a little lost, but there's a huge smile on his face. He knows where he is and who he's here to see. After a few moments Jake jogs back over to Ezra and wraps my brother in a hug. They exchange whispers and a quick peck, before getting back into the swing of things.

"Well, now it's my turn I guess..."

A few guests chuckle.

"There aren't any words for this moment, or none that really explain how I feel for you. Ezra, you saved me. You made me feel safe when I finally came out. Even if we were both too stubborn to fall in love, you never gave up on me. That alone is enough."

His words are short and sweet and has everyone reaching for their tissues. Mom and Dad are holding on to one another as they watch with proud eyes.

After the beautiful ceremony, Tony takes a ton of photos. I happily watch my brother and Jake fall in love all over again.

"Hey, what about them?" Ezra asks, pointing to Luke and me.

"Take their picture too. They helped make this day what it is," Jake says.

It's true. After our amazing proposal set up, Ezra and Jake appointed us their "wedding planners." It was fun, I'll admit, and on top of the photos it gave us great blog material. I can't wait to add this moment in too. It's been a huge success. Readers love my way with words, and clients absolutely love the stories of their magical days. Mostly, they love Luke's breathtaking photos. The whole project has made me love the craft all over again.

We take the spot where Jake and Ezra stood moments ago in front of the lake to the left of the arch. Luke wraps his arms around me from behind and leans in. "You're the most beautiful woman here," he whispers into my ear.

I turn my neck so that I can see his face; it's hard at this angle, but I'm still able to see the soft smile on his lips. The camera clicks several times, but I'm now ignoring it as I spin into his arms.

"I want one of these pictures for the living room."

"We'll go through them together and pick the perfect one. Maybe we'll catch an even better moment later," he says, winking.

I squeeze my brows together, and open my mouth to say something, but instead he plants a soft kiss on my lips.

THE FADING August sun lights up the sky a golden pink. People are dancing, dinner has been served, and its nearly time for cake. There aren't many of us, so we all sit at a long wooden rectangular table with matching chairs. Ivy and white flowers, like those wrapped around the arch, are intertwined through the backs of the chairs. It's very rustic.

Lanterns and tall black lamp posts brought in just for the wedding light up as the sky darkens some more. Ezra whistles, and everyone mingles on the dance floor in the center of everything.

I spend half my time on the dance floor with Luke and Nora too. She loves dancing and has even stolen Luke a ton of times for dances, which he looked totally awkward doing and kept fumbling over his feet.

"It's time for the D20 toss," the DJ announces over the microphone. "All the single ladies and gentlemen please head for the dance floor."

Instead of a bouquet Ezra and Jake have decided to throw the large blue D20 plush they used during the ceremony.

"That's you," Mom says.

"Um, I'm not single, remember, Luke?"

Mom grins. Her hands push me towards the group gathered waiting. "It doesn't count, you're not married. Go!" she urges again. She gives another shove, and I stumble onto the dance floor, knocking into Sean. It's not just ladies on the dance floor, it's every single person or unmarried.

"Fancy meeting you here." He smirks and bumps his hip into me.

"My mother made me do it," I say.

He chuckles. "Be prepared to fight, I need to find myself a girl soon. Everyone in the group will be married before me."

"Hey, nothing wrong with that. You'll find her."

"Yeah, Sean." Nora grins beside him. "You'll find her." She winks.

Sean's cheeks turn red, and I catch a glimpse of maybe something going on there. I hope so, they'd be good together.

I don't see Luke anywhere. I search the grounds, not wanting to leave the area. He should be here too since he's not married. Why did I get roped into this?

I find Mom and she and Dad are standing off to my right with Jenn, while Tony snaps a ton of photos. My parents are holding hands. Mom has tears running down her cheeks. I'm confused by her emotions. This is supposed to be the fun part of a wedding, not the sappy moment.

Ezra and Jake have their backs turned and are pretending to throw the die behind them. The DJ plays Forest Blakk's song "Fall into Me." Out of all the weddings I've been to with Luke I realize it's not a normal song for the bouquet toss. It's more of a first dance song. I heard it a few times and fell in love with it. Luke teased me for listening to it so many times in a row, but after a while he loved it too.

"Alright, guys, ready?" Jake shouts.

Everyone around me yells and chants. Where the heck is Luke?

"One."

I can't help my wandering eyes.

"Two." Jake and Ezra both shout, and bend at their knees prepping for the toss. "THREE!"

The guests part from the dance floor, leaving me all alone. I'm distracted by the movement and almost miss the plush, but shuffle to my right just in time to catch it. Ezra and Jake watch me, huge smiles on their faces. Their eyes are focused on something behind me. Ezra covers his mouth like he's attempting to hide his smirk.

A lantern floats up towards the sky. The candle flickering creates an orange glow behind its white fabric. It reminds me of the lantern—Luke? Something catches my eye, and I spin.

I was so busy looking up, I didn't notice Luke on the ground like he's tying his... holy shit he's not tying his shoes. I drop the D20 plush, and it rolls off the dance floor. In the corner of my eye, I watch as Sean picks it up and holds it above his head, like he's claiming victory. I only half smile because I'm in shock. My hands fly up to my face, covering my mouth.

On one knee he holds out a perfect square blue box resembling a TARDIS because let's face it, living with him I've had to watch every one of his favorite shows, and *Doctor Who* became a staple in our home. Leave it to Luke to add it to the proposal. It's so him, and I love it.

The box is open exposing the small diamond ring inside.

"Millicent Gibson," he says.

I search all the familiar faces surrounding us. Smiles all

around. Mom and Dad have tears rolling down their cheeks. But this is Ezra and Jake's day, what is he...

"Mill," Luke whispers, pulling me back.

The box in his hand trembles in his quaking hands. "Before you came back into my life, I had hit rock bottom. We had our differences and our opinions, but we conquered them all, and now here we are, and I couldn't be any happier. You woke me up, picked up the broken pieces, and kept them whole."

"What, me? Here? Now? What?" I stutter.

I make eye contact with Ezra again, who has snuck around to get a better view. He nods his head. "It's okay," he whispers.

"Millicent, you have captured my heart in ways I can't explain, and with the permission of your dad, brother, brother-in-law, and your mom, I'm on my knees in front of the people you love the most, asking for your hand in marriage."

"With me? Are you sure?"

Laughter fills the wide-open space. I'm not sure if I want to laugh, cry, or both. My eyes sting as they glaze over, making it hard to see Luke kneeling in front of me.

"I wouldn't be on my knees if I wasn't. Will you marry me?"

"I uh, I— I..." My lips tremble. I'm speechless and taken back that Ezra wanted this at his wedding. It's supposed to be his day, but the look on his face says it all, he was behind this.

"I— Yes. Luke, yes, a thousand times yes." My voice breaks as the tears fall.

I hold out my hand, it's trembling almost as bad as his, and he misses my finger a little. Both of us laugh, and I'm finally able to look him in the eye. His are filled with tears like mine, but there's so much adoration behind his beautiful emerald eyes. It warms my heart.

Once he slips the ring on, he stands.

"We're getting married?" I ask, still unable to process the moment.

"We're getting married," he repeats.

I squeal, the initial shock finally wearing off and wrap my arms around his neck pulling him into me. At first, I press my ear against his solid chest and listen to the sound of his heart beating rapidly. I let his lips touch my hair, and allow myself to hold him, and he holds me back, like he never wants to let go. Home. Luke has always been a part of this home.

"Can I kiss my fiancée now?" he whispers, his lips grazing my ear.

I lift my head from his chest. His hand rests on the side of my face. He presses his soft lips against mine and I immediately allow him in. The kiss sends a mix of shivers and heat down my entire body. My hands find his hair, I tug, he moans.

He pulls away only slightly with a Cheshire grin.

"I thought you weren't the one taking pictures today."

He narrows his eyes. "What?"

"Is that a battery pack in your pants or are you just happy to see me?" I smirk.

Luke laughs then pulls me into him again. His lips linger over mine.

"Leave it to the sex journalist to make a perverted comment at her brother's wedding while she's getting proposed to." He snorts.

"Ex-sex journalist, and you like it," I say, grinning.

He shrugs. "Yeah, I kind of do." He goes in for another kiss, this time it's sweet, but he makes sure to playfully bite my lip.

When we finally pull away my eyes land on Ezra. I race around Luke and right into Ezra's arms.

"Why did you do that? This is your day not mine."

"What better way to celebrate our wedding." He glances over at Jake. "Then to have my big sister get her happy new beginning with the man she loves."

"I love you," I say.

"Love you more, Mill." He hugs me tightly for a few seconds.

I go to Jake next, thanking him.

"It was all Ezra's idea. Luke tried to make it another day, but your brother insisted, and I couldn't say yes fast enough."

"You're both the best."

A slow song echoes through the park. The newlyweds dance, and after hugging Mom and Dad and them telling me how proud they are of who I've become, I waltz back over to my fiancé and take him in my arms.

"You're perfect," he whispers in my ear.

I hold him tighter and rest my head on his shoulder. We dance to three songs in a row and as we do I take in the world around me. There are no loud sirens, constant honking, crowded city streets, or people fighting at all hours of the night. Even with the music, it's quiet, peaceful, and perfect, and there's no other place I'd rather call home.

THE END

A NOTE FROM THE PUBLISHER

Thank you for reading this book. If you enjoyed it please do consider leaving a review on Amazon to help others find it too.

We hate typos. All of our books have been rigorously edited and proofread, but sometimes mistakes do slip through. If you have spotted a typo, please do let us know and we can get it amended within hours.

info@bloodhoundbooks.com